THE WATER BLADE

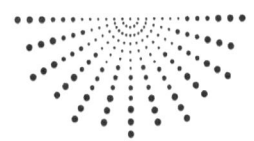

THE WATER BLADE

BOOK ONE OF THE RIDNIGHT MYSTERIES

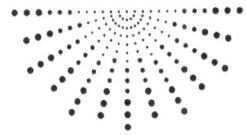

STUART JAFFE

Charlotte, NC

FALSTAFF
BOOKS

WWW.FALSTAFFBOOKS.COM

For Gabe
this one is your fault

PART I
AXON

CHAPTER ONE

Under the full moon, Axon Coponiv led her team towards the town of Heraldbund. They had defeated the Gibbons Gang with ease, and she knew Henlio and Pilot wanted to celebrate with the townsfolk. Particularly for Pilot, the female townsfolk. Henlio would settle in a chair, smoke a pipe, and drink while a gentle smile crept up through his thick beard. Bellemont, their witch, would most likely find a quiet place to be alone with her thoughts. After the party, Axon would find her with their horses, ready to go off to the next town. Xarad, on the other hand, might actually join Axon at the Cassunite Temple to offer thanks to the Cassun Nine—the gods and goddesses who ruled over all of life.

Axon's dark skin blended with her stallion and she liked the feeling of being a shadow in the night. As if she could become part of the land itself—solid, firm, unwavering. They crested a small hill, and Heraldbund appeared below, firelight flickering amber against the stone walls of the homes and shops. It seemed so tiny. So helpless. She would have to be the firmament beneath them, the walls against all dangers, the shadow of the King, stretching across the Frontier to protect all the little towns and villages.

She bit back a dark chuckle. If her mother could hear her thoughts, the woman would snap off a harsh word or two or seven. She would tell Axon that a Coponiv lady was meant for ball gowns and formal dinners. She should be courting a prince like her sister instead of traipsing around the countryside.

Tipping his wide-brimmed hat back, Pilot let the moonlight bathe his coal face. "Are we just going to stare at the town or can we get to the party?"

Axon looked up. The horses had come to a halt, and her team stared at her, waiting for her command. With a nod, she let them loose.

Pilot grinned and pressed his horse into action. Bellemont, dressed in the traditional Dacci garb of black strips of cloth and a veil covering her mouth, followed.

"We did well today," Henlio said, his deep, slow voice coming from somewhere behind his thick beard. He swung his robe back, allowing his armor to capture some of the moonlight. "You can let yourself relax a little."

Axon forced her lips to lift until he trotted off to join the rest. Only Xarad remained. He was young, a little naïve, but full of good intentions. Strong, too. If he had a title and a bit of money, Axon's mother might have approved of a match. Although she would also think Xarad too dumb for her daughter, too low class, but Axon wondered if her mother would forgo all her pride for that money and title.

"I'm going to the temple," she said, nodding toward the rundown structure off to the left.

Hiding a smile, Xarad said, "I never understood all that goddess stuff. My mama liked it, though. But I think I'm going to join the rest at the party. I just wanted to make sure you were okay."

"I'm fine."

"You say that, but you don't look that. I mean, we beat those Gibbons bastards hard. They won't be messing around with this town ever again. We did something good, but you look like we lost."

"Just in my thoughts."

"You sure? Because it seems to me—"

"Go join the party. Everything's fine."

Xarad gave a youthful shrug—he didn't know how to read people well—and headed down the hill. Axon shook her head. Even if he were smarter or more desirable in a host of ways, he was still too young, too foolish. And too randy. In the back of her mind, she knew he wanted to get to town before Pilot stole the prettiest girls.

She gave her team a few moments to gain some distance. A cool wind blew across the fields, and the distant rustling of trees sounded like a gentle ocean tide. She inhaled and let genuine peace fill her.

It would not last long, of course. She had a mission hanging over her, but that could wait another night. Just a little longer. Enough time for her to enjoy the world as she knew it—the rolling hills, the rich forests, the untainted lands. Farms and villages spreading across this beautiful, untapped country with all roads leading back to the great King Robion and the thriving cities.

Why did people have to ruin everything good? Why couldn't they simply see how perfect the Frontier was and leave it alone?

"Come on," she said to her horse, Weaver.

After tying the reins to a tree, she climbed the steps of the open-air temple, walked across the white stone path, and knelt before the nine statues of the Creators of All. She plucked a prayer cloth from an open container and placed the cloth atop her head. She bowed. To the Deities of Life—Tiq, Goddess of Birth; Ovlar, God of Childhood; Bieck, Goddess of Adolescents; Sazieck, God of Adulthood; Orlar, Goddess of the Aged; and Wiq, God of Death. To the Greater Deities, too—Tortu, God of Women; Pralma, Goddess of Man; and Qareck, the Lord of All Existence, Axon offered her thanks for her continued success.

"My apologies," a scratchy voice said. Off to the right, an old man wearing the robes of a Shul stepped out from a small shack. "I did not realize anybody had come to pray."

Axon touched her head to the stone in respect. "I didn't mean to bother anybody. I simply wanted to offer my gratitude to the Cassun Nine."

"Oh? You are with our town's heroes. I should be thanking you."

The Shul meandered toward her and settled at the foot of Ovlar.

Spending an entire life at this temple and leading prayers in the open had weathered his skin. Yet his eyes managed to offer her all the warm welcome she needed.

"It's only me. My team doesn't practice the faith."

"Yet you do. And that is plenty. It's not like when I was young. Not anymore. Back then, we would have to bring in extra benches to accommodate everybody. Now, we are fortunate if we receive one or two visitors. Unless it's one of the Holy Days."

"That's a shame. No, it's worse than that—it's wrong."

The Shul shrugged. "Change is inevitable. The Temple of the Cassun has always been tied to the King. And while King Robion has done a fine job, as have so many before him, I do not think the kingdom has much longer to last. If the kingdom falls, so does the Temple."

"Why would you say that? The kingdom is strong. All of the Frontier is strong." She wondered if he could hear her doubt.

"People don't follow the old traditions anymore. They question the institutions we hold sacred. In the East, they've done away with the monarchy entirely. They think they can do better on their own. In the West—well, we don't call that area the Feral Lands for nothing."

Axon placed her hand on the hilt of her sword. "As long as I live, I will protect this realm. The King, the kingdom, the Cassun Nine—it won't end here."

He patted her shoulder. "May the Lord of All Existence hear your words. Please, pray."

Axon lowered her head as the Shul settled in front of her with a groan. He took hold of her hands and bowed. Murmuring a prayer, his head lifted and lowered twice over her hands. Axon closed her eyes, bowed her head, and listened.

His hands were cold and damp like the statues after an evening rainstorm. And much like the calm following such a storm, Axon's tensions released. She thought she smelled fresh grass and new life. How her teammates could shun the incredible gift of the Cassun Nine, Axon did not understand.

The Shul stopped speaking mid-sentence. Axon felt a shudder

through his fingertips, and she glanced up. The blood had drained from his face, leaving behind a pasty pallor like bleached stone. In his eyes, his clear haunted eyes, she saw a struggle—as if he had two competing dreams battling for his attention.

She felt a jolt in the back of her head—like the one she had felt when ... but she didn't want to think about that. Her eyes focused higher up as fiery clouds formed in the sky. They billowed and tumbled until they obscured the moonlight. With her heart pounding, she tried to push away the horrible sights. Her skin blistered under the growing heat. The Shul had disappeared, and her body lifted from the ground. Her stomach flipped as the land left her. She rose, higher and higher, until she heard it behind her.

The Beast.

Her body turned and she stared into the blood moon eyes of the foul creature. Its serpent head sat upon a neck as long as a castle tower. Black, oily tendrils writhed along its surface. Axon gazed downward—all of the world below had become a sea of thrashing, oily shapes. She had to remember to breathe.

From deep in the waters, a blue light formed. Nothing but a small dot at first, it soon grew brighter, wider, until it broke the surface with blinding light. Beautiful and terrifying blinding light.

The Shul's grip on her hands tightened, and Axon's eyes snapped open.

The oily sea, the fiery clouds, the blinding light, and the Beast itself —all gone. She knelt before the Shul in the open-air temple, and her racing heart pulsed against her chest. The full moon cast its light upon them, creating gentle shadows across the stone.

"Please," she said. "Let go."

His grip tightened. "Your kingdom is a blasphemy."

"What?" She tugged at her hands, but the Shul refused to release her. "What's going on?"

With a vicious snarl, he bared his teeth, and in a voice not his own, he said, "The worthless below celebrate a victory while I am the foot that crushes you all."

The old Shul rose, never letting Axon free, and arched his head back to look at the sky. Axon fought the urge to knee the Shul in the groin and force his grip loose. Her mind swirled with the strange images she had seen, and part of her thought that perhaps the images had continued. Perhaps none of this really happened at all.

But then the Shul's head split open. A crack formed on his forehead and carved a jagged path down the middle of his body. He screamed like a beaten child until the crack cut through his throat. His voice diminished into a quiet gurgle. And then no sound at all.

Pushing out of the top of his skull, a dark creature spewed forth like an insect breaking through a chrysalis. But this was no delicate butterfly. This was a servant of the Beast.

The creature appeared to be composed of the waste and sludge of the world—its malleable body as foul as the stench floating off of its repulsive skin. As the Shul fell to the stone floor, Axon's hands were freed.

She jumped back and pulled her sword. Instinct and well-trained muscle memory kept her going. She learned long ago that luck often played a crucial role in battle. This proved no different.

The vile thing that birthed itself from the Shul's body made the mistake of raising its head toward the statues towering over it. Perhaps it thought they were creatures in their own right. Axon took full advantage.

As she launched forward and swung her blade across the muscular, foul neck of the creature, as its head tumbled away from its shoulders, as it slumped over and sprayed clumps of oily goo on the ground, she wondered if luck had nothing to do with it at all. Perhaps the Cassun Nine smiled upon her. Perhaps the blue light she had seen confirmed what she wanted to believe in—her true mission, her calling.

But those thoughts would have to wait. Screams cried out from the town below.

CHAPTER TWO

Leaping down the temple stairs two at a time, she looked toward the small grouping of buildings. People scattered like ants abandoning a destroyed hill. She mounted Weaver and galloped toward the danger. Bursting into the town center as frightened folks raced by, heading for their homes or the dark edges beyond, Axon hopped to the ground. Adrenaline fought off the horror of what had happened at the temple. She expected more fighting would help distract her further.

Henlio and Xarad ushered people toward safety while Pilot clashed his blade against the thick arms of a second sludge-like creature. Axon dashed forward, attacking from the side, and slid her blade into the creature's flank. Like cutting through thick custard, she felt no resistance of bone or muscle—just mass.

"Oh, good. You decided to join the party after all," Pilot said, firelight dancing across his brash face.

The creature wrenched to the side, knocking Axon back several feet. She glanced toward Xarad. Though he could be a good fighter when necessary, he looked as pale as the Shul had right before the man died.

"Find Bellemont," Axon said and Xarad rushed off.

Henlio lunged forward, his robes flowing behind him. He joined Pilot in another assault on the creature. The two fighters alternated attacks, but the creature matched these blows with ease.

A muscular woman pushing her way through the crowd halted and grabbed her head. She screamed with such intensity that a circle formed around her, giving her a large area to call her own. Axon knew what would happen. Before she could take more than three steps, the woman's head split open.

The dark cracks formed down her body. The skin and bone and muscle peeled away. Another creature formed, stinking of rot and waste. It crawled out of the corpse's shell.

When the nervous townsfolk trying to leave witnessed this horror, their fear ratcheted up. A full-on stampede broke out.

"Over here," Xarad called. He stood by Bellemont who knelt in the dirt. With both creatures advancing, Axon, Henlio, and Pilot gave ground—but slowly and making sure to strike with their swords as much as possible.

Axon snatched a peek back at Bellemont. She saw the Dacci witch dig out her special clamp. The young woman's strips of black fluttered as she took the small clamp under her veil and into her mouth. Barely wincing, she locked onto a tooth and yanked it free. Blood dripped from beneath the veil. She laid the tooth on the ground in front of her.

Axon heard the garbled cry of the creature. She lashed out with her sword before her head had turned back to the fight. The creature's arm took the blow, but it countered with a punch from its good arm, catching Axon in the shoulder. Henlio struck the creature from the side, saving Axon from a further attack.

"I'll handle this abomination," he said, launching into a flurry of blows.

She looked toward Bellemont again. From a leather pouch, the witch pulled out a decaying rat. She dumped the rat onto the tooth and placed her hands over the pile.

Xarad waved Axon over. "She's just about ready. Hurry."

Axon took one final swipe at the creature before tapping Henlio and Pilot to run. They sprinted across the town square, heading straight for Xarad and Bellemont. She could hear the thumps of the large creatures behind her. She could hear the thump of her own heartbeat. But she never heard the magic ignite. However, when they all reached Bellemont, the witch stood with her hands held wide.

"It's a shield," Xarad said.

Pilot wiped sweat from his face. "I didn't think she was making a giant hug."

The two foul creatures slammed into the shield, bits of their tar-like bodies spread against the invisible barrier, and they roared in frustration. Panting and sweating, Henlio turned his back on the creatures. He scratched under his beard and offered a short nod.

"How long can she maintain this thing?" he asked Xarad.

"Long enough for you to do something constructive." Xarad flicked a hand at Pilot. "Maybe you can find some way to kill those things. Y'know, like you're supposed to. Or maybe you need a hug."

Pilot said, "Maybe I'll throw you out there and you can act as a diversion while we leave. You might die, but that won't be a big loss."

Axon snapped her fingers at them. "I fought one up at the temple. I beheaded it."

"It seems they keep making more."

"Then a lot of heads will fall."

The two creatures joined hands which became a solid, muddy trunk between them. They charged forward and slammed their shared arm into the shield. The air around Axon vibrated.

Henlio wiped his brow with the bottom of his robe. "Even if Belle-mont can hold that shield a long time, I get the feeling they can break through it."

Pilot snickered. "Figured that all out, did you?"

"Why must you always make jokes when we're fighting?"

"Quiet. Both of you." Axon had no time for their nervous banter. She glanced at Bellemont. The Dacci witch had her eyes closed and her arms up like a sturdy wood carving. But her mouth twitched, her chin quivered, and the tips of her fingers shivered. She would not be able to hold on for too much longer.

The air within the shield grew humid. Axon saw Xarad break out in sweat while the others continued to pant hard. They should have regained their breath from the battle, yet that did not seem to happen. In fact, Axon noticed her own breaths felt labored in the thickening air.

To clear her thoughts, she looked off towards the darkened hills. She hoped to see the townspeople watching from safety. Instead, she saw a single figure wearing strips of black cloth and a veil like Bellemont. Another Dacci witch. A wide, white stripe had been painted from her forehead up, over her headpiece, and back. Dacci witches often painted themselves to intimidate.

It certainly makes them look fierce, Axon thought.

She locked eyes with the witch. Even with the distance between them and the night surrounding them, those eyes pierced straight through—even through the shield—cutting into Axon, striking an eerie touch at her heart. With her fingers tightened around the hilt of her sword, Axon bolted off toward the hill. She heard the confused calls of her teammates, but her focus on the witch pushed all else aside.

When she neared the bottom of the hill, the witch lifted her veil and smiled wide. She had cast so many spells that only a handful of teeth remained. Her mouth puckered inward as she let loose a cold laugh, one that promised to haunt Axon's dreams for years to come. It crawled out of the witch's throat like a mass of insects escaping a destroyed nest. The gnarled woman spit on the ground before running off.

Axon shot up the hill, her legs pumping hard, but she never made it to the top. From the town square, she heard the wailing shriek of the creatures. She stopped to look back and witnessed both of them blow apart like miniature volcanoes. Their oily, tar bodies spread across the town square, raining muddy sludge in small pieces.

Bellemont let her shield drop and fell to her knees. Pilot and Henlio raced around the town square to make sure the creatures would not reform. They poked the mounds of sludge with their swords and waited for a reaction. None came.

As Axon returned, so did many of the townsfolk. Cautious at first, but soon many people stepped out of their homes or from the fields. They lifted their voices to cheer on the heroes who had saved them once again.

But Axon halted. Her face dropped.

She could not hear the cheering. She could not see the smiles. The acrid odor of the dead creatures did not invade her senses. All of it vanished as her mind tried to understand what she saw before her.

Xarad. His body. Crumpled in a ball. Dead. From within Belle-mont's protective shield.

PART II
ZEV

CHAPTER ONE

Zev Asterling raised the new weapon up to his shoulder as had been described in the instructions that came with it. The backend, carved out of wood, sat firmly in place as he held the weapon straight out. The long metal tube reached further than his arms. Two prongs stuck upon the top acted as a method of lining up his aim. The weapon weighed more than expected, more than a sword —people would have to get used to that and build up some upper-arm strength.

He had set two glass bottles on a fallen log about twenty feet into the dead field. Double checking his aim, he inhaled slowly and then exhaled even slower. When he reached the bottom of his breath, he squeezed the trigger.

The weapon roared with a flash of fire. A chunk of the log, several hands' width to the left of the bottles, spit into the air. Zev lowered the weapon and glowered at the bottles as they mocked him.

With a tentative shake in his voice, Mayor Adler leaned forward from the porch bench. "Looks like it's getting better. You managed to hit the log this time."

Zev reset the weapon in the shoulder, took aim again, and squeezed off the second shot. He hit the log again—a little closer to the bottles this time. It would definitely take some practice. Rubbing his shoulder, he expected to be bruised by morning. Practice would help with that, too.

He walked back to the porch. Though his house lacked the fancy gables of most houses—for Bieck's sake, it lacked a second floor—it kept him dry in the rain and warm in the snow. Plus, during the hot months, the porch offered plenty of shade. He needed little more.

"That is a magical weapon," Mayor Adler said. The tubby man wore the embroidered blue vest and wide-brimmed hat of his office with pride. They marked him as a man of the town government. Zev thought that pride highly misplaced.

Fernbund was an inconsequential place filled with noisy and nosy people. Yet even this far away from town, they still managed to come to his door to pester him.

With a humble chuckle, the Mayor said, "I suppose you know why I'm here."

"No. Don't much care, either." Zev pressed the ammunition release and a small box slid out the left side. Next to the packaging the weapon had arrived in, a small container held several more rounds. He picked up two and reloaded the box before sliding it back into the weapon.

"Well," the Mayor said, "it's just that we have a small problem in town and hoped you would be able to help. But I can see you're busy with that incredible—what do you call it again?"

"I don't call it anything. But folks from the East call it a *rifle*. My brother sent it to me."

"I didn't know you had a brother."

"Why should you?"

"Yes, well, anyway, you see, normally I wouldn't bother you with such a thing—after all, we have the Temple Shul to handle our disputes and needs and such, except that Shul Farrar has taken ill."

"You're coming to me with a religious problem?"

"Not at all. This is about some missing pies."

Zev rested the rifle across one shoulder as he strode back for more target practice. "Not interested." He set the rifle in position once more and took aim. Then he waited.

Mayor Adler said, "I don't think you understand. These pies—"

Bang.

"That is to say, the person who made the pies—"

Bang.

A little closer but the bottles remained untouched. Heading back to the porch, he glanced up from beneath the brim of his hat—the Mayor sat there, waiting. "You're still here?" He reloaded the weapon.

Forcing a smile as he tapped his fingers against his knees, Mayor Adler said, "Believe me, Mr. Asterling, I would never have come out here if I didn't have to. These pies—they were made by Mrs. Byrne."

Zev stepped closer, towering over the Mayor. Gazing down, he said, "How about you start again—and this time, though I know it will be difficult for you, I want you to be honest."

Mayor Adler swallowed hard. "Like I said, somebody stole Mrs. Byrne's pies—cottleberry, if I'm not mistaken."

"Last chance—the truth."

"I am telling the truth. Her pies were stolen. And her husband asked me to come out here to talk to you about it."

Zev stepped back, set the rifle properly in his shoulder, and aimed it at the Mayor. "You're not here because of Mrs. Byrne's pies. You came here because her husband runs the bank that holds title to this farm. You were sent here because he's mad at me. He doesn't like what I've done with this place. None of you do."

Closing his eyes, Mayor Adler said, "You tried cattle for meat, osarrets for clothing—both died out. And based on how brown all of your crops look, your attempts at growing vegetables and grains are not going so well."

"So rather than do his own dirty work, Byrne sends you to try to intimidate me. Do I look intimidated?"

Keeping his eyes closed, the Mayor went on, "It's my job to look after the welfare of this town. We need all the farms to pull their weight. I'm sure Mr. Byrne is concerned about his investment, but I'm not here for him."

"One more dishonest word out of you and I swear I'll pull the trigger. You go back to Byrne and tell him this farm belongs to me. I'll make my payments to him and if I don't, he can come and try to take this place away from me himself. And as for you, nowhere in my purchase of this land did it say I had to actually succeed as a farmer. If the town can't survive without one farm, then the town doesn't deserve to survive. Now go tell him that. And then you should go home and pray to Ovlar and Bieck that I don't ever see you again like this."

With his head turned to the side and his face scrunched together, the Mayor said, "If you would please move the, um, the rifle away from my face."

Zev lowered the weapon and stepped back toward the front door like a sentry ready to block admittance. Mayor Adler stood and readjusted his vest and hat. Zev allowed the man to regain some dignity. As the Mayor lifted his chin and marched off, however, he stumbled twice before reaching his coach.

Once seated, he immediately snapped the reins at his horses. "I was only trying to help."

Wiping his brow, Zev watched as the Mayor drove down the dry, dirt road. Dust kicked up into the air and weaved between the dying crops. Zev wondered if Mayor Adler's horses knew how good they had it—wearing blinders to focus their attention forward. Always focused on the road ahead.

He set the rifle on the porch and entered his house. He liked the new weapon. A lot. If only it hadn't come from his brother.

Pulling the stopper off his last bottle of water, he poured the drink into a mug. He had hoped he could avoid going down to the river for fresh water until the morning, but the evening heat continued to rise. It would be a long time before things cooled.

He sat at his wooden table, tipped back the warm water, and closed his eyes. The letter from his brother that had accompanied the rifle sat on the table. He picked up a writing lead, pulled over a piece of paper, and wrote *My dear brother Marcel* at the top. Then he stared at the paper.

A dark grin crawled across his lips. He wrote—

I am no fool. While I find your gift to be charming, and out here a rifle has many practical uses that I can think of, there is no doubt in my mind that this so-called gift is no more than a bribe or, at best, a lure to bring me home. But I have had enough of kings and princes, corporations and business, money and banks. You and father have my blessing to continue investing in those new market exchanges, to continue politicking for another percentage point, to continue whatever it is you men think your lives are worth spent, but do not expect me to participate. For I am happy here on the Frontier. I've successfully raised livestock, grown crops, and have found a welcome home in Fernbund. I have peace in my solitude.

Zev crumpled up the paper and let it burn over a candle. He refolded his brother's letter and placed it back in the envelope. Crossing to his bedside table, he pulled out a wooden box and added the letter to the numerous other ones Marcel had sent. After placing the box back, Zev returned to the table and drank the last of his water.

Something gnawed at him—something about berry pie. A moment later, he pulled another clean piece of paper, picked up his lead, and wrote—

Dear Mrs. Byrne,

As I understand it, in order for a cottleberry pie to attain its special balance of sweet and spicy, it requires two days to cure after it has been cooked. I would expect that you set them out on your back patio table. You would not want the pies left out in any other room of the house, not with the risk that your children might knock them down, ruining the pies and staining your floors. And while the kitchen is a plausible location, it also varies in heat throughout the day as you cook your family's meals. This is not ideal for the curing process.

So, the back patio is your only sensible choice. Now, the back of your home is where your garden can be found, is close to the kitchen door, and is well fenced in. A perfectly reasonable place to let these delightful pies cure in the fresh air. As the banker's wife, you don't have to leave the house to work because he takes care of all your financial needs. So, again, I expect you were home and had the pies stolen from under you.

This means that your thief had to have access to the back part of your house at a time when he or she knew you would not be there or in the kitchen (from where you could easily see the pies). Whether you are aware of it or not, most people's daily habits are fairly predictable. Anyone who lives with or near you would know them intimately. In particular, Shul Farrar comes to mind. And since he participates in religious instructions at the schoolhouse, he would know when your children are home or at school, too.

Now, I'm not insensitive to the idea that accusing the holy Shul might cause some problems, but I guarantee that he is your culprit. No other person could enter your house without causing some kind of ruckus. But if you found the Shul in your kitchen one day, he could simply sit down and start praying with you, and all would be well. Plus, Shul Farrar lives next door and would have ample opportunity to acquire the pies. Furthermore, Shul Farrar is known to have a fondness for cottleberry pie. And finally, as I understand it, the Shul has been ill the last day or so which suggests he could not wait for them to cure properly and ate them.

One should never eat cottleberry pie before it's cured properly. I suspect if you look in on him you'll find his illness directly related to the pie—a slight darkening discoloration in the lips is a telltale sign.

Zev Asterling

He considered adding more to the letter—perhaps a few words to smooth over the harsh message he had sent Mayor Adler with—but he set the lead on the table. No good would come from it. Zev had known Mr. Byrne's reputation long before he agreed to take the loan for the farm. The man did not like missed payments.

Zev could still hear his father on the day he cashed out his interests in the various Asterling companies. "If you go out to the Frontier, you'll be wasting away your fortune. Don't think there will be more money coming from here."

Zev never answered his father. He took his money and left. At the time, it seemed more than enough to last two lifetimes. But failing with livestock and failing with crops had left him with no income.

Still, begging Mr. Byrne for leniency would only end with the man tightening the noose.

For Bieck's sake, Mr. Byrne would most likely take the letter to be a bribe. Doubtful that he expected Zev to actually solve the case—probably only cared that his wife got her pies back. But Zev did not write the letter to appease Mr. Byrne. At least, he didn't think so.

Shaking off his spiraling thoughts, he stuffed the letter into an envelope, scrawled on the address, and headed to the post drop at the edge of his property. As he slid the letter into the drop slot, he heard a distinct clapping in the distance—a galloping horse.

A dark woman on a darker horse raced towards him. She wore the armor of a warrior—thick and protective yet with enough give to keep her agile in the heat of battle. She had a sword strapped to her back, a shield tied to the side of the horse, two daggers in her belt, and at least one other strapped to her calf.

Behind her, attached to her saddle, she had her kit and a large, glowing blue blob slung across like a body. Magic kept it locked tight to the horse—perhaps the fortunes of a good hunt. It barely bounced with the rhythm of the hooves.

She thundered down the dirt road and pulled the horse hard to halt in front of him. Blazing eyes glared down as she looked him over. "I'm told you are the best at solving crimes."

Shaking his head, Zev turned back toward his house.

"For the safety of our realm," she said, speaking in that restricted tone of somebody raised within the kingdom walls, "for the honor of our great King Robion, I ask for your help."

Over his shoulder, Zev said, "Not interested."

The woman kicked her horse into motion. She trotted up behind him. "This man has been murdered."

Zev paused. He looked back and saw that, indeed, the blue blob contained a man locked in a magic-induced stasis. Placing one hand on the horse's rump to avoid startling the animal and accidentally getting kicked, Zev stepped closer to the body. A quick glance told him enough.

The man wore a plain cloak and his hair had been cut close to the skull. A squire, perhaps. Hard to tell with the blue swirls of magic obscuring his view. If not a squire, then a Shul's apprentice. Whatever the case, this woman would not be the only one Zev would have to deal with. A simple letter to solve the matter would not suffice.

He lifted his head and looked directly at the woman. "No." He walked away.

In a loud, yet clearly disappointed voice, the woman said, "You'll be paid. Quite well."

He swore he heard the jingle of a coin purse. *Crap*, he thought and then chuckled—his mother would have had a heart attack if she knew he even *thought* such a foul word. Turning back to the woman on the horse, he shook his head and pointed toward the barn. "I'll take a look at him in there."

CHAPTER TWO

Zev opened the barn doors—their rusty whine bothered the horse—and gestured to an empty stall. Though the building could house six animals, all the stalls were empty. As the woman walked in, she kissed the palm of her left hand—a sign of respect toward Sazieck, God of Adult Life.

The woman removed the horse's saddle and set the animal up with some hay and water. Zev created a makeshift examining table from several large planks of wood and two sawhorses. Together, he and the woman lugged the body over for inspection.

Once the body hit the table with a thump, Zev put out his hand. "I'm Zev Asterling."

"Axon Coponiv."

"Coponiv? With the King?"

She nodded. "On private order. I don't belong to his official Guard."

"That probably works better this far south on the Frontier. Nobody cares about kings and such. You'll find people are more about religious laws than royal laws out here. But I guess that probably suits you well."

She folded her arms across her chest and jutted her chin toward the corpse. "Shall we get this started?"

The shadows of the barn made it difficult to read her dark features. She had a strong build, that much anybody could tell, and Zev had no trouble noting her sharp, angular bones. But like all people, she wore a mask—yet hers truly covered what lay behind her eyes. Most people could not do that. At least, not to Zev.

He stepped over to the body. With a glance back, he gestured to the table. Axon joined him, pulled out a green stone and pressed it against the blue stasis field. Like fat sizzling in a hot pan, the blue field burned away. The smell, however, was far from appetizing.

Zev flicked open his work knife and cut away at the victim's clothes. As he sliced the coarse fabric, he sought any sign of an entry wound. Knowing what direction the attack came from might be important.

"His name was Xarad," Axon said. She paced near the head of the table like an angry jaur ready to bare its teeth at first provocation.

"You are a warrior of some sort, right?"

Axon halted and puffed up her chest. With her eyes lifting up as if she could see through the barn into the wide sky, she said, "If we succeed in our mission, then we will be far more than a group led by a warrior. My team is filled with trained fighters and more, but we are not mercenaries nor do we roam around the land simply searching for a fight." She had a small pouch at her side, and from it, she pulled out a flask. Tipping back the metal container, she drank and winced. "Never mistake me or my team for mere warriors."

"Meant no offense. I simply noticed a lot of scars from long ago on Xarad's body."

"He's been with me for many years."

"I guess that's why you've gone to such lengths to have his death resolved."

"What do you mean by that?"

Zev straightened. "Warriors—whether insignificant or legendary—make their living by getting into dangerous situations that could cause their deaths. Surely, you have had members of your team die before. If not, then you are either novices or never get in any kinds of fights. The only other option is that you are the greatest warriors of all time to have never lost a single member of your team, and if that were the case, I would certainly have heard of you. Everybody would have. So, why is Xarad's death so important? Were you lovers?"

Axon snorted a laugh. She tipped back her flask one last time before returning it to her pouch. She moved in close to Zev—close enough that he could smell the sting of alcohol on her breath. "The Beast of the West is no longer content in its own country. There have been reports of it and its people testing our borders once again—after all these years. My team is going to see the King to get the Water Blade."

He got the clear impression she expected him to marvel at this declaration. "And?" he said.

"The Water Blade—so that we can destroy the Beast that threatens all of us. Losing a member of my team is a tragedy under any circumstance, but this is the greatest mission we've ever been charged with."

"But you're on the way to see the King?"

"That's correct."

"Yet you're saying you were charged with this mission. Who charged you, if not the King?"

"How can you not know the story of the Water Blade? It rests in Ridnight Castle. It is protected by magic. Only one worthy enough to fight the Beast, only one who actually has a chance of defeating the Beast, can take the sword. All others will be hurt by it."

Zev returned to Xarad's body. "So nobody has charged you with this task. Not yet. You hope to see the King, try for the sword, and get your mission."

Curling her top lip, she tossed the pouch of coins on the table and turned away. "This was a mistake. You can't possibly be smart enough to solve this crime when you don't even understand the basics of our people. I heard you were new to this country, and I see it's true. You should return to the East."

Zev hunched closer to the corpse. He didn't like that she kept mentioning the Beast. Because nobody in the East had ever seen the creature, it became fodder for nightmares. Descriptions of it varied greatly—a tentacled monstrosity, a giant snake oozing bile, a muscular creature with ten horns and a whipping tail. It went on and on. Growing up, it simply meant the unknown dangers lurking in the shadows. But now—Zev wondered if living in the Frontier meant he might actually find out what that thing was.

With a shake of his head, he focused on the dead man's neck. It had a puffiness that he had attributed to the distribution of weight from Xarad being on his back—but now he saw something else. "Crap. This wasn't simply a matter of dying while fighting. Xarad was murdered."

Whirling back, Axon's eyes widened. "That is exactly what I thought." She broke into a lengthy description of their final battle—of the Beast's creatures that they fought, of the protective spell Bellemont cast around them, of the way that no weapon from the outside could possibly have hurt Xarad, and of her realization that one of her own team had murdered the man.

"Do you understand?" she said. "The only way we will ever succeed in taking down the Beast, in protecting the Frontier, is if my team is a solid, unified force. But if there is a murderer among us, then we have failed before we can even begin."

"It's not quite that simple." He pointed at Xarad's neck. "This man was not attacked within your protective shield as you think. He was poisoned. Probably two or three days earlier. That is, if the poison is one of a handful I think the killer could have used. The swelling in the throat suggests a reaction to something ingested. Have you stopped to eat at an inn on the way? Come in contact with anybody who joined you at a fireside perhaps? Anything like that?"

She shook her head. "For the last week, we have traveled up through the Osbor Plains. We've seen nothing but a herd of cattle and, of course, the creature we fought. But that town—Heraldbund—that was the first contact we've had with other people in days."

"How long were you there?"

"Less than a day. The bandits they fought came upon us before nightfall."

"Then you certainly have a murderer within your ranks. I'll need to inspect Xarad more closely. Perhaps I can find the delivery method or even the specific poison used. I'll warn you that my knowledge of poisons is limited, but I'll do my best to offer some explanation by the morning." Zev paused, his work knife in hand. "You may not want to watch this next part of the examination."

"Oh?"

"Different poisons act differently upon the skin and organs. If I look inside his neck, I'll be able to narrow down the possibilities."

"But you just said—"

"I may not know all poisons but I know some."

Axon's face tightened as she raised a warning finger. Turning away, she tapped her chest as she paced. She wore a necklace of nine twined strands, each strand with nine beads. A devout Cassunite, then.

Zev did not interrupt her. He had his own behaviors when weighing, calculating, and planning his decisions. If praying to the Cassun Nine worked for her, then best to let her go through whatever process she required.

At length, she said, "You cannot cut him open. He must be brought back with me so that he can get a proper burial. To mutilate his body would be an insult to Wiq, and I will not insult the God of Death."

"If I can't look inside him—"

"How many times have you looked inside the body of a man? I doubt any. You are a terrible farmer who ran away from the East. I doubt you are a healer, nor do I think you will discover anything within him. You simply want to do this to further your own curiosities. That I understand. That is the reason you were recommended to me. You have a natural curiosity and you're probably quite smart." Axon plucked the knife out of his hand. "There are other ways to gain answers, and I have the fullest confidence you can do it without sacrilegious insults."

Folding his arms, Zev stepped back. "You obviously have something in mind."

"Tomorrow my team heads for Ridnight. You could come with us. I can concoct a plausible story that justifies you having joined our team. Perhaps as Xarad's replacement."

"You want me to pretend to be part of your team so that I can question the different members and find out who the murderer is. Is that it?"

"Looks like you are smart, after all."

Zev chuckled. "I am not a warrior. And I don't belong anywhere near a team like yours."

"Only until you reveal the killer."

"I'll be happy to examine this body all night long. If you let me, I will take a look deeper in him to figure out whatever I can. But I'm not going anywhere, and I'm certainly not going to face the Beast of the West while trying to accuse one of your seasoned fighters of murder. If you're into suicide, you go right ahead. But you'll go without me."

"You won't have to face the Beast. I only need you until we reach Ridnight. That will give you a few days to interview my team and figure out who the murderer is. Once at the castle, I will get the Water Blade and the rest of my team, the ones who are innocent, will join me and head toward the Beast. But you—you will be free to do what you want."

"I think I'd rather kill off some more crops and go hungry."

She sighed. "Just when I thought you were intelligent. Don't you think the King would be grateful? You were happy with the little bit of money I can give you here, imagine how much King Robion will give you for solving this problem."

"Why should the King care that I helped some traveling warrior?"

"I told you I'm not a mere warrior. But, unlike you, the King cares about the entire realm. How am I supposed to go fighting the Beast and saving the realm on behalf of the King if I have to keep watching my own back because one of my team might murder me? You solve this, you will have helped me, and thus, you will have helped the King. You will have helped the entire Frontier. What King wouldn't reward such a thing?"

Zev could not stop himself from peeking at the pouch of coins on the edge of the table. Money aside, he knew he would do better interviewing the team. His threats to cut open Xarad's neck had been silly.

He had never done such a thing before and knew little of what he would find inside a human body—at least, in terms of understanding a poisoning agent. He wasn't even sure why he had said those things. Perhaps she had been right. Perhaps his curiosity pushed him. Or maybe he hoped the horror of the suggestion would have sent her away. But that pouch at the end of the table—that spoke a lot more truth.

Frowning, he nodded. "It's just until we reach Ridnight."

At that moment, Axon did something that Zev would rarely see again—she smiled. "Thank you. You may have just saved everyone in the Frontier." She strode over to her horse and began the process of saddling her. "If you want, I'll leave Xarad's body here, in case you need to examine him some more. But don't cut him open."

"I won't touch him."

"The rest of my team is in town at the Inn."

"The Spring Bloom or the Long Neck?"

"This little town has two Inns?"

"Well, the Long Neck is more of a tavern with two rooms upstairs. Spring Bloom is a proper inn with a full floor of rooms. They're owned by a married couple that split up and, well, it's a long, boring story."

Axon finished prepping her horse. As she swung into the saddle, she said, "I don't know which one they picked. But after recent events, they'll need some rest. I'll bring them by tomorrow morning to pick up you and Xarad. Be ready."

With her orders given, Axon rode out of the barn and headed back to town. Zev swept the pouch of coins off the table before closing the barn doors and heading back to his home. He didn't need to see the body anymore—though he suspected he would slip back later that night to look it over again.

As he stepped onto the porch, he paused. A dark thought gurgled in his bowels. If the killer ever suspected Zev's role on the team, then the closer they got to Ridnight Castle, the more dangerous that person would become. Especially to Zev.

The coin pouch in his hand suddenly felt very light.

CHAPTER THREE

The next morning, after closing up the house, Zev brought his Eastern workhorse out from the pasture. Though not truly a horse, the Eastern workhorse looked close enough to have garnered its name. Bulkier with muscle and covered in thick, shaggy hair, Stick had the strength to pull a plow or carry a heavy load with ease. Zev had not been able to stop his herd of cattle from succumbing to disease nor could he keep his crops healthy and strong, but he had no problem taking care of Stick. The workhorse was more than just an animal to him. More than a pet, too.

As he cinched the saddle on the animal, a gentle breeze passed over the farm. For the last year, every morning began with that gentle touch as a reminder that he had freed himself from the ridiculous demands of the world in the East. That breeze often calmed him like a meditation. He inhaled the fresh air, let it fill his body, and readied to face whatever challenges came at him that day.

Stroking Stick's thick fur, Zev said, "This is going to be fine. We'll travel to Ridnight City, get to see the castle, maybe bring a killer to justice, and be done with it." Stick snorted and Zev snickered. "You think? Well, with the money I'll get from the King—oh, yeah—I'll be able to pay off Mr. Byrne. Then it won't matter what I grow or don't grow in my fields. And don't worry, I'll always make sure there's food enough for you."

He heard the rumble of four horses approaching—unmistakable as it closed in like the unwelcome crash of rock fall. Up the main road from the house, he spotted a cloud of dust, and moments later, Axon appeared with three other riders.

Zev tightened his hold on Stick's reins. Ever since they first arrived at the farm, Stick had been the only workhorse. Zev did not want him to spook when surrounded by so many other large animals.

Axon led her team right up to Zev. Glancing down from her horse, she said, "I'm going to get Xarad loaded up. I'll leave you to introduce yourselves." She trotted off and disappeared inside the barn.

Climbing down from a dappled horse with a braided mane, a sturdy-looking man approached. He wore a mixture of Eastern-inspired leathers with the Frontier version of vest and hat—though, he had the sense to wear deep green instead of blue. The stubble on his dark-skinned face and the twinkle in his bright eyes suggested he knew how to be charming as well as dangerous. "Axon said your name is Zev. Pleasure to meet you. My name's Pilot."

"Thanks for letting me join you."

"Look at this," Pilot said, patting Stick with a firm hand. "Not a bad looking Eastern. I've seen bigger back home, but this boy has a fine coat. Looks strong, too."

"He's done a good job for me."

Pilot tipped the brim of his hat as he gazed across the farm. "From the looks of it out there, he wasn't enough. You're in desperate need of us. No way to make a living growing dead plants." He glanced back at his teammates, but they did not laugh.

Sitting atop a large bay, another man nodded at Zev. This one wore a traveling robe, and a thick beard covered most of his face—made it difficult to tell where the mouth began. "I'm Henlio. Feel free to ignore Pilot. We all do."

"Very funny," Pilot said. "You're all poking fun until it comes time to swing a sword. Then everybody's happy to have Pilot hanging around."

Henlio did not take the bait. He remained quiet, leaning forward on the pommel of his saddle, and watched Zev closely. A few feet further away, a young woman rode another bay. She wore the distinct black trimmings of a witch from the West.

Though standing in the open air, Zev suddenly felt the world closing in. "You're a Dacci. Aren't you all servants of the Beast of the West? I thought he was your god."

She turned her head towards him, a black veil covering her mouth. The Dacci needed to use their own teeth to cast spells—the less teeth one had, the more experienced the witch—so they all wore veils to keep their skill level from being public knowledge. She said, "I have been with Axon for a long time. I have served her in the party well. I can cook, heal wounds, and more. But you have no right to question my loyalty."

"I didn't mean—"

"Don't worry about Bellemont," Pilot said, slapping his arm across Zev's shoulder. "She's just upset that Xarad's dead. We all are, of course, but she's the one who created the magic shield that was supposed to protect us all."

As Zev watched, Bellemont turned her mare and headed for the barn. Stick snorted, and Zev turned his attention toward calming his workhorse.

Henlio continued to stare at Zev, clearly assessing the new teammate. "It's the money, isn't it?"

"Excuse me?" Zev hoped he hid the startle in his voice.

"I'm trying to comprehend why you want to go off fighting the Beast of the West. Looking at you and this poor excuse for a farm, it is clear that you've got nothing here. Unless you're secretly rich, you owe money on the farm. Isn't that true of all you farmers? So, it's the money."

Before Zev could reply, Pilot stepped in the way. "Doesn't matter why he wants in—Axon says he's in. Besides, we can always use another fighter."

As Pilot uttered the word *fighter*, he lunged toward Zev while his fists cut back. Two body blows crumpled Zev into a ball. He rolled on the dirt, gasping, trying to relax his stomach muscles, but they gripped tighter and tighter, pulling his legs in.

At length, Zev managed to roll onto all fours. Coughing, he said, "I'm not a fighter."

"Really? I couldn't tell," Pilot said.

With a bored tone, Henlio said, "Help the man up."

Pilot put out his hand. "Sorry about that. Just wanted to see what kind of fighter you were."

Zev took Pilot's hand, and as he rose, he brought his fist right up into Pilot's gut. He pulled back his other fist ready to strike Pilot in the head, when he heard Axon's voice call out, "Enough."

All eyes looked up at their leader astride her horse, the deep scowl on her face. "Zev is our brains. He will help us with strategy and tactics. He's a smart man." Leaning closer toward Pilot, she added, "Not everybody needs to be strong enough to wield a sword."

"That's good," Pilot said, "because he won't be any use with a sword."

Pointing to both men, Axon said, "Mount up. It's time to go." She moved ahead and turned her horse to address the entire group. "Do not make the mistake of thinking this is just another job for us. We've done good work in the past by helping towns and people fight off those they can't fight themselves. But now, we are heading to Ridnight to see the King, to take hold of the Water Blade, to strike out West and destroy the Beast before it can invade the Frontier and destroy us."

As Zev mounted Stick, he peeked at the others, trying to gauge their reactions to Axon's speech. Pilot and Henlio looked bored—they must have heard these words before. He lingered on Bellemont's face but could not get a good read.

Axon continued, "Losing Xarad is tough. We all cared for him. Zev is not a replacement. But he is part of the team now, an important part, and we must treat them as such. Especially because our success relies on all of us working together. And it is in that manner which we head off to Ridnight Castle. Together." Axon wielded her sword and held it high in the air. "Together."

Pilot, Henlio, and Bellemont all raised their fists in the air and said in unison, "Together."

Nobody bothered to see if Zev had joined in.

Axon turned down the road and trotted off. The others followed in line. Except for Zev. He thought about Bellemont's eyes—they had squinted and turned away when Axon mentioned Xarad. She did not want him to see her thoughts. Not that he could, but it did not require brilliance to see that either she blamed herself for Xarad's death or she was to blame.

He dismounted and scurried onto his porch. Fumbling a moment at the door, he burst into the main room and grabbed the rifle and box of ammunition. Back outside, he mounted Stick. The ammunition box fit easily in the saddle bag. The rifle fit on his back—his brother had been kind enough to purchase the shoulder strap accessory.

"Okay, Stick, let's hurry up and join the group." Applying light pressure to his heels, Zev urged Stick onward.

CHAPTER FOUR

As they headed northward along the dirt road, as Zev's farm receded in the distance, he kept his eyes locked forward, fighting the itch to look back. The rolling hills of other farms with corn growing high and herds grazing on healthy grasses teased him with their success—but also with a sense of longing. As if his agricultural ambitions drifted behind him, too.

A short time later, a woman coming the other way drove a horseless cart. Marcel had mentioned these new contraptions in his letter accompanying the rifle, but Zev did not think he would be seeing one so soon. It consisted of four large wheels made of a light, metallic material. The wheels connected at the corners of a wood base typical on any cart, and it boasted a flatbed in the back and a special seat near the middle of the front for the driver.

Pumping her legs against a series of wheels and pulleys, the woman slipped by on the road and offered a pleasant wave. Her delightful smile brightened as the wind blew her hair back. Zev marveled that she moved with the speed of a trotting horse yet appeared to require little strain or effort.

He noted Axon's shudder and decided to use the moment as an opportunity for his investigation. Anything to stop himself from smelling the morning flowers that reminded him home waited nearby. He pushed Stick forward until he matched Axon's pace. "First time you've seen a horseless cart?" he asked.

"You'll see more the further north we go. Ridnight is not some backwoods town. They get influenced by trade with cities all over the world—including the East."

"But you don't like these machines."

"There is good and bad with all new inventions. I simply don't want to see the good of our country fade away. I don't want us to become some version of what happened in the East. It starts with losing our relationship to the land, to these animals, to an honest and hard day's work. Those changes trickle upward. We've seen it happen. The East once had kings and queens and great powerful families. Now? Governments with so many people screaming for what they want that nothing gets done. People with no lineage becoming wealthier than families that have been around for centuries. Doesn't make any sense to me."

With a bitter chuckle, Zev said, "My family would bristle at what you've said—even as they might agree with it."

"You have a lineage?"

"A long line of shoemakers and tailors. Nothing that would be considered noble. But the Asterlings have always been among the best in their trade—enough so that the Asterling name became one sought by kings all over the world. These changes that you decry have been very beneficial to my family."

"I've never heard of you."

"Unless you're working for those who clothe the King, why would you?"

Axon sat straighter in the saddle. "I suppose there will always be some who prefer these changes. But they are going to ruin this kingdom."

"I take it that your own family is connected to the kingdom? You don't strike me as the kind to have come from those living on the edge of the Frontier, farming the land without any law."

"My father worked for King Michael the Second. My mother was a wetnurse for the court. I have a sister—she grew up as a lesser-princess, eventually married a prince, and now she lives on an estate off toward the eastern border." Axon's eyes narrowed. "I have a brother, too. He's a well-educated man, and I don't get to see enough of him. He spends most of his time teaching at the University."

"Doesn't that make you a princess, too?"

"I took to fighting early, and my father understood. The rest of my family saw me as an oddity, but my father worked hard with me. I suppose he hoped that by indulging my interest in combat, he might sweat it out of me, so that I would eventually become a proper lady. But that was no life for me. Of course, being a member of the court meant that I could not join the military. It would be unseemly toward my family. So I contracted as an Enforcer of the King's Royal Laws."

"And that eventually brought you to my doorstep?"

Axon turned her head to face Zev fully on. In a strange tone, one that nagged at the back of his head, she said, "Yes. Exactly that." Before he could ask another question, she snapped her fingers toward the back. "Henlio, come here."

"What do you need?" Henlio asked as he trotted Baha up to the side.

To Zev, Axon said, "I have been friends with Henlio for many years. We even fought in the Battle of Alapia together."

Zev tried to keep from looking impressed. The Battle of Alapia marked the first attempt by the Beast to attack the Frontier. Just west of the small town of Alapia, a group of Dacci witches and soldiers marched through the night with the intent of attacking the town at dawn. A group of the King's Guard teamed with some of the Frontier to fight them off, and despite terrible losses, they succeeded. Zev had never met anybody willing to admit they had been in that battle. Until now.

Axon turned toward Henlio. "Xarad's death is a small crack in our armor right now. But if we do not mend it, it may destroy this team."

Spotting opportunity, Zev spoke up. "I agree. Henlio, how would you assess the rest of the team?"

Henlio's eyes fell upon Axon. She gave a slight nod, and he glanced over his shoulder at Pilot and Bellemont.

"Pilot's a product of the East," he said. "He enlisted and served with the Easterners for several years—until they unlawfully attacked the Frontier. Strange to think of it now. That Axon and I fought together against the Easterners, and that Pilot was somewhere fighting on the other side. But when that war ended, when we fought off the East and sent them back home defeated, Pilot did not join them. He left the military and stayed in the Frontier. Eventually, he met up with us. He's a solid soldier, an excellent fighter, and a true horse's ass. But I highly doubt that the death of anybody would cause him trouble within the group." Henlio's hand reached back and patted his saddlebag. "Besides, Pilot and Xarad were not close. Especially after the Lowbund Harvest Festival."

"Lowbund? What happened there?" Zev asked.

"Foolishness. Nothing more."

"Something must've happened. Are you saying they had a falling out there?"

"I said nothing."

Axon said, "It's no secret. At the festival, Pilot and Xarad both drank too much. They fell for the same woman, and you can imagine that it did not matter which one she chose—if she even chose one, I'm not sure—but it was doomed to end poorly."

Again, Henlio fidgeted with his saddlebag. "It always seemed like more than simple jealousy. But you'd have to ask Pilot about that. And to be honest, I would not recommend it. At least not until you've been with us for a while. He acts very joyful and friendly, but he's not about to open up to you. And if you try too early, you'll regret it."

"I appreciate the warning." Zev's gaze turned to the Dacci witch. "And Bellemont? How did you all end up with her?"

"She's one of the Stolen."

"What?" Zev's skin prickled. "I thought that was propaganda."

Axon said, "No. It really happened."

According to the stories he had heard growing up, for several years, raiding parties from the East and from the Frontier would sneak into the Feral Lands of the West and steal children. If Bellemont was one of the Stolen, she would have been brought back to the East to be raised as a proper and dutiful wife. Those responsible thought they were doing a great service—saving these children from becoming witches, from learning magic and being forced to lose their teeth and their souls in service of the Beast. How she went from an arranged marriage to a practicing Dacci witch would be a fascinating story. One that Zev knew he would have to learn.

Henlio shivered and looked away. "If there's any weak link, it's her. But the real test will be at Ridnight. If you fail to get the Water Blade, I expect that Pilot and Bellemont will abandon us."

"I know," Axon said.

Zev said, "But don't you think—"

"Leave us." Axon made a slight wave with her hand, never letting go of her reins. "I'd like to speak with my friend alone."

Zev backed away, settling Stick between the two groups—Axon and Henlio up front, Pilot and Bellemont at the rear. He knew he should have been pleased. Just a simple conversation had already unearthed plenty of information. But all he felt was the pressure of Pilot's and Bellemont's eyes on his back and the knowing belief that up ahead, Axon and Henlio plotted against him. Especially because Henlio once more glanced down to check his saddlebag.

CHAPTER FIVE

Z ev had not eaten freshly caught meat over a campfire in ages. In the East, he had lived in the city. Food came in on carts, displayed in the open market, bought for a few coins, and was prepared in a kitchen. He had read about those people on the Frontier, roughing it, living off the land, but he never experienced it until he left his home for good.

After that moment, he received more experience with the hard-scrabble life of being on the Frontier than he expected. Eating meat off a spit over a campfire was hardly the worst. And in the right company, it could be a warm and close experience.

But this wasn't the right company.

This group spent most of their time eating in silence. Pilot had hunted a few small animals and Bellemont skinned them for cooking. But other than a couple of comments about their quality work, the team ate and let their eyes watch the darkening night.

If he intended to actually do his job, Zev had to say something to get them talking, but his mind could not find a way to get the conversation moving. He felt like he aimed for glass bottles on a log and didn't even have a heavy rifle to hold. Just throwing stones blindly.

"I was wondering about the battle you all fought before hiring me," he said and instantly regretted the words. That wasn't throwing stones blindly. That was throwing knives at his own throat.

All eyes fell upon him. Nobody ate further. Even their chewing stopped.

At length, Axon said, "We faced minions of the Beast. Creatures made of foulness. And a witch, too."

Henlio puffed his chest out. "You've been hired for your brains—to help us with tactics and such. I certainly hope you're better at reading a battlefield than you are at reading this group."

"I've got to agree with fur-face," Pilot said, "and I hate to agree with him. If you're smart, you'll apologize, shut up, and eat your meal. I kind of hope you're an idiot, though. We might have some real fun cutting open your corpse."

Zev lowered his head slightly. "Sorry. I meant no offense."

"Don't let it ruin your meal. I wasn't serious about the corpse thing. That's way too macabre for my taste."

Though Pilot chuckled, Zev remained still. He stared at the remnants of small game still cooking on the spit. That seemed a better place to be at the moment.

Tossing his bones into the fire, Zev let out a short sigh. He had thought that with just a few words, he would discern all the important information, toy with it for a short time, and deduce who had murdered Xarad. In all the situations he had helped the town, that seemed to be the way of things. He had never come across so many people trying to obfuscate their own history. But not only did he have to struggle for every bit of information he required, but he could not forget the most important fact—one of these people gnawing bones around the campfire, one of them was a murderer.

He watched the eyes of each member of the team. He searched their faces—as much as he could see of Bellemont's—but found nothing that gave away the solution. How could he? Every single one of them had killed something or someone before. They all had that same cold-bloodedness needed to battle monsters. Only one of them had taken it beyond and turned the blade on their own.

"I'm going to sleep," Henlio said, rolling on his back.

And with that, everyone settled in for the night.

The last time Zev slept under the stars, he had just purchased his new farm. Back then, the night had been cool and the small house humid. So, he stretched out on his porch and slept with the moonlight. The air had been fresh with the minty scent of marmol trees mixing with the musty odor of ten head of newly-purchased cattle. He listened to the soft grunts and moos and fell asleep with dreams of all the success his farm would soon have.

This time, however, he stared at the moonlit sky and the failures trailed behind him. The cattle, the crops, the financial ruin of the farm —it all added up to nothing. Instead of cows mooing with potential, he listened to Axon and Henlio snoring. Instead of crops standing firm, Pilot stood guard with his back to the dying campfire. Even the pleasant smell of smoldering wood did little to comfort Zev.

They had pitched camp near the edge of the Garnic Forest. A large boulder gave them some protection, though they did not expect bad weather that night. More than weather, Zev understood that the boulder blocked one side of attack. They only had to guard against the other three.

And Zev couldn't help but think that if not for a prized pig, he would be at home, snuggled safe in his bed. He chuckled. The prized pig.

He had been a farmer for less than two weeks when his neighbor, Mr. Borenby, caused an uproar in the town—somebody had stolen his prized pig, Myrtle. Plenty of evidence pointed to those from the Feral Lands. While in town to purchase some supplies, Zev heard the story and thought it too conveniently obvious. As far as scapegoats went, the Dacci made easy targets—they were looked down upon, thought of as sneaky and untrustworthy, and feared for their mysterious powers. But from what Zev had read about them, he knew they were smart, careful, and strategic. If they wanted to steal a pig, they would not have left anything behind to implicate themselves.

Without any law enforcement around, Zev worried things might get out of hand fast. He knew people often reacted first and thought later. Spouting off his concerns, several people in town listened carefully and challenged him to come up with proof that the thief could be anybody else. At the same time, Mr. Borenby and several others gathered weapons to form a war party.

Zev went to Mr. Borenby's home, looked over the pig stall, and found the answer pressed into the pig's droppings. A man's left footprint—probably too large to be Dacci and definitely of a Frontier shoe —and next to it the clear hole of a wooden peg. Mr. Merrick, a pig farmer from one town over, had lost his right leg in the Battle of Alapia.

And that was it. From that moment on, the people of Fernbund anointed Zev as the smartest man in town. Whenever they could, they dared to visit his farm and beg for his help to solve their problems— no matter how minor. No doubt, that reputation had caught the ear of Axon and brought her to his farm, as well.

And Axon brought him to the point of sleeping under the stars, on the hard ground, with the slim hope that he would solve a crime based on little evidence and with little time left.

Sitting up on his elbow, Zev glanced off to where Bellemont sat facing the fire. He had never managed a good look at her. During the entire day's journey, she had hung in the back, and once they made camp, she hurried off to hunt small game for dinner.

But watching her stare into the fire, he focused on her eyes. Her Dacci veil covered the rest of her face, anyway. Those eyes, though— they held both a soft allure and a frightening intensity. He thought of the old tales of the wooly gareth. People often would stumble upon a mother with its cubs by accident. Supposedly, the mother gareth would stare with that same mixture of calm and caring blended with vicious threat. If true, then Bellemont's eyes would be the closest Zev would ever come to witnessing such a thing. The wooly gareth had been extinct for several centuries.

"I can't sleep either," he said.

Without moving the rest of her body, Bellemont shifted her head slightly in his direction. She held his attention for a few seconds before returning her gaze upon the fire.

Zev lowered back down, rested his head on his rolled-up pack, and tried to sleep once again. But sleep would not come. If his mind did not tumble over his past, then it rushed through what little he knew about his current search for a murderer.

He heard a rustling. Keeping his eyes closed, he perked his attention toward the sound. He heard it again. Probably just an animal foraging near the edge of the woods. Probably.

But then he heard a stick snap. He sat up. Pilot did not seem concerned by the noise. Zev settled back down and closed his eyes.

Three more sounds interrupted the quiet. Zev scrambled to his feet and headed toward Pilot. He never got to warn the man. The attack came from three different sites.

Two Dacci witches emerged from the tree line like living shadows stepping out of a dark cave. Both wore the black strips of cloth and face veils, but one witch had a white line running down the middle. On either side of the camp, two armed soldiers appeared. Dacci soldiers constructed their armor from the bones scattered throughout their country—carrion, loved ones, and, of course, their enemies.

Zev was so focused upon the arrival of this threat, he never noticed Axon and Henlio waking. When Axon spotted the witch with the white line, she brandished her sword and shield, yelled, and charged forward. Pilot, Henlio, and Bellemont all drew swords as well. They stepped into balanced fighting stances and prepared for the attack.

In the seconds all of this transpired, the animalistic side of Zev's brain assumed control. Adrenaline flashed through his veins. He bit his bottom lip as his eyes searched for the safest place to take cover.

Axon swung for the witch and the team let loose a loud warcry before charging their opponents. Zev grabbed hold of his rifle and ducked behind a pile of equipment—clothing, food stores, and everything else the horses hauled during the day.

He clutched the rifle against his chest hard enough to leave an indent. He struggled to breathe. A muscle in his neck convulsed. Just on the other side of the barrier, Axon and her team fought.

He listened to the clang of swords, the grunts of punches, and the shrieks of soldiers being wounded. He had to help. He knew it through his bones. But he had never been in a fight like this before. Two fistfights—that was all he had experienced in his life. One in a tavern; one as a schoolboy.

With a slow breath, he forced his fingers to relax. Fear crawled up his throat like a parasite attempting to overtake its host. But he swallowed it back down.

He rolled onto his knees, swung the rifle atop the supplies, and scanned the battlefield. On his left, Pilot and Bellemont traded blows with two soldiers. To the right, Henlio clashed swords with two soldiers as well. And straight up the middle, Axon stood with her sword held high. She appeared to be locked like a statue. In front of her with a cocky glint in her eyes, the Dacci witch with the white stripe stood.

Zev wanted to help Axon, but his lack of shooting ability suggested a nearer target would be more successful. He turned his focus toward Henlio. If a bullet could wound one of the soldiers, Henlio would easily handle the other. But lining up a shot that kept moving proved far more difficult than staring at glass bottles on a log.

Forcing himself to be patient, Zev waited until the soldier stood firm. Following the procedure from the rifle's instructions, Zev exhaled and squeezed the trigger.

Wherever the bullet hit, it did not hit the target. The loud report of the rifle, however, shocked the soldiers. The horses reared back and neighed with fear before galloping into the night.

During the seconds that the soldiers tried to understand what kind of magic made the loud sound, Henlio took advantage. He leapt upon one distracted soldier, slicing across the man's back. As blood splashed into the air, Zev dropped behind the supplies.

He heard Henlio's roar followed by the other man's cry. But the second sound cut short. Thoughts of the soldier's death flooded Zev's mind. Wincing, he shoved those gruesome images away and buried his focus on reloading his weapon.

Flicking the release mechanism, he pulled out the ammunition box. But he used too much force and the entire piece fell to the ground. With shaking hands, he fumbled the box from the dirt and back into the rifle.

"Pilot!" Henlio's low voice called out. A screech of metal against metal responded.

Setting his weapon down, Zev lowered to his hands and knees and crawled toward his saddlebag. However, when he pulled out the fresh ammunition, three bullets jingled out of the bag and rolled off on the ground.

Zev closed his eyes and cursed. He heard Axon bellow commands but the words made no sense. Pilot responded with guttural noises. The entire fight played out like an orchestrated piece of music but one built on dissonance, chaos, and terror.

As he gathered the bullets and stuffed them into his pocket, his eyes fell upon Henlio's saddlebag. Zev had not been brought along as a fellow warrior. Axon had never expected him to fight in any form. He had been brought for one purpose—solve the murder.

He crawled back toward his rifle and peeked over the supplies once more. Two soldiers were dead—one on either side of the camp. Zev could not locate the two Dacci witches and suspected they had run off. If he intended to inspect Henlio's bag, he would have to do so immediately. Axon and Henlio alone could handle the last two, but they also had Pilot and Bellemont. The battle could end at any moment.

Zev hustled back to the saddlebag and opened the flap. The smell hit him first—a ripe, rancid odor. He closed the flap to check that he had not accidentally opened Bellemont's saddlebag. Dacci witches always carried foul-smelling ingredients in order to cast spells. But he had the right bag after all.

A quick search, while breathing through his mouth, found many expected items—bits of bread, some snacks for the horse, sword sharpening kit, a small journal, some clothes. But one item was not expected—the split skull of the trubrat. No bigger than a thumb, the skull had been tied intricately into a pouch that connected to a necklace. Zev wondered if Henlio and Bellemont had a deeper relationship. This necklace might be a gift for Bellemont or even from her.

The fighting continued, though the number of sword clashes had diminished. Zev shoved the skull back in the bag and closed the flap. As he scooted back toward his rifle, he saw Pilot's saddlebag.

With a fast motion, he dug into the back and found a clear glass bottle stoppered with cork. Inside, it had been filled halfway with a dark, oily goo. Even with the stopper, Zev could tell the horrible smell originated from this substance.

"Come on," Henlio said. "We can catch them."

"Nobody leaves," Axon said. "Zev? Come on out."

Zev's face wrinkled as if he had bitten into a sour turnberry. Emerging from behind the supplies, he carried his rifle in one hand. Despite knowing he had nothing to feel guilty about, that all the members of the team knew he was not a fighter, that Axon knew his real purpose for being there, he still felt pangs of shame over his poor performance during the battle.

Axon gestured to the dead body at her feet—one of the soldiers. "Time to make use of your brain."

Though Zev had spent over a year living in the Frontier, he had never seen a soldier from the Feral Lands up close. In many ways, the man looked stranger than the Dacci witches.

For one thing, the Dacci soldier wore armor fashioned from animal bones. The armor had a thick texture, and though it protected the soldier from many serious attacks, Zev suspected it would not stop a bullet. Someday, the Eastern government would get fed up with playing nice. Someday this armor would become a relic of a dead society.

Despite the rather primitive nature of the armor, Zev found the man's physique and hygiene to be sufficiently modern. Clearly, Dacci soldiers kept themselves in prime condition. The man's taut skin and muscular frame spoke to that. Unlike the Dacci witches, the soldier had no definitive odor. Apparently only the witches carried rotting flesh on their person.

Pilot said, "Is he just going to stand there?"

Without looking away from the body, Zev said, "First step, visual inspection."

"It's a dead Dacci soldier. What more do you need to see?"

"For a start, his skin is notably unblemished. Not much in the way of scratches or cuts—other than those inflicted in the last few minutes. Is it possible this was his first battle?"

Henlio said, "Anything's possible when you're dealing with the Feral Lands. Those people spend so much time scraping by to survive, they don't understand what real civilized people do."

Before Pilot could start complaining, Zev went ahead and patted his hands on the clothes of the corpse. He found a few coins in one pocket, several colorful stones in another pocket, and in the last he found a folded piece of paper.

Even before he plucked the paper loose and opened it up, instinct warned him this would be bad. After opening it, he found instinct had been correct. He stared at a hastily drawn map of the area. A single line traced around from his farm all the way to Ridnight City.

Showing the map to Axon, Zev said, "That is the route we're planning on taking, correct?"

She nodded.

"Then they knew we'd be here."

Bellemont stared at the paper map. "How could they possibly know our route?"

"That's a good question," Henlio said, folding his arms as he leaned toward Bellemont.

"Your insinuations do not make me nervous. I have nothing to hide. I certainly did not betray this group."

"I said nothing. It might be that you are feeling guilty about something?"

Axon stepped forward. She folded the map and tucked it in her pocket. "Get our horses and pack up. Fast. We leave now."

CHAPTER SIX

Stick had always been a strong creature willing to work through long hours of the day. But on the farm, the work ceased when the sun went down. The tough animal had never been on a forced march before, picking his way through the darkened woods with only the horse in front to guide him. Zev stroked Stick's neck and hoped his favorite workhorse would be okay.

He tightened his coat against the nighttime cold and lowered his head to avoid getting hit by branches. Stick's heavy scent brought a little comfort of home, and Zev patted the animal again. Though his hands had stopped shaking from the attack, he could still hear the horrible sounds of fighting and dying. He inhaled Stick's musty aroma once more and sighed.

Trying to clear his head, Zev turned his focus to the murder. A morbid smile drifted across his face at the idea that he found pondering a murder the best way to calm his nerves. But nothing else that went on in the party did not involve him. If he solved the murder, he could get paid and go home. Besides, the challenge of it got his heart pumping and his brain firing off like nothing else. Unfortunately, with what little information he had gathered so far, he could not draw a definitive conclusion.

Pilot had disliked Xarad and competed with him for female attention. However, the entire team knew that. Not a good way to go about killing somebody when everyone knew your motivation. Plus, Pilot did not strike Zev as the kind of man who would go for the subtlety of poison.

Henlio, on the other hand, had a healthy balance of viciousness and self-control. He exhibited the former when battling two soldiers at once and displayed the latter with his close counsel reserved for Axon. Zev found it easy to picture—Henlio could identify a target, muster the hatred necessary for murder, and the patience to use poison. He also had some kind of relationship with Bellemont that may have gone beyond being in the same fighting unit—whether it was hatred, love, or a weird combination, Zev could not figure out. But Henlio lacked any strong motivation against Xarad, and his long friendship with Axon made it difficult to believe that he would undercut her efforts by sabotaging the team.

As a Dacci witch, Bellemont had plenty of marks against her. However, Axon trusted the young woman and believed in her loyalty. If Bellemont was actually one of the Stolen, though, she may have had strong reason to betray the group. She also, quite simply, might not be all that sane.

Stick snorted, and Zev placed a hand on the animal's neck once more. "I agree. Looks like they're all suspect."

Out of the darkness, Axon appeared, riding her horse up alongside Zev. Strands of moonlight cutting through the canopy glistened upon her dark skin, transforming her with an ethereal glow. Back in the East, Zev had met many bosses and managers. They relied on financial incentive and lust for power to motivate. Not Axon. She exuded the confidence, capability, and intelligence that molded true loyalty from her team. She was a born leader.

Which made this murder even stranger.

"Sorry about the night march," she said. "We'll end up at the castle quicker, but you'll lose time to do your job."

"It's all about getting as much information as possible. Once the information is there, then I simply have to figure out how the pieces are connected."

"You've examined the body and you have my team at your disposal to question. Is there something else I can get for you? Tell me what you need."

"If I knew what I needed, I'd already know who killed Xarad. That's why it's important to get as much information as I can. Even things that don't seem important."

Axon licked her lips as she stared ahead into the dark forest. Zev decided not to prod her. The little he knew of her suggested that if he pushed, she would resist. Better to let her choose to open up. And if she chose to shut down, instead, that might tell him a lot, too.

They stayed silent for a while, and he could feel her tension growing. The longer he remained quiet, the more pressure she seemed to feel upon her shoulders. He swore he could see her hunching over from the weight.

With a defiant turn of her head, she said, "I have something to say. I only tell you this because I want Xarad's killer discovered. I don't know for sure if it matters, but I cannot bear the thought that the killer might go free if I stay silent."

"I understand."

"You are to keep this private. Nobody knows what I will tell you, and if it becomes important for your investigation, then I would appreciate you keeping as much of it private as possible. Is that clear?"

"I'm not here to cause you problems. You're the one who hired me. If what you tell me does not influence the solution of Xarad's murder, then it will be as if you never told me at all."

Axon's shoulders eased back slightly. "Are you a religious man?"

"Haven't had much use for it."

"But you know of the Cassunites. The Cassun Nine, yes?"

"Of course—it's the predominant religion throughout the kingdom. Except on the Frontier border. We tend to be more atheists and agnostics."

"The Cassun Nine are with us our entire lives. One deity for each of the six stages of life, one for each of the sexes, and one deity who lords over all the rest. That one, Qareck, provides our lives with balance, with meaning, with a knowledge that we are part of a greater whole. While the other gods and goddesses are connected to life for a specific time, it is Qareck that sees everything from beginning to end. There are many who believe Qareck can see beyond our lifetime—far into the future and far into the past." Axon narrowed her eyes upon Zev. "Have you heard of the Godwalkers?"

He tried not to choke on his words, but he did not expect her to be so devout as to follow Godwalkers. "They're a sect of mystics who think they can learn to do what the Dacci witches do."

"The Dacci showed the world that magic exists. Godwalkers want to use it for good. They hope that by honing their magical skills, they might someday be able to connect with and speak to the Cassun Nine. Walk by their sides."

"You went to one of these Godwalkers?"

"Her name was Enola. Many of the soldiers I knew would visit her before going off to battle. They'd ask her to commune with Qareck, to peer into the future and let them know if they would survive. I often thought of it as harmless reassurance. Enola never told anybody they were going to die. Not good for business. But the number of inventions coming from the East, the number of changes to the way life is done, it has been speeding up every year. Our kingdom holds firm, but if the Beast were to strike at the same time as the East, we would suffer. And they will attack. Both of them. At some point."

"You fear the kingdom won't survive."

"I wish I were so generous." She looked down at her hands gripping the saddle. "My interests were more selfish. I wanted to know if I would be the one to destroy the Beast. If I would become a legend." With a sharp inhale, she lifted her chin and stared ahead once again. "To reach the level of being a legend, to be immortalized in history, to know that my name would be taught to every young student in school, would be the greatest honor someone like me could ever achieve."

Zev let her words hang in the darkness. They filled up the night yet echoed with emptiness at the same time. "I appreciate your candor," he said, "but I'm not sure how this connects to Xarad."

"Because the Godwalker did not give me a clear answer. Instead, she told me that the answer would come when I was ready to hear it. At the time, I thought she didn't want to commit to an answer because it might prove that she was a fraud."

"That obviously has changed."

"The night Xarad died, I visited the town Temple to pray." The muscles in her neck flexed. "It was there—I had a vision. I saw the Beast. And at the moment the vision ended, the attack that took Xarad's life began."

"That doesn't make you responsible for his death."

"Of course not. But in my vision I could see the Beast, and I felt sure that it could see me. If, through the magic of the Godwalker, I am going to see the future, then it stands to reason that the Beast could also look into the future. I can see him and he can see me."

Zev crossed his arms as he thought. "This evening's attack—you think the Beast did that to stop you. That it killed Xarad and is coming after us because you might actually be the one to destroy it. So it wants you dead before you can kill it. Is that right?"

"I do not think the Beast killed Xarad. I did not have the vision until the attack came. And had it not been for Bellemont's shield, then I would blame the Beast for taking out all of them. And as you have discovered, Xarad died from poison. But the Beast is influencing the world around us. It is coming after us."

"I think your problem might be closer to home. I'm not denying your vision or anything you suggested, but there is still a killer among us, and that means you have among us one who has betrayed you. It's clear to me that the same individual who murdered Xarad is also feeding information to your enemies. The Beast might see into the future and know where we are going, but why would it scrawl a map on paper? Why wouldn't it use its magic to send a vision of its own to its witches?"

She looked over her shoulder. "I cannot believe that any of these three would betray me."

"Yet you hired me, nonetheless."

They traveled on through the night with little more said. Axon remained by Zev's side, and he wondered if his presence gave her some weird comfort—perhaps letting her believe that no further betrayal would occur with his intellect working on the problem. Perhaps she simply didn't want to push her horse any harder.

Zev chuckled at himself. Understanding the motivations of a leader like Axon meant understanding the world of soldiers and warriors in battle. Shooting his rifle once in the midst of a skirmish did not qualify him to make such judgments.

But he did believe she intended to go after the Beast. Her chances of success would increase substantially if he could put her mind at ease. Before he had completed his thoughts, he said, "We'll be arriving at Ridnight soon, yes?"

"By the dawn. Don't worry—King Robion will pay you regardless of your success."

"If it's acceptable, when we get to the castle, I'll stay and continue to search for your killer—until you leave on your mission after the Beast. That should give me an extra few days to solve this."

Though her face remained stoic, Zev sensed a lighter tone to her words. "That would be greatly appreciated," she said.

Up ahead, Zev spotted Pilot rushing back towards them. He had not realized the night had passed, but being able to see Pilot showed him how lighter the sky had become. Axon halted and Zev reined in Stick. When Pilot arrived, Henlio and Bellemont also joined.

"Scouted ahead," Pilot said, through panting breaths. "Made it all the way to the forest's edge, right where you can see Ridnight City."

Axon leaned forward, her face darkening as her brow lowered. "What's wrong?"

Pilot paused to catch his breath. "The castle is under attack."

PART III
AXON

CHAPTER ONE

By the time they reached the tree line, the morning sun pressed across the open fields leading to Ridnight. The city walls formed a stone hexagon with a tower at each point, and each tower had been sculpted to represent one of the six Deities of Life. Three more towers, the tallest towers in the city, rose from the middle of Ridnight Castle and depicted the Greater Deities—especially, Quarek, the Lord of All Existence.

Whenever she approached the city, Axon had always marveled at the mind-boggling vision and years of toil required to have built such a majestic tribute to the Cassun Nine. This time, however, her attention drew toward the ground. Her stomach cramped at the sight of the Beast's encampment. A barrier of filth stretched around the city like an extra circle of city walls. From the distance, it appeared to be the same horrible substance that made up the sludge-like creatures. It certainly smelled like them. At the front, a wide gap bracketed the main road. Standing in that gap, Axon saw two dark forms—Dacci witches. Finally, in the fields, she glimpsed two soldiers lining up the bodies of citizens who had attempted to escape.

After a short time, it became clear that the Dacci had shut down the city. Nobody dared leave the city walls, and if anyone had tried to approach the city from the outside, they were most likely being buried with the other bodies. Word must have spread fast. Not a single merchant or farmer, entertainer or traveler could be seen. Normally, the road leading up to Ridnight bustled with as much activity as the city itself. But Axon heard only the birds chirping and the breeze against the grass. The city had been turned into a mausoleum.

"Disgusting," Henlio said. He stood firm off to her right, peering out at the enemy and awaiting his orders—a good soldier.

Bellemont sat on her horse and snacked. Smart. No telling when they would next get a chance to eat in peace.

And Zev—he paced a circle nearby, stopping only to mutter to his workhorse. Despite their varied reactions, Axon could see that they all needed the same thing—a plan forward. They knew her well enough —even Zev—that the idea of turning away would not be acceptable. An attack of some type would be coming soon. But Axon would not placate them with false ideas nor would she waste her energy planning out strategies without full information.

So, she waited.

Well before the sun hit the top of the sky, Pilot returned from a more intensive, deeper reconnaissance. The entire group encircled him to find out what they faced. Axon, however, did not rush over. She had seen Pilot's grim expression as he galloped toward them.

After riding around the entire city perimeter, Pilot confirmed that the sludge wall formed a complete circle. Like the front section, there were several points in which the wall broke and a Dacci witch stood in the gap. Though he had risked discovery, he figured gleaning every last bit of information he could manage would be the best choice— especially because he did not want to have to scout a third time. So, he slid off his horse and approached on foot in order to confirm his suspicion—the witches sat on the ground, each working hard at maintaining a spell.

To Bellemont, Axon said, "Does that mean they have to keep casting for the wall to stay standing? If we dispatch the witches, will their wall fall?"

"It depends on the witches," Bellemont said. "A strong, seasoned witch might be able to hold the entire wall herself. If she's willing to sacrifice a lot, and if she has a vivid imagination, she could make the wall and have no further need to work at keeping it together. The other witches could be casting other problems for us, too."

"That last part is probably what's happening," Pilot continued. "For one thing, I was able to see some of what they have on the other side of that wall. It's not good. Near each opening, there are two armored soldiers, but they're huge. Unnaturally huge."

"Did any of the witches have a larger sacrificial mound than the others?"

"Maybe. I didn't notice. The few I've seen you make are small enough to fit under your hands."

Bellemont said, "Then at least one witch is conjuring guards while another keeps the wall up. If we were dealing with a witch that could create the wall and walk away, the sacrifice would have started with a large animal. At least."

"I didn't see anything like that. Oh, and our friend with the white stripe is out front."

Axon glared back at the wall. "Of course, she is."

"The good news is that they aren't attacking. They've got the city locked down but that's it. And here's a strange part to all this—I heard people begging out the windows and from the top of the wall, wanting to know the demands of the Dacci, but no answer came. From the things the people were saying, I'm sure they've been asking for a long time. But from the Dacci—nothing."

Henlio said, "Why wouldn't they attack? They can't be planning on starving an entire city. There's plenty of food inside the city walls. Our people could last for months with ease, and that would give them more than enough time to mount an attack or sneak out a messenger for help or something."

"You don't listen," Bellemont said, and Henlio scowled as he looked away.

Zev said, "Well, this is the most I've heard you talk, so please, don't stop."

"I want to hear, too," Pilot said.

Henlio snorted. "The day you are willing to listen instead of flapping your mouth is the day the Beast will sing a song of peace."

"Maybe if you bothered to let me sit in on a strategy talk—"

"If we let you sit in on strategy, we'd never get anywhere. You talk more than any man I've ever met."

"Be still. Both of you." Axon waited until she had command of the group again. With a subtle shift from stern ruler to concerned equal—no more than a change at the corner of her eyes—she settled next to Bellemont and said, "You know I listen to you. But I never want to put you in a position where you feel you must choose between our group and the Dacci. That's why I don't pry."

Bellemont's eyebrow rose. "Yet here you do exactly that. I have told you before—especially you, Henlio—that I will not betray you, but I will not betray my birth people, either."

Axon hated to put any of her team in this position, but she hated it even more for Bellemont. The poor girl had suffered enough tragedy. From the day they first met waiting for a coach to Oric City, where Axon had noticed how agitated Bellemont seemed and worried the girl meant to harm those on the coach—she was dressed in full Dacci witch regalia, after all—only to learn that she was one of the Stolen and had risked escape, to the loss of Xarad and how Bellemont wore her guilt as blatant as a prisoner's forehead tattoo—always visible, always a reminder of failure—the dark touch of Quarek colored her world. But despite her fortuneless life, despite Axon's wish to never force Bellemont into this dilemma, they needed her to choose sides. The city, the King, and possibly the entire Frontier depended on it.

Perhaps Bellemont had read the struggle on Axon's face. Perhaps her loyalty over the years proved itself yet again. Perhaps Bellemont truly cared more for the kingdom than some imagined reunion with those she lost as a child. Whatever the case—and Axon knew better than to inquire—Bellemont dropped her head yet managed a nod.

"Make sure Henlio pays attention. I will never say this again."

Axon snapped her fingers at Henlio, and the man turned back with a gruff scowl. Pilot paid attention, of course—he was thrilled to have some input. And, most importantly, Zev listened. Perhaps Bellemont would reveal something of value to both causes—saving the kingdom and justice for Xarad.

With a deep breath that fluttered her veil, Bellemont said, "Nualla, the Beast, lives in the ground. Deep in the Western lands, the Feral Lands, he *is* the ground. He feeds on that which all living beings leave behind. Nothing is unwanted to Nualla. From our bones to our brains, our flesh to our waste, from fallen trees to dead insects—all that the world wishes to rot away becomes part of the world again through the might of Nualla."

Henlio snorted. "Sounds like the ultimate carrion feeder."

Axon punched his arm hard enough to bruise. "Not one more word."

With her head remaining down, Bellemont went on, "Nualla is the world, and he gives life to all of us Dacci. We sacrifice to him and in return, he grants us the ability to cast our magic. Thus, all Dacci are part of Nualla and Nualla is part of all Dacci."

"Meaning what?" Pilot said.

"That Nualla can see through the Dacci. Nualla spreads across the Feral Lands, reaching out to wherever his followers exist, and through their sacrifices, he can be with them, be where they are, touch the world around them."

"And he can do this to you?" Zev asked.

She shook her head. "That honor was taken from me when I was ripped from my home. The connection takes years to build and it begins at birth. All of the Stolen lost that opportunity the day they were abducted."

Axon rested a hand on Bellemont's back. She wanted to hug the girl and apologize for yet another tragedy, but she had learned long ago that she had no power to alleviate such pains for Bellemont. She could only listen.

"The giant soldiers Pilot saw on the other side of the wall," Bellemont said, "were once regular Dacci. But they have now become elite forces—soldiers who have given themselves over to Nualla completely—and Nualla wields them like vicious puppets."

"How do you know?" Henlio said, ignoring Axon's admonishing

glare. "You were probably still fouling your pants when you were taken away. How can you tell what the Beast is capable of?"

"How do I cast spells? How do I know what to wear? How can I recite the proper prayers? I was older than most when I became one of the Stolen. I had been with my Dacci family long enough to begin the connection with Nualla. He taught me."

Zev crossed his arms. "If I understand you, it's like an exchange. You said the Dacci and Nualla are part of each other. You sacrifice to him and he returns by giving you power. So, if these soldiers are willing puppets of Nualla, then he must give them something in exchange."

"Strength, size, the distinction of being chosen by Nualla. They will spend the rest of their lives revered by all Dacci."

Henlio kicked at the ground. "I've listened to you babble on about these dirt lovers, but I've yet to hear you explain the actual question—why aren't the Beast's soldiers attacking?"

Axon felt Bellemont's back tighten and wanted to erase the last few days. Before Xarad's death, the team worked together with all the grace of a well-balanced blade in the hands of a master swordsman. Since that horrible day, however, the fractures continued to form. They tore and cracked and mutated the team, and soon, Axon knew there would be little left.

Before she could intervene, however, Zev spoke up. "You may have been listening, but you did not hear what she said."

"Wonderful," Henlio said with a snort. "Nonsense riddles from the new man."

"Pay attention. Nualla—"

"The Beast."

"Okay, the Beast is a massive creature under most of the Feral Lands. It devours the dead for energy. But we know the Beast doesn't spring out of the ground in the East. Or, for the most part, here in the Frontier. Which means it's not large enough or strong enough to support reaching out across that large a distance."

"Except the bastard is right out there, right now."

"But it must be stretched so far, it must be using so much energy to maintain what it has at the moment, that it cannot attack. To do so would mean abandoning this quasi-siege it has created."

Bellemont straightened and closed her eyes in appreciation. "Nualla lacks any strong points in the Frontier from which to extend."

Axon swallowed hard. She had been right to bring Zev along, but his insights would not alter what she already knew. What her vision had shown her—the Beast might be weak this far from its own lands, but it held back the attack for a different reason. The city was not its main objective. It wanted her.

Axon stood, gazed over her team, looked out at the enemy, and nodded. "We're too small a force to battle them with a frontal assault. If we're going to accomplish anything, we'll have to be smarter than that. Henlio and I will sneak beyond the sludge wall and take out the altered soldiers. Hopefully, we'll manage a significant number before an alarm is cried out."

Bellemont rose. "What kind of spell do you need?'

"Are you sure? I don't want you to—"

"I am part of this team, and my most useful function is casting spells."

"But your teeth."

"This will only be the fourth spell I've ever cast for you. I'm young. I have plenty of teeth remaining."

Axon could not hold back her pitying gaze. She hoped Bellemont would not be offended. "Pilot and Zev—I want you to stay here with Bellemont. You will protect her. If this connection with the Beast is like she remembers, then it will know that she is casting a spell. It may send forces to stop her."

Pilot patted his sword. "Nobody will even breathe on her."

"And the spell?" Bellemont asked.

Axon smirked. "How many dead things do you need for a big one?"

CHAPTER TWO

Henlio dropped two more tree-rats on the pile of dead animals accumulating in front of Bellemont. "That makes ten," he said, shaking his head. "Enough already?"

Bellemont dug into her pouch and topped off the pile with half of a gezzit. "This should be adequate."

While Henlio and Pilot had spent the last few hours hunting small woodland creatures for the spell, Axon sat with her back against a tree and mentally prepared for the coming fight. She could have helped, of course, but she wanted to keep Bellemont under watch. With Xarad's killer still among them, Axon figured this split provided safety for everyone. Neither Henlio nor Pilot could kill the other, or even attempt to kill the other, without immediately giving away their guilt. As long as Axon watched Bellemont carefully, nothing could happen here, either.

Besides, Axon had to admit that she trusted Bellemont the least. Not because Bellemont did anything deserving of doubt but simply because Bellemont came from a dark world with an unstable environment. How much of her life had been distorted because of the lenses she had lived through? Pilot wanted to fight and be useful. Henlio had been at Axon's side for ages. Plus, she didn't think he had the brains to learn about, handle, and administer poison. But Bellemont—

"May I ask you a question?" Zev said, approaching Bellemont with his brow scrunched tight.

Henlio and Pilot settled after their hunt—guzzling water and rubbing sore necks. Axon peered up from her thoughts as Bellemont knelt before the pile of corpses. They made a macabre tableau.

"When you cast this spell," Zev continued, "won't that bring Nualla right over here?"

That caught everyone's attention. They all stared at Bellemont and waited.

"It hasn't yet," she said.

"But you said these sacrifices call Nualla to create an exchange."

"I've never sensed him being with me. Maybe he does come and I don't know it. Or maybe being stretched so thin makes it difficult for him."

"Then how can you perform magic? Don't you need Nualla?"

Bellemont shrugged and returned to preparing herself for the spell.

The lack of an answer troubled Axon. On the one hand, she could not expect Bellemont to know every aspect of Dacci culture—especially considering the girl was Stolen. But the way Zev focused on Bellemont, the way his mouth tightened as he considered her, the way his eyes tried to cut through her murky walls—it left Axon more concerned. Could Bellemont truly be Xarad's killer? If so, then by trusting Bellemont's magic, was Axon setting herself and Henlio up for death? Plus, Axon trusted Henlio, and his clear dislike of Bellemont suggested he knew something about her. Perhaps just sensed it. Whatever the answer, Axon still had to lead her team into an attack on a superior force.

She walked over to Zev and gestured with her head for him to follow. Once they were secluded from the others, she said, "Is it her?"

"Bellemont? Maybe. I can't say for certain."

"But if it's her and we let her cast this spell—"

"I don't think you have to worry about that. Bellemont is very loyal to you."

"Would that loyalty surpass self-preservation?"

"Self-preservation will keep her from doing anything drastic. If she is the murderer, she doesn't want to be discovered now."

"Why?"

"I'm not sure. But she's had opportunities to run away from us and rejoin the enemy. She hasn't done that. So, either she's loyal to you or she still has work to do." He raised a single finger to stop her from speaking. "If Bellemont wanted to kill all of us, it would already have been done. In fact, I'd say that if she is guilty, she probably killed Xarad because he stumbled upon whatever larger purpose she has."

Axon did not know if she felt better or worse. But Bellemont called them over, she was ready to start the spell, and Axon buried all her fears. Too late now. She gambled on Zev's analysis, and gripping one strand of her necklace, she mouthed a quick prayer to Orlar, Goddess of the Elder Years, to look over her so that she might live to see her hair turn gray and her skin wrinkle with delight.

As they walked toward the pile of animal corpses, Bellemont bowed before her sacrifice. "After I make the final offer, one of my teeth, I will mix it with the dead. Then I will close my eyes, and I must picture what I want the spell to do. The clearer the picture, the stronger my conviction, the more real in my mind that I make the image, then the greater the results of the spell."

Leaning on his knee, Pilot said, "Why not just imagine the sludge away? And the witches and soldiers, too?"

"Where would they go? What would that look like—lifted into the sky, burnt away in flames? What?"

"Who cares?"

"I have to be specific about every detail or the details become something other than what I want. It's not a static picture in my mind. It's more like coming up with a play that covers every nuance and answers every question about the story. If you want a spell to lift a boulder, it's easy. Not a lot of questions surround that. If you want to be King, it's an immense number of factors to juggle. Plus, the greater the spell, the larger the sacrifice."

Zev crossed his arms. "That's why the Dacci don't simply cast a spell to destroy all of us."

"Something that big would require more Dacci than exist, an unfathomable sacrifice, and should even one of them fail to get the image correct, the whole endeavor would turn into something far different."

Axon recalled the corpses the Dacci soldiers lined up for burial outside the wall. From the shadowy crevices of her mind, the thought struck her—she had Xarad's corpse still. If they added him to the sacrifice, Bellemont would have substantially more power. Since they could only call upon her magic a few times—she only had so many teeth—each spell should be utilized for its fullest potential. With Xarad's body, Bellemont might be able to end this without any risk to the rest of the team.

Bellemont pulled out her clamp and faced Axon. "So? What do you wish?"

Axon pushed off her darker thoughts. Though she regretted the thoughts in the first place, at least she banished them with ease. Desecrating her allies would never be the path of a legendary warrior. And doing so on the off-chance that Bellemont could make a sacrifice large enough while having the skill necessary—foolishness.

"We can't attack straight on," Axon said, "There aren't enough of us. We'll need to be secretive. Can you make us invisible to our enemies?"

"That I can do." Bellemont's veil lifted at her cheeks, and Axon assumed she smiled. "I warn you that the spell will only last a short time—especially if you and Henlio do not remain close together. The further apart you go, the more difficult it will be on me."

"Do your best."

"Always."

Bellemont bowed her head toward the sacrifice and closed her eyes. Axon had seen a few spells cast but still found the process captivating. When they reached the point where Bellemont extracted her tooth, Axon observed with a mixture of horror and respect—even wincing as blood dribbled from the young woman's mouth.

Zev jumped and Pilot's mouth widened. Both gasped as they stared at Axon.

"That's amazing," Pilot said.

Zev appeared more impressed. "I've grown up hearing about magic but to actually see it happen—incredible."

Henlio laughed. "You can't see us, can you?"

Pilot's smile faltered. "Don't you do anything to me."

"I could walk right up to you and—"

"And nothing. It won't last forever, so if you do something, there will be retribution."

Axon glanced at her hands—she saw them fine. She gazed across at Henlio—she saw him fine as well. But clearly the others did not see them. "Pilot's right. We have a short time. We can't waste it."

Hefting his sword onto his shoulder, Henlio grunted. "Ready when you command, ma'am."

Axon decided not to reiterate her orders to Pilot and Zev. They understood their duty. And if Pilot proved to be the killer, Zev could stop him from causing her or Axon trouble. She hoped.

"Let's go," she said, pulling out her sword and marching toward the foul wall.

CHAPTER THREE

Axon crouched low as she and Henlio crossed the rolling darrus fields to approach the sludge wall. Each time she instinctively bent down, she forced her back straight. She was invisible—reshaped into a ghost. For now. No reason to hide in the tall grass.

As they neared the high wall and the two soldiers burying the dead, Henlio fanned off to the right. Axon put out her hand to stop him. Normally, she would welcome his flanking maneuver, but Bellemont said they had to stay close together. With a nod of his shaggy head, he did not widen the gulf between them.

Axon's speed picked up. A dozen blue-black gezzits, picking at morning seeds and bugs, fluttered into the air. The two soldiers paused their work to gaze at the sight, but neither took notice of the two threats racing towards them.

With a simple, fast strike, Axon cut one soldier's throat as she ran by. She slowed, turned back, and finished his life with a thrust of her sword. The other soldier stared as his friend convulsed and blood spurted out his neck, yet there was nothing he could see to cause the sudden spasms. Lost in his confusion, the other soldier never heard Henlio's blade. Probably never understood how he had died.

Not a sound was made.

As Axon scanned the area for anybody that might have noticed, Henlio rolled the bodies into the mass grave the men had been digging. The breeze blew across the grasses. The clouds drifted by the sun. But nobody came running. No alarm call rang. Bellemont had truly molded them into the air. They were the wind and the clouds. Unseen but certainly felt.

"I have to give the little girl her due," Henlio said as he stepped next to Axon. "This spell is mighty."

"Let's hope it holds up when we sneak by the witch."

They headed toward the nearest gap in the wall. Axon wanted to sprint, but while the spell made them impossible to see, they were not impossible to hear. The soldiers had been easy—they were focusing on backbreaking work and their grunts and grumbles masked any noise Axon and Henlio could have made. But the witches sat still, focusing on their spells in the quiet.

And there was the magic.

Now that the initial rush had passed, Axon noticed an odd sensation dancing along her skin. It rolled up her arms and down her back —a tingling like her limbs going numb followed by her skin prickling as if in fear, yet warmth washed through her muscles as if a thick blanket protected her from a winter wind. And then it started over again. At first, she found the different phases disconcerting, but as her adrenaline kicked in and her confidence being in battle focused her thoughts, she found the feeling of magic somewhat pleasurable.

The question, though, circled back to the witches. If Axon could feel the magic that surrounded her, that made her unseen, could the witches feel it as well? Magic made it easy to drop one's guard. She would have to stay alert for any sign of discovery.

Shoving those thoughts aside, Axon raised her hand to halt Henlio. Just ahead, she spotted the break. With careful motions, she moved alongside the wall. The wind shifted, and the thing's vile odor hit her hard. Compared to the noxious fumes that assaulted her, an outhouse used by stomach-sick children and closed up on a sweltering day would have been a delightful aroma.

Henlio gagged. Axon froze. Once he regained control, they remained still like the statues of the Cassun Nine. Each passing moment gave her the relief that they had not been heard coupled with the pressure of knowing that Bellemont could not keep them invisible for too long.

Once they started moving again, they reached the gap in short time. The Dacci witch stationed there sat on her knees before a pile of horse manure sprinkled with white chips of bone. Axon held her breath as she gingerly crossed the ground like crossing her creaky bedroom floor when trying to sneak out of the house as a youngster.

One step. The next. Small, quiet movements.

She swallowed back the temptation to remove the witch from the world. Once the witch died, she would no longer be able to cast spells —a clear and positive outcome. But Axon understood the real threat at the moment was the giant soldiers. They would be difficult to take down once they were riled to any danger. Axon and Henlio needed to kill as many of the giants as they could manage while stealth befriended them. Any action that threatened to expose them had to be avoided.

The witch's eyes snapped open, and Axon held still. The witch lifted her head, turned at an awkward angle, and stared straight at Axon. The winds shifted once more, and as the change in sounds reached them, Axon wondered if that would be enough to assuage the witch's suspicions.

Henlio had stopped several steps back. Axon saw his fingers roll closed on his weapon. She risked flexing one finger to warn him off.

The witch sniffed the air, but Axon did not think anybody would notice one stench over another when the stomach-churning odors of filth swirled around them all. But the witch's eyes widened, and Axon prepared to spring into an attack. With a loud rumble, the witch passed gas. Her eyes relaxed, she lowered her head, and returned to her spellwork.

Axon waited three nauseating breaths before moving again. But the witch did not stir. With Henlio carefully stepping behind, they slipped beyond the sludge wall and into the grounds leading toward the Ridnight walls.

As they moved on, Axon marveled at the immense scope of what the Dacci witches had accomplished. Without an army of thousands, a handful of witches created a barrier that stopped anyone from escaping the city. While the majority of the city walls went unguarded, should anyone slip out, they might think they had reached freedom, but they would eventually have to deal with the sludge wall or a witch herself. Either way, an alert would go up, one that would bring a giant running—and a running giant could cover a lot of ground quickly.

Axon wondered why the witches had chosen to cast their wall so far from the castle. But then she snickered. Casting magic like this took too long. If those witches dared move any closer, the city archers would have had plenty of time to line up a perfect shot. Arrows would have been sticking out of Dacci skulls. Instead, the wall sat back two full lengths of an archer's range. The witches took no chances.

With the sludge wall at her back, Axon paused. For a brief moment, Axon could forget the threat against her beloved city. Part of her embraced the sensation of warmth that flooded her heart whenever she approached her home. Those city walls did not speak of threat or protection from danger—they were merely structures that defined the space she considered most important to her life. As sacred as any Temple of the Cassun.

But even without the witches behind her, Axon saw through the façade. The city no longer held the luster it once bore. The mounting pressures from the East and the West chipped away like harsh weather taking its toll on the stone.

Henlio's hand pressed down on her shoulder. In a sharp whisper, he said, "I think that's one of them."

Following his gesture, she saw a small mound in the distance. "I've been seeing these fields my whole life. I know them well. That does not belong there."

"Then I have an idea. Since we can't split apart too far, we should lure that monstrosity someplace that will isolate it from any of the others. If we're lucky, we'll kill it before any others take notice."

Pointing to the left of the mound, Axon said, "Just over that hill is a small pond and some trees."

"It should do nicely."

"You okay to run the distance? We probably don't have too much time left from Bellemont."

"I'll run all day, if you want me to."

"Just make sure you have enough energy to fight once we get there."

Turning across the darrus fields, the grass split beneath them. With any luck, the giant would see the trail of trampled grass forming and follow out of curiosity. Axon soon found that luck did not wish to grace her at all. When they finally reached the small grouping of trees around the pond, the giant had yet to stir.

She decided to risk taking a few extra moments to catch her breath. Though he did not say it, she could tell Henlio appreciated the respite. Glancing off in either direction, she did not see another mound to indicate a giant—they were certainly out there, though. Either these things moved extremely fast or the witches could not get the Beast to stretch its influence far enough to create extra giants.

"We might have a chance at this, yet," she said.

"Aren't you full of optimism?"

Axon drew her sword, and Henlio followed. Good. They were ready.

She reached down for a large stone and threw it in the direction of the giant. She then had Henlio run between the trees as if trying to hide. It took them four more tries before the magically enhanced soldier lumbered towards them.

Axon shifted toward her right, drawing the giant's focus. With a short motion, she commanded Henlio to climb a tree. The soldier's footsteps thumped like a building crashing down. She did not want to ever face a full army of these things. Their marching alone would topple cities.

Despite being invisible, Axon still took a position behind one of the trees. No point in unnecessary risk. Especially with her beloved city at stake.

As the soldier barreled closer, Axon finally got a clear look at the thing. He stood at least two people tall and probably a full person wide. Axon guessed the soldier was male by the copious amounts of hair poking out between the crevices of his armor. But perhaps a witch's spell did other things to the soldiers besides make them grow big.

This one trampled through the grass with blind rage painting his face. His body had been mutated, and Axon suspected his mind had been as well. But the poor fool would not have much time left to worry about it.

As the giant thundered toward the pond, racing straight by Axon, she lunged across the way—slicing the tendons at his heels. The mighty soldier cried out like a babe in need of mother's milk. Momentum stumbled him forward, each step throwing jolts of agony through his body. Axon could see his muscles tense as he cried out with each step.

When he stopped, he turned to his left, his brow knitted in confusion. Then Henlio struck. The burly man leapt from the tree with his sword aimed downward. Landing on the giant's back, Henlio thrust his blade through the nape of the giant's neck. Axon watched as the metal sliced out from the front, sluicing blood across his chest.

The giant's eyes froze open, and his arms flailed upward. But Henlio had already pushed off.

With a sword sticking through his neck, the giant could not make a sound. The rage drained from his face, leaving behind a child who struggled to understand what had happened. Something had cut his feet and a sword had sliced through his neck, yet he saw nobody. Tears trickled down his cheeks. Axon hated to admit it, but a tinge of pity poked under her skin.

Henlio's sword did more than silence the giant's speech—it blocked the airway. With each missing breath, panic ensued. The giant flailed behind and found the hilt of the sword. He tried to pull it out, and his augmented strength managed the task with ease—but not without problem. The blade caused more damage coming out than going in. The giant nearly severed his own head.

Blood lumped out of his neck, covering his armor like red molasses. He had only time enough to stare at the sword before his eyes rolled up and he fell over. The sword bounced onto the ground as his enormous body slammed into the pond. Water splashed high and sent waves rushing outward.

Retrieving his sword, Henlio said, "Didn't think that would go so easily."

"We ambushed him and we're invisible. I'd have been angry if it was any harder. As long as we can keep that up—"

"I don't think that's going to be an option." Henlio gazed off into the distance.

Three mounds grew larger, rushing towards them like stampeding horses. The vibrations thumping from the ground shivered up Axon's leg.

Henlio said, "They still can't see us. They'll come out here, see their dead friend, and stop to figure out what's going on."

"And if there was only one, we could take him easily. But three of them? And there might be more on the way."

"I'm not saying it'll be without problems, but isn't this our plan? Take out these big threats first?"

"You know plans fly away the moment a battle begins."

Henlio kicked the feet of the giant. "We took care of this one, we can take care of more. What other choice do we have? We're not running away."

"Of course not." Axon surveyed the area, searching for anything that might improve their odds of survival—let alone winning. How much longer would Bellemont's advantage work for them? Taking down one or two more giants only to be killed by a third served no purpose. It would not stop the attack on Ridnight. It would not save her King. And perhaps worst of all, she would die not knowing who had killed Xarad.

Her eyes came to rest on the slain giant. With his body at a sharp angle—the top half of him underwater, the bottom half stretching out into the grass—he looked more like a fallen tree than a man. What she next saw tore through her skin with the icy blade of fear—the cuts she had made upon his tendons were nothing more than fading white lines.

She knew she had cut him through. She had seen the blood, heard his pain-soaked cries, watched him stumble. Yet only a faint scar remained. In the time between her strike and his final act of removing the blade to sever his own throat, the damage she caused had healed.

"Magic," she whispered.

She watched the giant in the water. How long had he been under? How long before he could no longer heal?

"Running out of time," Henlio said. "Are we fighting?"

Axon stepped away from the giant to gaze out towards the sludge wall—towards the gap. "It's the witches. I assumed they were here to keep the wall up and act in support of the soldiers and giants. But it's all them. They created the giants. They created it all. They control it all like game pieces."

"You want to kill that witch we walked by to get in here?"

Axon stared back at the approaching giants. "I don't think we can make it."

"We're invisible. They're going to stop at the pond and check out their dead friend."

"Only if we stay invisible. We've taken too long as it is."

"You don't know that. I may not like her all that much, but Bellemont's tough."

"I have no doubt, but it won't be enough. I can feel the change on my skin already. Surely you can, too."

"It's just the rush from fighting wearing down."

"We're wasting time debating. You can feel the giants getting closer —feel it in the ground."

Henlio shoved Axon. "Go. Run. I'll do what I can to stall these horrid things."

"You can't sacrifice—"

"I'm going to live. They can't see me. The moment they can, I'll be long gone. But it won't mean anything if you don't kill that witch. So go."

Henlio turned away, and Axon knew she had no choice. Not to

follow through meant squandering the opportunity Henlio planned to create.

She bolted off, making no effort to hide the noise of her weapons and armor. As adrenaline shot through her body, she bared her teeth. Well-toned muscles hurled her along the tall grasses like a famished animal chasing down its prey.

The gap in the wall grew with each step closer. Fearing she would hear Henlio's warcry followed by his voice cut down with his body, she blotted out the world behind her. Soon—soon she would reach that gap and the witch that sat there.

All her focus shifted forward into running, running, running. Sweat slid down her back. Her years of training had once again paid off—her breathing remained steady and strong, and she could endure this full-on sprint as long as she needed.

The distinct sound of a metal sword crashing into armor sliced into her attention, warning her that at least one giant had reached Henlio. It would be difficult for Bellemont to keep them both invisible the further Axon ran off. If only she could hold the spell for—

As if unseen hands reached down and twisted her skin, her body heated up. *Not yet. Not yet.* But the sensation washing over her left no room for doubt—Bellemont's spell had fallen completely away.

Up ahead, she spotted the witch. The dark-shrouded woman lifted her chin and leaned forward. Maintaining her run, Axon reached across and pulled out her blade. The fighting continued behind her as she narrowed her focus on the witch in front.

A guttural scream from behind tripped Axon up. She tumbled forward, popped, and whirled around. In the distance, she saw Henlio hack through the leg of one giant as another attempted to get around the third in order to reach his target. But Henlio never stopped moving—always keeping the injured giant between him and the other two. The tactic would work for a while, but eventually Henlio would tire—long before the giants.

Spinning back, Axon broke into another sprint with renewed vigor. Up ahead, the witch rose to her feet. She lifted her arms out wide as her eyes locked onto Axon.

The ground in front of Axon erupted and a twisted spike of muck shot up through the soil. Dirt and rock sprinkled the air. She pivoted to the left and continued, but another spike broke through. And another. They shot out at odd angles with no discernible pattern like random fists punching through the ground. Axon jumped left, swerved right, rolled to one side, then the other. All the while, she moved forward. Ever forward. Never losing sight of the witch.

And the witch moved. Just a slight motion of the head, but enough to confirm Axon's racing thoughts. The witch was in trouble. If Axon could believe everything Bellemont had said about casting spells, then the witch used a sacrifice to control whatever spell her part in this attack was—but also in the oily spikes. That slight motion of her head —the witch searched for more dead material to cast a new spell.

Axon dug in hard, pushing her legs faster, the taste of victory wetting her lips.

The witch lowered her hands and shifted toward the wall. She dug out awful, muddy clumps of it and slapped the rancid goop onto her old sacrifice. She dared to glance up, the worry filling her eyes.

Axon adjusted her grip on her sword.

The witch pulled off two more clumps of wall goop to form a knee-high mound. With a mournful outburst, she ripped off her veil revealing a young but distorted mouth.

All sounds drifted away for Axon. Only her breathing echoed in her head.

The witch shoved two goo-covered fingers down her throat and vomited on top of her sacrifice. With a smooth, well-practiced motion, she produced her tooth clamp and rent free one of her teeth.

Axon wanted to go faster. She was close. But though she would not slow down, she found no other reservoir of energy within.

Spitting blood upon the sacrifice, the witch hunched over and thrust her tooth into the mound. She closed her eyes, lifted her head back, and let blood dribble from her open mouth.

In that moment, Axon understood why Bellemont always wanted somebody standing guard over her when casting a spell. As if lost in some warped dream, the witch before Axon had no defense.

And no time left.

Axon slammed her blade through the witch's gut, splattering the mound off to the side, skewering the witch, and lifting her into the air from sheer strength and momentum. With one fast swipe downward, Axon pitched the witch into the dirt. The motion caused the blade to slice the witch's gut open further.

Spinning back, Axon looked toward Henlio. With the witch dead, two of the three giants collapsed and died as well. The third giant paused in confusion—a mistake that Henlio had no trouble capitalizing on. With a huge swing, he slashed open the giant's belly. Smartly, Henlio ran off toward Axon. The giant tried to follow, but after a few steps, it tripped on its own innards and tumbled to the ground.

To Axon's right, part of the sludge wall collapsed as well.

Axon and Henlio shared one breath to nod at each other. Before the next breath, however, a Dacci soldier on horseback charged through the breach of the wall. Her long hair flew back as the horse galloped toward Henlio. She held a spear and lowered her body in the proper position to gain the most penetration when she struck.

Axon could do nothing but watch. Like a spectator at a sporting challenge, she clenched her fists, tightened her jaw, and refused to blink—not wanting to miss a single moment. She tried to will her confidence into him, tensing her gut as the soldier neared.

It happened fast—Axon expected no less. Henlio swung his sword while the soldier thrust her spear. The horse galloped by. A moment later, Henlio remained standing, the horse slowed to a gentle walk, and the soldier flopped to the ground. Before Axon could sigh relief, Henlio whirled back and rushed to catch the horse. He vaulted into the saddle and hastened for Axon.

Sheathing her sword, Axon positioned herself to leave plenty of room for the horse. She raised her left arm and widened her stance for good balance. Henlio raced forward, leaning over with his arm out, and in a smooth motion, their arms clasped. Henlio held firm like an ancient oak as Axon pulled herself up onto the back of the horse.

Leaning her head forward, she said in his ear, "Head to the gap that leads to the city entrance."

Henlio raised an eyebrow. "The white-striped witch?"

"We should have killed her first thing."

With a smart kick, Henlio pushed the horse faster. The thundering hooves satisfied Axon's bones. She understood this world—swords and blood and horses. She knew what to do.

When the next gap finally came into sight, she spotted the white-striped witch. But this would not be as easy as the last one. Though they approached much faster than Axon had on foot, the white-striped witch spotted them with plenty of time to cast a new spell—and her sacrificial mound of death and bile stood nearly as tall as the witch herself.

Raising one hand in the air and her fingers splayed wide, the witch stepped forward. Axon wondered what this new stance would bring, but she did not have to wait long for an answer. The witch thrust her arm to the ground, and the sludge walls melted down as if they had become nothing but liquid.

Henlio reined in the horse. Two more giants in the distance fell to their knees. Several small, black-clad figures darted off toward the forest, their dark clothing fluttering behind them. The witches were running away. Before Axon could comment, she watched the white-striped witch lift off the ground. The horrible woman floated back-wards, always keeping her eyes on Axon. As she made her escape, she spit a mouthful of blood onto the ground. Based on the woman's cocky wink, Axon guessed she meant the blood as a final insult.

"It's over then?" Henlio said.

"Almost." Axon gestured toward the remaining soldiers—living, breathing, non-magical soldiers. Less than a few twenty.

Cheering erupted from the city walls. Axon could see small figures jumping up and down. Screams echoed across the fields, but for a change, they were screams of joy. The city gates opened, and the King's Guard burst out on horseback. If the Dacci soldiers remained to fight, they would certainly be slain.

"Now it's over," Axon said.

Henlio turned the horse toward the city. "Strange strategy. Cut off the city, bring in a small amount of troops, and do nothing. Then when the first real resistance comes and takes out one of their witches, they all run. What's the sense of that?"

"It was a warning."

"Of what? Surely the King already knows the Beast is out there."

"The Beast is warning me—it knows I'm coming."

CHAPTER FOUR

Over the years, Axon received plenty of thanks from the small towns and families that she had helped across the countryside, but she never received a true hero's welcome like that ordered by the King. Riding through the city gates with the King's Guard marching in front and her team keeping pace behind, Axon experienced a symphonic explosion of praise. People of all ages lined the city streets. They cheered and cried. Hats were thrown in the air and other garments fluttered like flags, pendants and ribbons filled in the gaps. Everywhere Axon turned, she witnessed colorful jubilance and celebration.

Musicians, both single and in bands of four or more, formed circles in the side streets, doling out fancy rhythms and danceable tunes. Children crowded around a miniature proscenium as a puppet Axon and a puppet Henlio saved the kingdom. Axon even caught glimpses of animal acts deeper within the city.

Later, after the thrilling parade and after the local politicians had made their less-thrilling speeches, the crowds broke into smaller groups that continued to dance throughout the night. Delicious aromas drifted from one street to the next, and as Axon walked block by block, she discovered the world's cultures slamming together, promising delightful and new culinary experiences.

She caught sight of Pilot surrounded by four attractive, young women. As he tipped back his hat and winked, she suspected that at least two of them would be joining him later that night. Elsewhere, she found Henlio sitting at a table with a large mug of ale. People wanted to hear a retelling of his adventures and how he had helped defeat the giants. As long as they kept supplying the ale, he would keep talking. Axon wondered how much of the story would end up being true, but then, the truth did not really matter to these people—this was an exciting show and a celebration of relief to the end of a terrifying conflict.

Zev, on the other hand, appeared determined for some truth. Axon had overheard him questioning several of the city leaders. He wanted information on poisons, but those in charge brushed him off—at least, for the evening. This was a time to rejoice, and no politician wanted to miss out connecting themselves with the good feelings of the city's people.

One block further down, Axon found Bellemont sitting alone with a half-full mug of ale. While nobody challenged her, the public kept a wary berth around her table. After all, the city had just been threatened by several Dacci witches and their magic. Only being part of the heroic team kept Bellemont from serious danger. Watching the way people eyed her, however, made Axon wonder how long that restraint would last.

Grabbing an ale from a server passing by—free ale being one of the benefits to the heroes of the day—Axon strolled over to the table and sat opposite Bellemont. They drank their ale without saying a word while revelers and lovers, musicians and magicians, and every other form of celebrating citizen continued to cavort around them.

At length, Bellemont said, "There is no need to be gentle. I know I have failed you."

"Failed me? How?"

"What kind of witch am I that I can't keep a simple invisibility spell going long enough for you to be safe? You and Henlio could have died."

"We could have died regardless."

"The fault is mine. I know that I do not belong with you anymore. I accept that."

Axon knocked her fist on the table. "Nonsense. You're one of the Stolen. How are you supposed to get trained properly when you've had none of your own kind to guide you? You've taught yourself every aspect of being a witch and done a remarkable job at it. Besides, you can see that Henlio and I are fine. Your spell gave us all the time we needed to succeed."

As a new quiet settled upon them, Axon watched Bellemont's evasive glances and wondered what questions Zev would ask in this situation. Because despite her kind words, Axon's faith in Bellemont did hold strong. In the matter of Xarad, Bellemont had the most access to the man—when fighting, he often was tasked with protecting her while she cast a spell. And though Bellemont suggested her failure with the invisibility meant that she should no longer be part of the team, though Bellemont appeared contrite and ashamed, Axon saw how it all could be interpreted quite differently.

One variation—Bellemont could have killed Xarad and then purposely failed the invisibility spell early in hopes of getting Axon and Henlio killed. When that also failed, she figured the idea of being ineffective made an excellent excuse to leave the group so that, in actuality, she could escape before being detected and brought to justice.

Another variation—Bellemont could have poisoned Xarad but did not expect the man to die within her shield. She then deduced Zev's true purpose within the group and began plotting some way to protect herself. She could not kill Zev without causing even greater focus on her situation, but if Axon and Henlio died on the battlefield, that would put an end to the inquiry. When that failed, she floated out the idea of leaving with the hope that either she could escape or that her actions would make her appear innocent.

Axon rubbed her head. Was this the kind of thinking that went through Zev's mind all the time? It could drive one mad.

She considered asking a few pointed questions, but the crowd behind Bellemont parted. An overly-dressed page entered. He jogged right to Axon's side and bowed. "His Majesty, King Robion, requests your presence."

Axon tried to maintain a calm exterior as she stood. She set her mug down and looked at Bellemont. With her firmest leadership voice, she said, "You are not leaving the team. Nobody leaves the team." To the page, she added, "Show me the way."

As she walked off, she nodded to herself. She had made the right decision—for the time. Until she knew who had betrayed her, she could not let any of them leave. It was that simple.

Strolling under the portcullis did not fill Axon with awe or fear. She had been within the castle walls before—her parents had been part of the court for many years. But when the page ushered her into the King's throne room, the weight of royalty pressed down upon her.

She had never met the King before. The King. Her King. And a private audience, no less.

She offered a quick prayer to Bieck that she not embarrass herself —the Goddess of Adolescence would know plenty about embarrassment. To be safe, she tossed in a prayer to Ovlar and Sazieck, too. When the page did not stop in front of the throne but rather guided her to a door in the back—one that led to the King's private receiving room—her stomach flipped.

Part of her wanted to tap the page's shoulder, stop him, tell him that she did not deserve such an honor. Part of her thought it would be rude and ungrateful. Of course, part of her jumped around like she did as a little girl when given her first sword.

The page opened the door, stepped in, and before Axon could follow or object, she heard the page announce, "Ms. Axon Coponiv."

Trying to control her breathing as she would in battle, she straightened her shoulders, lifted her head, and entered.

The plainness of the room startled her. Unlike the throne room, this place had no gorgeous tapestries, no paintings by the great Frontier artists, no gold-trimmed furniture, not even a statue or beautifully carved shelving. Instead, she found a simple stone room with two windows letting in the moonlight. A small fireplace and several sconces provided flickers of warmth. A wooden table dominated the room. At the head of the table, she found King Robion. He wore a gray tunic open at the chest and a thoughtful frown. Sitting at the corner next to him, Axon found Zev.

She stepped forward, curtsied, and bowed her head. "Please, sire, call me Axon." As she rose, she caught Zev's shocked frown. He probably didn't think someone as uncouth as a warrior knew how to curtsy.

King Robion gestured to the chair at his left. "Very well, then. Come join us, Axon. I hope our celebration is making you feel properly thanked for the wonderful feat you have done for us all."

"It's a bit overwhelming."

He chuckled and scratched his tight beard. "I imagine so. Well, your friend here has been telling me a bit about his past and what he remembers of the East, but what I really want to understand is how he thinks."

As Axon sat, she noticed Zev shifting in his chair. "I've known him for only a short time, but I must admit, I wonder the same thing."

Zev reddened. "Oh, I'm nothing special. Just a failed farmer."

"Such modesty." The King beamed and she found him difficult to read. Was he amused, proud, cautious, truly interested, or merely doing his job as politely as possible? The King continued, wagging a finger at Zev. "I've been hearing about your judicious handling of certain matters in your little town. And if those matters reach my ears, then something special must have happened. For instance, explain to me about the Harvest Festival and the Coru thieves. As I understand it, a group of men were traveling town to town, terrorizing the villagers, and causing all kinds of vandalizing. I even sent a unit of my men to roam the streets in that area. I hoped they would catch this gang, but no luck."

"I didn't know that. In fact, I had never heard of the Coru thieves during all of that. Not much news gets out to my little farm."

"Yet after an incident in the town of Treebund, things got quite ugly at one of the taverns, and three men were arrested by one of my guards. The only problem was that the guard could not figure out which men belonged to the gang and which had just been traveling through. Is that correct? They came to you for the answer?"

Zev squirmed in his seat again. "Some in the town council thought I might be able to help and offered to discount my livestock feed costs for a month. I wish I could tell you I did it for more noble reasons."

"All people deserve to be compensated for their work." King Robion leaned toward Axon, and with boyish glee, he said, "This part is what amazes me. Zev asked for each man to be taken into a room separately, he asks them each the same three questions, and then comes out and points to the one man that belongs to the gang. Not only is he correct, but the guilty man confesses out of fear that Zev has some magical powers. He gives up the rest of his gang and a level of peace is restored to the area."

Axon raised her eyebrows. "What were the three questions?"

"That's exactly what I want to know."

"You'll be disappointed," Zev said. "There's nothing magical or particularly impressive. Before I formulated my questions, I spoke to a few of the locals to understand the situation. All three men claimed to be traveling merchants who frequented this route. All three claimed to have been heavy drinkers and, in fact, all three acted quite inebriated. But according to one of your guards, the Coru gang did not drink while committing their crimes. It was part of what made them difficult to catch—they stayed clear headed and sober, saving all of their rowdy behavior for more private times and more private locations."

"So you felt one of them was faking."

"I did. Now, the first man I took in, I chose because he reeked of ale. I asked him how many ales he had at the Treebund Tavern. Then I asked him how many he had at The Pigsnout. And finally I asked him how many he had at Town's Edge."

The King drummed his fingers on the table. "That's it? You asked all three of them those same questions?"

"I did."

"I fail to see how that solved the problem."

"Merchants are creatures of habit. They live a nomadic life and become particular about their preferences as a manner of controlling their difficult-to-control world. When I asked the first man about the third establishment, the Town's Edge, he told me that he drank no ale there because the owners watered it down. Whenever he goes there, it's for the food—which is quite excellent. For drink, he only orders water. Of the other two gentlemen I questioned, one of them gave the same answers. But the other one did not know about the poor quality of ale because he never drank there because he was part of the Coru gang, which never drank on the job. If he was a merchant like the others, if he frequented the route like the others, then like the others, he should've known."

The King clapped his hands. "Brilliant. Absolutely brilliant. I thank you for helping my people. And I thank you for your help with Axon's success in saving all of us in the city. Now, I must speak with your leader for a bit, but please make yourself comfortable in our city and if there's anything I can do—"

"There is one thing," Zev said as he stood. Axon thanked the Cassun Nine that she had not been drinking or eating at that moment —she would have choked.

"Oh?" the King said, a smirk crossing his lips. "What do you wish?"

"The court has a chemist?"

"Of course. A fine woman with the finest mind."

"If you could make her available to me, I have been pursuing some inquiries which her expert knowledge might be of great assistance."

"She will be glad to help you." The King snapped his fingers at one of the pages. "Please escort Mr. Asterling to our chemist."

Zev fumbled a bow. "Thank you ... your Highness."

King Robion waited until Zev had left before slapping the table and snorting a hearty laugh. Axon watched the display, unsure how he expected her to react. When he finally comported himself, he said, "I apologize. There is not often much opportunity for levity, and watching Zev flounder in front of me was amusing. But you've grown up in the courts. I doubt I'm too intimidating to you."

"Intimidating enough."

"I truly doubt a man like me can ruffle you. After all, you are here because you faced down numerous giants, soldiers, and witches." With another snap of his fingers, the remaining page fetched a tray of cheeses and breads. Taking a bite, he gestured toward the platter, but Axon did not move. "This is some of the finest in the Frontier."

"It's been a long day," she said. "I don't think I could eat anything right now."

As if she had spoken profound words, the King waved his finger toward her. "I'm interested in knowing exactly what happened on the field today. Tell me your strategy, what tactics you used, everything you can. It's important."

Axon had not expected this, but she was encouraged to find a concerned leader in this man. Warming to the subject—she had never been one to dwell upon war stories, but for her King, she made an exception—she broke into a detailed account of the battle. Starting from her thoughts when Pilot first scouted the area all the way to the final moments as she watched the white-striped witch float away, she gave the King as much of an analysis as she could provide, given that she had barely time to digest the day's events. Throughout it all, King Robion stayed deeply focused. He rarely interrupted and only to clarify a term or moment he did not understand. When she finished, he sat back and scratched his beard.

"This is not the first time the Beast has attacked the Frontier," he said. "The pressures from the East are also increasing. Something will eventually break, and the single-mindedness of the Beast suggests it will break violently. If the Frontier is going to survive, we must be prepared."

"I absolutely agree."

The King studied her face. She had to admit, she found him handsome. Happy that her dark skin hid any blush, she waited as his gaze continued to fall upon her. She could not recall any man ever looking at her like that. Nor woman, for that matter.

At length, he said, "I called you in here and listened to your recount of the battle because I thought you might be the one to lead my army."

Axon could not hide her surprise. "Do you mean the King's Guard?"

"No. I'm considering raising a new army to prepare for the Beast. It will be costly and may cause hardship upon my people, so I don't take it lightly."

"Surely you have capable soldiers within your Guards' ranks."

With a soft breath, the King said, "I'm not offering you the position. I thought I might, but I can tell from listening to you that you don't want the job. You would certainly accept, and I suspect you would perform admirably, but you don't want it. Not yet, at least. Yes, you saved the city. You're not afraid of battle. And certainly you fight for the Frontier. I simply can't figure out how it is you wish to fight for your King."

Perking up, Axon straightened in her chair and laced her fingers on the table. "That is exactly why I came to the castle in the first place. I have a unique way that I can serve. I wanted to meet you so that I may try my hand at taking the Water Blade."

The page standing by the door audibly gasped. King Robion did his best to not betray any emotion, but Axon saw him flinch.

"In all my years as King, I've only ever administered the test once. The results were not good. It is an awful thing to see, such madness, and I'm sure a far worse fate to experience. Please, I beg you not to do this."

"But you will honor the request if I make it."

"I cannot deny you. I simply don't want to see such a fine soldier and such a beautiful woman destroyed by this thing."

She reached over and grabbed a knife off the tray. Stabbing a piece of cheese, she said, "I have had a vision. The Great Deities have sent me here as one step on my path toward destroying the Beast. I cannot turn away from that. Even if Qareck appeared before me and told me not to do it."

"Why?"

"Because it's the right thing to do. Because it will save our people." She ate the piece of cheese.

Pushing away from the table, the King stood. He paused, and she thought he might try to dissuade her again. In the end, he offered a soft shake of the head. "If you survive this, the Water Blade is yours."

"Now?"

King Robion's bitter smile chilled her. "If I had my way, then yes. I'd rather see you die tonight than grow to like you and watch you die when I might really care."

"But?"

"I would never deny a mother or a father their chance to be with their daughter before such a treacherous undertaking."

Her stomach dropped. "My parents?"

"You will have a final meal with them, and you will have a few hours to rest. I will send a page to call on you late tonight and you will have your chance for the Water Blade."

She barely heard him. "I have to have dinner with my parents?"

CHAPTER FIVE

T he last time Axon had stepped foot on the family estate, she could barely hold a sword properly. She knew how to ride a horse but lacked the strength and confidence to guide any animal into battle. She had been an ache in her father's side and a sheer disappointment to her mother.

The ostentatious dining room—overly-high ceiling, long, stained windows, beautiful tapestries on the wall space between, and the great fireplace set in the back—grew higher, bolder, more intimidating as she approached. But seeing their faces as her footsteps echoed, witnessing the love and adoration beaming off them both, Axon had to wonder if the King had informed her parents of her plan to try for the Water Blade. Perhaps they knew this might be the last night of Axon's life. Perhaps they wanted to encourage her, give her nothing to fear, and fill her with their love.

Her mother, always dressed to perfection with her hair set flaw-lessly, tapped a long fingernail at the empty setting to her side. "Come, Axon. Sit. We are so proud of you."

As Axon approached the table, she had to concentrate on walking without tripping. She had never heard such words before. "I thought you'd be angry. Here I am off fighting, getting dirty, doing the things you used to yell at Father about when he let me do them."

Her mother laughed before snapping a finger at her servant standing in the back corner. "We're ready to eat now, Darcy."

Darcy bowed. "Very good. I'll have the food up immediately."

To Axon, her mother said, "Don't simply stand there looking like a fool. Sit, sit."

For his part, Axon's father never stopped smiling. A big broad smile that reminded her of all the times he watched her compete and win. Though his tight, curly hair had grayed since she left, his boisterous voice boomed his deep love for her ever the same. "You saved an entire city. How can we be anything but proud of you?"

Her mother said, "Especially because you got this big parade and time alone speaking with the King. I admit I was against your way of doing things, but now it is clear that your value has increased tremendously. There will be quite a lot of princes interested in seeing more of you."

As Axon sat, her heart dropped. "Princes?"

"Don't worry your pretty head about it. I will handle everything. You wouldn't know the proper way of doing things anyway. Trust me and I'll see you connected to one of the best families in all the Frontier. In fact, I already have set up one of the most eligible men for you to enjoy lunch with tomorrow."

"I don't want to have lunch with some stuffy prince I've never met. I'm not interested."

Axon's mother tapped the table—a soft but firm sound. "Don't be ungrateful. You had several years out there roaming around the world against my wishes and better judgment. The fact that it turned out well for you is wonderful, but that is no excuse for the disrespect you have shown me and your family." Her lips curled into an approximation of a warm smile. "But now you're home. It's time to put away the silliness with swords, dress like a proper woman, and join the rest of society."

"You still won't listen to me."

"And you still only think of yourself. You can't expect to do everything exactly the way you want without any repercussions to others. All of your traipsing has hurt the rest of the family. How do you think it affected your brother at the University? He's probably been denied several promotions when they found out he had a fighter for a sister. And thank goodness your sister got married when she did or she would be looking at a life alone by now."

Axon looked at the empty table settings. "Where are they?"

"We had no idea you would be coming here," her father said. "The University is over a full day's travel and Jess sent a message that she is feeling a little under the weather."

Her mother said, "Jess is giving a polite excuse because she doesn't want to be in the same room with somebody who wishes to lower themselves like you."

Darcy returned with several other servants carrying trays of food. Axon could smell the salty and rich aroma of pala stew—her favorite growing up. As the servants walked around the table and set things down, poured wine, and made sure everything looked properly perfect, Axon struggled to understand the situation. She had thought the King provided her with a final family dinner before risking her life, but it was evident that her parents knew nothing of her plans. Otherwise, why would her mother set up a lunch for tomorrow?

And her father—sitting in his fine suit with his heavy waistcoat and fur-lined collar—he should be straining to hold back his tears. He blubbered when she went off to school the first time at age five. Knowing she faced death should have him full of non-stop affection.

As she set her napkin in her lap, she noticed that she had not had time to change her clothes. She still wore her full traveling outfit. Partially out of habit, she said, "I'm sorry. I swear I did not wear this to insult you."

"Didn't the King give you enough time to find a dress? Your father and I have been worried about you for years, haven't had the chance to see you, and this is how you come to our home. You didn't actually speak with the King wearing that, did you? I can see you have a lot of learning ahead of you if you want to fit in."

"Now, now. Never mind about all that," her father said. "We have plenty of time to get reacquainted and accustomed to the way things are. For now, honey, we want you to know that we love you and are so proud of your accomplishments."

Axon could not hide her bitter tone. "Just so long as I stop wearing this and put on a dress. Just so long as I marry myself off to some prince. Is that it?"

"Are these such bad things?" her mother asked. "Do you hate this kingdom so much?"

"I have fought for this kingdom. I still fight for it. What do you think I'm doing out there?"

"That's the problem. Orlar only knows what you could get up to out there."

Axon popped to her feet, her wine glass spilling a little. "I fight to preserve our world. You live behind the city walls and the walls of this estate. You have no idea what is out there. You have servants and money and all the food a person could want. But the world is changing. Do you know in the East they've done away with kings? Just got rid of them. They try to govern themselves now. It's insane. And out in the West, there are monsters that want to destroy everything you have. And what stops them?" She leaned over the table. "Me."

Despite all she had been through in her life—all the training she had endured, all the fights she had won, all the dangers she had faced —her mother's stern eyes and cold, narrow mouth still held the power to force her back into her seat. A quick glance from her mother sent her father muttering some excuses as he kissed Axon's cheek and hurried away from the dining room. A snap of her mother's fingers and Darcy ushered all the servants out of the room as well. Axon tried to keep her knees from bouncing. She failed.

"Eat your dinner before it gets cold," her mother said.

"I'm not hungry." At least her voice held firm.

Axon's mother set her fork down with a sharp clink. "I see you have every intention of being as obstinate as possible. Very well, then. Since you have apparently lost all good manners on your travels, I will lower myself to be blunt."

"When have you ever held back your opinions?"

She closed her eyes, and Axon knew her mother made a quick prayer to Sazieck for parental strength. "Since you were little, you've always wanted to be noticed. You were never satisfied being part of the group. Everything about you centered around trying to make a name for yourself. If there was a race, you had to be the fastest. If there was a ball, you had to be the best dancer or wear the prettiest dress."

"I've always been competitive, so?"

"Oh no, my baby, you do not strive to be the best out of a sense of competition. You simply want the title. You want to be singled out. Special."

"Then why can't you understand that I'm not interested in marrying just any prince who happens to take interest because I'm becoming well-known?"

"You are the one that does not understand. You have this thing about you, this need to be seen as special, and so when you tell me how you fought off the bad creatures and saved everyone, you did not do it out of a noble reason of helping people. You did it for the fame. This is why you don't want anything we have to offer. Our family name has value. But not to you. You are all about yourself. You see, when you participate in society, when you marry well or do anything that brings honor to our family name, you immortalize the family. That's far more important than us as individuals. The family name will go on long after both of us have died. But you don't value that."

"What do you know of what I value?"

Gesturing to the door, her mother said, "If you truly value the family, then when you walked in here, you would have been so excited to share your honors as a member of the family. It would not be *I saved everybody,* but rather *look what it's done for the family.* You would have been thrilled that you have restored some of the value to our name which you took away when you went off in the first place. I'm honestly amazed that you were able to get anybody to follow you into battle. I should think those in your group will figure out soon enough that you'll gladly sacrifice them at any moment if it means gaining more fame for yourself."

"But Daddy—"

"Your father is a wonderful man with a generous heart. Do not try to bring him down into this. You've done enough damage to this family as it is." Axon's mother pushed her chair back and stood. "I think you're right. I don't have much of an appetite, either. I'll see that Darcy leaves the information about tomorrow's lunch in your bedroom. And when you attend, please wear a more appropriate outfit."

Axon wanted to argue more, but her mother walked away. Part of her wanted to run off and find her father. He would hug her, kiss the top of her head, and let her feel as if everything her mother had said was wrong. But one aspect of her mother's words stung of truth—Axon's actions did reflect poorly on the family. At least, as far as society considered it.

If she died in her attempt to get the Water Blade, the King would make sure all knew of the sacrifice she had made. Perhaps that might help restore some of the damage she had done to the family name. But if she succeeded, there would not be time for fancy lunches with hopeless suitors. If she succeeded, the Beast of the West would be her next task. And if that horrible vision in her mind spoke the truth, then the Beast awaited her as well.

She lifted her fork and shoveled in the salty stew. Though she had become accustomed to eating whatever fare came her way on the road, she had to admit, every bite of this wonderful meal brought joy into her mouth. She ate faster.

CHAPTER SIX

When Axon was little, she often wandered away from the nannies watching over the court children. She would explore parts of the castle, parts of the city, and on a few occasions, she managed to wander outside the city walls. Once when this happened, she had stowed away on a farmer's cart and ended up in his barn. Afraid she would get caught by an angry farmer, she searched for a good hiding place and discovered a door that led to the cold cellar. Though only a few feet deep and not much wider, her steps into that dark and chilly place left her with nightmares for months to come. Following King Robion down the stone stairs, spiraling lower and deeper until she knew they were underground, prickled her skin with that same sensation—a touch of cold, a touch of dank, a touch of dread.

The King had stopped speaking as if the dark pressures around them made speech difficult. Axon flexed her fingers and repeatedly took deep breaths, but she could not ease her tension. She had asked for this. She wanted it. She trusted her sense of purpose. She trusted that the Beast's repeated attacks only proved its vulnerability—it knew she could destroy it. Yet none of that could stop this growing suspicion that she should have listened to the King. That she might be stepping into the greatest mistake of her life.

At the bottom of the stairs, they walked through a tight corridor and entered a large circular room. Torches burned in sconces around the perimeter. The ceiling, shaped like a dome, reflected torchlight off a circular pool of water in the center. Despite the cold of being underground, this room felt warm. A little stuffy, even. Gesturing to the pool, King Robion said, "You begin in there."

Axon walked to the edge of the water. She gazed in—clear and cool, no fish, no algae, an entirely unnatural purity. Fighting the urge to glance back at the King, she stepped in and waded toward the center. The water lapped against her thighs and splashed higher the faster she moved. With her heart hammering and her fingers tapping the pool's surface, she stopped at the center and turned around.

While she had made her way in the water, a page had entered, and the young boy whispered something into the King's ear. With a nod from the King, the page scurried away.

"The Godwalkers will soon arrive." The King took a tentative step closer. "Once they enter, the test will have begun and I cannot stop it. If there is the smallest sliver of doubt within you, then be honest with yourself and stop this now. Any doubt, no matter how small, may result in madness or even your death."

Raising her chin and speaking loud enough that her voice thundered in the echo, Axon said, "If I were to stop now, then those who have died to get me here will have died for nothing. I am ready."

The King lowered his head. "Very well."

As he stepped back toward the wall, nine cloaked figures entered the room. The first six wore floor-length white cloaks with black trim—one for each of the Deities of Life. The next two wore cloaks of red with white trim—in honor of the God and Goddess of the sexes. And finally, one entered in black with white and red trim—the one Lord over All Existence. A design had been embroidered on the right sleeve of each figure. These nine Godwalkers spaced evenly around the circular room.

The black-clad Godwalker representing Qareck, Lord of All Existence, stepped forward and pulled back the hood. Axon saw a woman, elderly and blind—her eyes covered with a dried mucus. White and red lines had been painted on her face. The old woman spread her hands as if feeling the warmth from the distant campfire. She hissed, and the other Godwalkers took off their hoods. They alternated men and women corresponding with the sex of the deity they represented. They were different colors and different cultures, but all of them were late in their years and blind in their eyes.

Only when King Robion spoke did it hit Axon how quiet the procession had been. Despite their age and their clothing, their movement in an echoing, cavernous room had made barely a sound. These were nothing like the Godwalker she had dealt with before, and she worried that woman may have been a fraud. If so, then all of this was a mistake.

As the woman in black stepped back to the wall, King Robion came forward. He cleared his throat, and Axon knew he wanted to offer her another chance to escape. He would not do so, of course—that time had gone—but like any good King, he did not want to see harm come to one of his subjects. Especially one he seemed to value.

"Long ago," he said, his voice small at first, "back when most of these lands had yet to be settled, back when Ridnight was little more than a town with a good leader and a loyal community, there came a threat from the West. A creature born from darkness, an unseen force filled with evil that only dreamt of devouring those who dared to make the Frontier their home."

One Godwalker stepped forth. The design embroidered on her sleeve—a baby in utero—represented Tiq, Goddess of Birth. Her right hand stretched out from the long sleeve, and she tossed a red powder into the water.

As she returned to her spot, King Robion continued, "Our ancestors had never seen such a creature before and had no understanding of how to deal with it. It is thought that our first overtures were of friendship. But I do not believe that. Being King has taught me that most people make decisions and act from fear. But whether friendship or violence, an overture was made, and the creature that we would later call the Beast attacked and destroyed."

The next Godwalker moved to the edge of the pool. On his sleeve, the shining sun design of Ovlar, God of Childhood. Putting out his hand, he spread a brown powder into the water before returning to the others.

"The leader at the time was a young woman who would later become the first of the royal line, Queen Lorraine. But back then, she was nothing more than the daughter of a farmer."

The third Godwalker took her turn. Her sleeve bore the design for Bieck, Goddess of Adolescents—clashing swords. With a swift motion, she tossed in a purple powder. As she eased back, Axon noticed the clouds of color under the water billowing toward her.

"For many years to come, the settlers worked hard to maintain their town, the farms, and their families. Every few years, the Beast would come and take as many lives as it could. Though the people of Ridnight fought back, they learned fast that they could not defeat the Beast. They could only annoy it until it would finally leave."

The Godwalker representing Sazieck, God of Adulthood, stepped forth and with an arc of the hand, tossed a blue powder into the water. Axon saw that his sleeve bore the image of a healthy, strong tree. The water swirled with colors, and where it touched her skin, she felt a soothing warmth.

"By the time Lorraine had become an adult, she could no longer accept this pattern of struggle and death. She had heard a rumor that far in the mountains to the north, was a wellspring of magical properties. And despite the assurances of her parents and the town Shul that this was nothing more than myth, she embarked on her own adventure to find this wellspring in hopes that its magic might save them from the next time the Beast attacked."

Another Godwalker stepped forth—Orlar, Goddess of the Elderly. Her sleeve depicted a setting sun, and like those before her, she threw her powder into the water. Green this time.

"Nobody heard from Lorraine again. The parents buried a box of items representing their lost daughter and life went on. But, the next time the Beast showed, as it threw its evil upon the growing town, a figure appeared in the street—an old woman carrying a sword made of water. She fought the Beast and based on all accounts, she would have killed it, but it ran off. It cowered back to the West where it has remained ever since. Lorraine became Queen and she quelled the desire of some to race into the West and finish the Beast. As long as the Beast stayed in its lands, there would be no problems. We would honor the border and all would remain in peace."

The last of the Godwalkers representing the Deities of Life stepped forward. On his sleeve, the bone design of Wiq, God of Death. He spread black powder into the water.

"Before she died, Queen Lorraine set the Water Blade beneath the castle and charged the Godwalkers with its protection. She believed that someday either the people or the Beast would forget this peace. Someday another would have to come along and claim the Water Blade."

The three Godwalkers representing the Greater Deities stepped forth and in unison spread white powder into the water. Axon shook her head, trying to push off the sudden fuzziness that clouded around the edges of her thoughts.

Raising his voice, the King said, "Only these Godwalkers know the test Queen Lorraine has devised. Only they can tell if you have passed. This test is not some arbitrary group of games the Queen put forth, but rather it is the very test she had to endure in order to get the Blade originally. Be careful. To fail is to be destroyed. I wish you the greatest of luck."

Like actors in a play, the Godwalkers moved forward in unison and positioned at the edge of the pool. Axon had not noticed it before, but each time one of the Godwalkers had spread their colored powders into the water, they did so with their right hands. The left hands remained hidden under their long sleeves. But now, each one of them pulled their left hand out and placed it into the water. Every single Godwalker bore a left hand twisted and knobby, charred and weathered. A few were missing fingers while for others, white bone could be seen.

With their hands in the water, Axon felt a strange jittering along her skin as if hundreds of tiny fish nibbled at her. She looked up and spotted King Robion in the back. They locked eyes, and she saw in his face that he already prepared a eulogy for her.

The world melted away. It began on the walls—the orange fire of the torches seeped toward the floor slow and thick like lava. The stone slid downward, filling in the gaps and cracks of age, creating a solid gray wall. And the faces—the Godwalkers and the King dripped like wax under a hot fire. As this liquefied world disappeared beneath her, Axon found a mesmerizing blend of colors that swirled and swooped. Reds that pulsed like heartbeats while lazy greens swung to and fro. Ambers and violets rolled by like fine ribbons on a new dress.

"I am the Godwalker that speaks for all."

Though Axon could not see where the voice came from, she had no doubt that this was the Godwalker dressed in black—the one connected to Qareck, the Lord of All Existence.

"To be worthy of the Water Blade, you only must find your way back. Fail, and you'll forever be lost."

She heard nothing more, and after a short time, she sensed that the Godwalker had disappeared. With that thought, the hypnotic swirls of color settled and took form. It happened fast, barely giving her brain time to register what her eyes witnessed. When it finished, she stood behind the castle, on the training grounds for new recruits.

All she had to do was get back to the pool. But she was no fool. It could not be that simple.

CHAPTER SEVEN

The training ground had not changed in all the years since her days as a young and eager beginner. The running courses, the muddy pool, the fighting dummies, the balance tests, and even the endurance portions of the field could have been plucked from her memories. Though she had been allowed to participate, though she trained every bit as hard and long as those destined to be in the King's Guard, they denied her the honorific of being called a cadet. Despite the slight, she would pass the courses with honor and dignity—part of the reason King Robion allowed her to patrol the Frontier in his name.

She wondered if she would catch the latest batch of recruits going through their routines. The air smelled heavy of spring flowers—a bit late in the season for such things. Very late, in fact.

She did not hear anyone nearby nor did she see anyone. Perhaps the cadets were on a forced march to build up their stamina. No matter. She was not here to reminisce. According to the Godwalker, all she had to do was get back to the pool beneath the castle. That meant getting back into the castle.

Trying to remain alert for any attack, she headed away from the field. But after three steps, she heard a heavy voice from her past.

"Just where in Wiq's name do you think you're going?"

Axon slowly turned back to find the dark, muscular form of Master Kallinog—the man who had taught her how to fight, her first mentor. A man who had been dead for eleven years.

Pointing to a group of seven young trainees, he said, "You know the rule—nobody leaves the field until everybody has succeeded. What? Do you think you're above us all?"

She could feel her body shrinking under his gaze. His powerful voice regressed her to the days when she barely knew how to hold a sword.

"Don't make me repeat myself."

Before she could process her own thoughts, her legs jogged her body towards the group. But even as she came closer, she could not make out their faces—they were blurry with features just on the edge of recognizable like a name she knew but could not pull from her head.

"Sorry, Master Kallinog," she said, keeping her gaze low. "I've been summoned to the castle."

Under normal circumstances—normal for over a decade ago—she would never have lied to Master Kallinog. But she had no idea what the rules were for speaking to a dead man, and since the only rule she had been given was to get back to the pool, she decided lying would not be unacceptable. Unfortunately, Master Kallinog did not agree.

He stepped closer, her face only coming up to his broad chest, and with his nostrils flaring, he said, "You are my trainee. Mine. You do what I say, when I say, and right now I say you stay here until the whole group has succeeded."

Axon looked over at the group of cadets—one sat on the ground nursing her ankle. *Her?* How did Axon know the cadet was female when she couldn't see their faces?

Donya. That was the girl's name. As it entered Axon's mind, Donya's face took shape—serious brown eyes, straight auburn hair, pert nose, uneven teeth. Axon remembered her well. And she remembered this moment, too.

As Master Kallinog yelled on about duty and loyalty and teamwork, Axon stepped away and looked across the course. This wasn't just the training ground—this was *her* training ground. The irrigation ditch on the far corner had only lasted a few years before the King had it moved. And the fighting dummy in the middle had a face one of the cadets painted on it—but over five years ago, that dummy had been replaced. None of this was current. None of it was real. It had been ripped right from her memories.

Which meant that she knew exactly how to get away from here.

She stepped before the group of cadets, all their faces slowly taking shape as she remembered them. "Listen up," she said, and those faces stared right at her. "We have a mission to finish. All of us need to get through this course to the other side of the pit—including Donya. This isn't that complicated. Everybody takes a turn carrying her, and when we need to, we carry her together. Let's go."

Taking the lead, Axon cradled Donya and headed off down the course. Three steps in, the world melted away.

When it reformed, she stood in the middle of a private study. Dusty volumes lined the walls, statues of the Cassun Nine filled in the vertical gaps between bookcases. A wooden desk filled with yellowed papers and melted candle wax took up the back of the study while several old, somewhat comfortable chairs had been placed haphazardly throughout the room.

While she had been in this study only once, she would never forget it. It began with her parents arguing. They wanted her to wear more dresses and attend more balls. They wanted her to act proper and attractive. They wanted her to marry. She overheard them discussing her future—overheard her mother chastising her father for letting their daughter ever pick up a sword.

"She has such beautiful, dark skin," her mother had said, "but all any man will ever see is her armor and her sword and the bloodlust in her eyes."

Axon ran off with the delusion that she would escape the city, escape any search, and become a great warrior wandering the countryside, helping the people. Looking for a quiet place to cry, she found this study. She did not know which chemist it belonged to—or perhaps it belonged to someone more dangerous—but the arcane nature of the texts on one wall and the religious texts on another told her enough.

As it had when she was a child, the room unnerved her. She had the constant sensation of being watched. She felt like the subject of an experiment.

Axon shivered and tried to toss aside the memory. Because in the past, she had backed up to the door, slipped into the hall, and ran off. The danger of the room, the sense of unseen eyes lurking amongst the books, unnerved any sense of her future. She would be crazy to defy her family when the court had rooms like this at their disposal.

Later, she returned home and received a sound thrashing from both parents. She would still go on to be a fighter but not by running away. She trained under Master Kallinog and got her position through legitimate channels.

But here, in the conjured world of the Godwalkers, none of that would happen. She turned around to leave and found the door had vanished. A solid wall had taken its place.

She paused, closed her eyes, and listened. She heard no footsteps. No breathing. No sign of the rest of the castle. While the Godwalkers had pulled the room from her memory, they had not created the rest of the surrounding building. They had not populated it with a castle full of servants and entertainers and royalty. It was like a stage play with no other actors and no script.

She looked left and right, half expecting to see the wings of the theater. But she found only the walls of the study.

Walking behind the desk, she thought about how she had escaped the training ground—helping someone in need. But she was the only one here. There was nobody to help.

She sat. So many books—hopefully, she wouldn't have to read them all in order to get out. That would take the rest of her life. With a touch of her hand to her necklace, she recited a quick prayer to Tortu, God of Woman.

Why here? This seemed like an odd memory to pull her into—assuming, of course, that the Godwalkers had a choice in which memories they activated. But if it was random, then there would be no logic to use in trying to solve her escape. Better to go with the idea that this location, this memory, had been chosen. So, why this one?

The answer would have nothing to do with the room itself. Axon had only been here one time and only for a few moments. Perhaps then the memory had to do with what she was running from—her parents' design on her future.

She had wondered from time to time what might have happened had she not disappeared for so many hours. If she had stayed in her room and let her mother tell her what they had decided for her future. Would they have forced her to give up the sword? Would they have insisted she wear a ball gown and seduce a suitor? Or, if she had given them the chance, would she have found respect and understanding and love? It was possible. After all, her father had introduced her to swords in the first place, and despite the beating, he rallied for her to train properly. He even had a hand in gaining her the position under Master Kallinog. Perhaps her parents would have found a compromise. Instead, she angered them, took a beating, and vowed never to become a lady of the court.

She never regretted it, but if she were honest with herself—and she tried to always be so—she had to admit that she lamented the loss of her more womanly side. Plenty of women became fighters and soldiers, but few ever delved into the world she had. It's one thing to be part of the King's Guard, but to fulfill a fantasy of walking the countryside to help people, to be a wandering warrior, that was unusual. And despite how much she disliked the term *warrior,* she had to be honest—that's what she was.

"I never would go back, though," she said, letting her voice echo upon herself. "No matter what small part of me enjoyed the dresses, the music, the dancing, and the romance, I would never go back. Holding a blade is what I was born for. Fighting to protect the country I love and its people. No regrets."

With a soft clink, the wood door reappeared in the wall where it belonged, and it opened.

Afraid the door might change its mind, Axon jumped to her feet and hastened out of the room. The colors of the study broke and blended until they reformed once more into a new location. This time, she stood in a dark forest.

Her heart skipped and her breath froze. Her skin prickled as a lump formed in her chest. She knew this place. This was not pulled from one of her memories.

It came from her nightmares.

The air grew colder, and the thick mist rolled in through the trees. Moonlight poked its way to the ground creating strange shadows of twisted forms twined around each other. Leaves rustled, twigs snapped, and strange breathing echoed through the trees.

Axon stood still. Part of her could not move as her body recalled the heart pounding terror she had felt whenever this nightmare plagued her. But more, she did not move for a darker reason—in her nightmare, no matter what she would try, no matter what action, nothing would let her escape these haunted woods.

The Godwalkers' previous tests had been based on real events, real memories. But this—this had been conjured by the bleaker fears in her brain. There was no way out, never had been. So how could the Godwalkers expect her to get back to them?

First thing she needed to do—calm down. The panic clawing under her heart was a reaction to her memory of a nightmare. But those horrible dreams attacked a little girl. Not the woman who stood here now. Not the warrior who could handle herself in any conflict.

Axon closed her eyes and inhaled deeply. As she exhaled even slower, she opened her eyes and centered herself. She could handle this.

In the nightmare, she never escaped—never except for one way. She would wake up. Only upon waking could she end the terror of that forest.

As if in response to her thoughts, a deep growl erupted from behind the copse of trees to her left. She did not flinch. Didn't even blink. She would not let spooky sounds and shapeless shadows harm her.

She bit her bottom lip. Hard. When that produced no result, she slapped her cheek. Finally, she pinched the soft skin under her arm. But none of these resulted in waking her.

Because I'm already awake.

From nearby, she heard the gentle mewling like a newborn graypot—a small, tubby creature that ate seeds and often resembled its name. Such an innocent sound amongst all the dark threat. Perhaps she had to protect that creature, that little babe. Perhaps in doing so she would open up a passage out of this place.

Tracking the sound had been easy, but she did not find a little graypot or even a newborn creature at all. The woods had tricked her. She stepped out into a shadowy clearing, and in the center, Axon found Xarad—on his knees, head down, sweat drenching him.

She rushed over, pulling out her sword in case somebody attacked. When she reached him, she saw his unmoving body. No—she saw breathing, shallow breathing. He was alive. But whatever had been done to him, soon he would be dead. Again.

She dropped to her knees and wrapped her arms around him. Holding his head to her chest, she stroked his hair, hoping she could offer some comfort in his final moments. "I'm so sorry. I've failed you again. I failed you when you died the first time because I didn't know how to help you. I failed you this time because it took me too long to find you." The words bubbled out of her, and she could not stop them. "I'm trying. Please, believe that. I'm doing what I can to find out who killed you. I'll see that they pay. I will do whatever I must so that your soul can rest. I promise you that nothing will stop me from finding who's responsible."

From behind, she heard the creature enter the clearing—heavy steps accompanied by a deep growl. Moving as slow and nonthreatening as she could manage, she rested Xarad on the ground and rose to her feet.

Looks like I have to protect someone after all.

Easing her sword into a ready position, she glanced down at Xarad. Still alive. This was the test, then. Kill the creature and save Xarad. Do it right this time.

The ground rumbled as the creature emerged.

CHAPTER EIGHT

An alabaster monstrosity ambled from the mist. Legs grew out of its undulating torso, reached ahead, and pulled its mass forward, retracting its legs in the back. Its pale head sat atop the torso like a shell covered with a thin row of eyes and a sharp-toothed mouth. Snarling and growling, the creature snapped its jaws as it circled Axon.

Setting her feet in a sturdy and balanced fighting stance, Axon held her sword at the ready. Her heart hammered against her chest as she swallowed down the childish whimper creeping up her throat. She knew this thing. And it knew her, too. It had haunted her many nights while growing up.

She kept her eyes locked on this creature. It smelled of rotten eggs and mold, and Axon forced herself to breathe only through her mouth. From the way it maneuvered around her, she could tell that its interest rested in Xarad's body. Perhaps it sensed he was dying and wanted an easy meal. Perhaps it was a carrion feeder and simply sought the first taste before other scavengers arrived. In her nightmares, she had never lingered long enough to find out. No matter the case, Axon would kill the creature long before it had a chance for even one nibble.

Another step and the creature launched into its attack. It barreled forth like a tumbling boulder. Legs whipped out and retracted. Axon watched this white billowing form with sharp teeth coming her way.

Timing her move for the last possible moment, she held her ground before leaping into the air. As she angled off to the side, her blade came down hard on the passing creature. The steel made contact, and the strike reverberated up her arm.

Landing on her feet and in complete control, she spun around and readied for another attack. But the creature looked unharmed. Not even a mark.

It also looked disoriented.

Axon charged forward to take advantage of the creature's lack of focus. She blasted by its side, raking her sword across its skin. She heard a satisfying moan.

Placing herself between the creature and Xarad, she held her sword up, lowered her body, and sent a blistering glower at her enemy. But as the creature faced her, she did not see a scratch on it. No blood, no marks, nothing.

"Impossible," she whispered.

Snorting, the creature broke into another rampaging attack. Though she did not hold much hope for landing a wound, she planted her feet and prepared to repeat her maneuver. There was not time for another plan. As the creature opened its mouth, as it neared, Axon calculated the timing and launched into the air at an angle.

But the creature had learned. It slid to a halt and shot out two milky-white appendages that latched around Axon's legs and threw her to the ground.

She managed to turn in time to protect her head, but her side took a hard hit. Rocks and sticks on the ground dug into her while the impact shot the air from her lungs and rattled her head. Struggling to her feet, she felt a short breath of relief—she still held her sword.

But the creature did not relent. Two pearly legs kicked her in the gut and side, knocking her to the dirt once more. And the thing jumped onto her. As if being trampled by a stampeding herd, the creature's numerous legs appeared, stomped on her, and retracted. Over and over.

Another appendage snaked out of the creature and wrapped around Axon's waist. It hurled her into the air, and unspooling as it went, spun her as far as it dared to let her go. The world circled around her until she felt the ground smacking into her back. She rolled along the dirt, coming to rest against Xarad's still form.

Axon lifted her head and peered across the clearing. The limited moonlight and roiling mist made it difficult, but she saw the form of the creature waiting for her. Despite the wobble in her legs, she planted her foot on the ground and tried to stand. Her knee shifted to the side and she fell forward, the brunt of her weight smashing into Xarad's gut.

The alabaster creature screamed.

Axon bolted to her feet, ignoring the pain and uncertainty of her legs, and held her sword tight. She saw the creature had bent slightly with two of its legs rubbing what might have been its stomach—as if soothing its pain. She glanced down at Xarad, at where she had fallen on him.

No. That would be sick.

Even the thought of testing the idea turned her stomach. But she could not simply stand there and wait for this creature to attack again.

Fighting back the urge to vomit, she placed the tip of her sword against Xarad's leg. In a fast, shallow motion, she sliced downward— nothing that would harm the young man but enough that she might see the results. The creature screamed as a crimson line appeared along its side.

She knew the solution, knew what the Godwalkers wanted, but she lifted her sword and focused on the creature. With a warcry erupting from deep within, she sprinted across the clearing, rage in her eyes, spit flying from her mouth, her legs pumping faster, faster, as she held her sword overhead, ready to strike. She focused on the wounded side. Focused on the blood. And though the creature had plenty of time to react, its attention had been drawn to his own injury.

Twisting her hips and torso, she put all of her weight behind the swing of her blade. She landed a clean hit on the open wound. Axon saw the row of eyes on the creature's head widen one by one in rapid succession. The corner of her mouth curled up—part smile, part snarl.

But her moment of victory vanished. The creature's shock came not from pain but simply surprise. It adjusted fast.

New limbs shoved out of its torso, took hold of Axon, and pummeled her into the ground. It smashed three successive body blows before pausing. Once it decided she would not move again, it limped off to lick its hands and press saliva into its wounded side.

With the heel of her hand, Axon rubbed the tears from her eyes. She got to her feet and limped back towards Xarad. She had tried. Even when she knew what they wanted of her, she still tried to attack that creature head on.

But this—Xarad—this was wrong. To make her kill him. To make her deliberately kill him.

She poised over his body, held her sword up, her muscles aching and its weight heavier than before. Gazing across the clearing at the creature, she shook her head. If she kept hacking away at this creature, kept trying to find an alternative, the creature would simply survive. It would hurt her but never kill her—at least, not until she had nothing left to give.

Her eyes drifted down to Xarad once more. "You're a sacrifice. I know you're not real. The real you died already. But if you were real, if I stood over you with this choice to make—could I? I think that's what this is about."

It had been easy to tap into the noble part of her that wanted to help an injured cadet finish the field course for the team. It had been easy to face the questions of her past, of who she could have become in a life she could have led. But that was not the real test. This decision was what the Godwalkers wanted all along. Could she face the true nature within herself—the part of her that would do anything to get that Water Blade?

Yes, she could.

She thrust her sword straight down through Xarad's chest. She felt a slight resistance of bone and kept pushing. Blood spurted out as she punctured his heart. She did not stop until the steel broke through his back and into the ground.

Across the clearing, a volcano of blood erupted from the creature's deformed torso. Black and crimson stained its horrid pale skin. It wobbled, unsteady on its numerous feet. With a gurgling growl, a sound empty of all threat, the creature toppled over and moved no more.

She looked back at Xarad and as blood dribbled from his chest, the world dribbled away around her. She did not care to look up, to watch the fantastic display of melting colors. She simply watched Xarad until he melted away, too.

When her eyes adjusted to the new room, her mind took longer to understand what she saw. At length, she lifted her head.

She stood in the middle of the pool surrounded by the Godwalkers and King Robion. She had returned. Her sword—the sword she had used to kill Xarad—stuck straight through the water and buried deep in the ground below. Yet she held another sword in her hand. Gazing down, her heart shuddered and she uttered a short cry.

The Water Blade.

She held the Water Blade.

It glistened blue and shimmered in the light. It looked solid as steel yet rippled like liquid. As she slowly sliced it across the air, bright blue droplets fell in its wake. She could see through it, the image distorted but visible. Perfectly balanced, perfectly weighted, it felt as if she did not hold a weapon at all but rather a work of art.

She heard splashing and wheeled around with the Blade held at the ready. The King rushed towards her, his hands out.

"It's just me," he said. In one hand, he held a scabbard specially designed for the Water Blade. Made of three deep-blue leather strips that had been weaved together, the scabbard also had a silver tip. With a formal bow, the King presented the gift to her.

Half-dazed, she accepted the scabbard and placed the Water Blade inside. She then bowed to the King in return.

"The Water Blade is yours," the Godwalkers said, still hiding which ones spoke. "It will always be as strong as you. The more you give to it, the stronger it will be."

"Rise with me," King Robion said, as he straightened. A bold smile filled his face. "I never thought I would see this." He stepped forward and wrapped his arms around her, holding her tight to his chest. She could feel him shaking as he said, "You will save us all. You will be a legend."

PART IV
ZEV

CHAPTER ONE

Zev crossed his arms tight against his chest as he stared out the guest room window. Ridnight spread before him, its people busily going through their day, their constant activity reaching up to the castle as a gentle murmur. Far in the distance, far beyond the clear sunny skies, Zev knew a dark storm gathered. To the West, to the East—violent change would soon be upon them. Yet looking at Ridnight, no one would suspect anything unusual or wrong awaited.

He tried to shake off his maudlin thoughts. No good would come from it. He crossed his large room to a beautiful carved table and a generous basket overflowing with fresh fruits. Biting a sweet yet tangy grava, his face tightened into a scowl. He did not deserve this treatment.

What had he done? While Axon and Henlio infiltrated the sludge wall, attacked the giants, fought off the witches—what had he done? Bellemont had cast the invisibility spell. Pilot possessed the skill and strength to protect her if any of the witches and soldiers had attacked. Zev merely stood out of the way.

And if it had ended there, that much was fine—he knew he was no warrior. But then the parade. Then the celebrations. Then the free drinks and food and music. Then the luxurious guest room in the King's castle with its abundance of fresh fruit that somebody had to spend the morning gathering up. If he had identified Xarad's killer—the thing he had been hired to do—then perhaps he would not feel so undeserving.

But he had failed in that. His disguise of being part of the team was meant to give him access to the team members. But he barely had a chance to question any of them. At least, the King's chemist, a brilliant woman named Andilee, had been able to help him to some degree.

She turned out to be a petite woman with a sharp, clipped way of speaking, and a methodical way about everything she did. She wore a colorful outfit and had a broad, bright smile. Her large workroom with its double doors and numerous worktables reminded Zev of an old schoolroom—albeit clean and organized far beyond any school he had ever visited.

He liked her from the start.

"In order to accurately identify this poison," she said as she carefully put away several instruments she had been using earlier, "we require a sample from the victim."

Zev leaned against a table. "That might be a bit tricky. Axon, the leader of our group, does not want Xarad's body disturbed. Desecrated. She's expecting a formal burial soon."

"That is not our concern. We are trying to determine what killed the man."

"I understand. I agree with you. But she—"

"I am the King's chemist. We'll have the deceased body delivered to us right away."

She exited the large room and returned a few moments later.

"You play cards?" she asked.

"Cards?"

"It will take the pages a little while to get the body over here. I thought we might play some cards."

Zev chuckled. "I have a suspicion that if I play cards with you, I'm going to lose a lot of money."

With a barking laugh, Andilee said, "I heard that you were a smart one. Clearly that's true."

Seeing he would not be lured into gambling, she turned to a stack of books at one desk. Zev crossed the room to examine one of several bookcases. He had never seen so many volumes in one place before. Many of them were histories. "I guess you study more than just chemistry."

"Absolutely. I don't believe in letting the mind wander aimlessly. There's too much to learn to waste time."

"Yet here we are wasting time until they deliver Xarad."

As if to mock him, the double doors leading into Andilee's workshop opened and two men entered with Xarad's body on a stretcher. Andilee indicated a wide table for them to place the body on. With a bow, both men left.

Without preamble, Andilee walked straight to the body and looked it over while holding a sharp, small knife in one hand. Zev hurried to her side.

"Please, remember that Axon does not want the body mutilated."

Glancing up at Zev as if she looked upon an imbecile, she said, "You seem to think I do not understand my job."

"Not at all. I meant no offense."

"Perhaps you best be quiet and observe, instead."

She turned Xarad's head to the side and placed a mirrored tray against the back of his neck. With the knife, she scraped bits of the skin onto the tray. When she finished and with his head turned back, nobody would spot the mark she had made.

Zev tried to ignore the cocky smirk on Andilee's face. He pointed to the discoloration on Xarad's lips. "I thought that perhaps we were dealing with subber leaf. Given the gestation period."

"Not a bad guess—for an amateur. But subber leaf would have also produced either a rash on the arms or further discoloration on the fingers and toes."

She took the tray over to a workbench where she laid out five small drinking glasses. In each one she placed some of the scrapings. She then poured liquid from several different vials into each glass.

They waited.

Eventually the reactions began. Andilee nodded at one glass, huffed at another, gave a thoughtful mutter at a third, and finally raised her eyebrows at the last. "This is not good," she said.

A strong, thudding knocked against the guest room door, snapping Zev's focus back to the present. He had no doubt that the knock belonged to Axon. He let her in, praised the Water Blade at her side—something she still sought compliments for—and offered her some of the fresh picked grava.

"My team heads out tomorrow morning," she said, taking a bite. "I need to know whatever answers you have."

Though his gut knotted at the admission, he had to be honest with her. "I still don't know who killed Xarad."

"That's it? It's been two days since I earned this sword. I've got Henlio resupplying and getting the horses ready. I can't wait any longer."

"Why the rush? You don't even know how to use the Water Blade, let alone what it can do."

"It's a sword. I know how to use it."

"It's obviously more than that."

"The great Queen Lorraine figured it out as she fought. If needed, so will I. But I can't get very far unless you tell me what you know."

Zev wanted to argue the point further, but instead, he said, "I've found out some information that might help, but it's not an answer. Not yet."

She bit into the grava with more force than before. "And?"

"Well, it's about the poison. I met with the King's chemist, and we took a sample off Xarad before his burial." He saw her bristle, but before she could throw out a bunch of useless objections to something already done, he pushed on as fast as his mouth would allow. "We identified the poison. Well, she did. It's called hookroot—mainly because it's a long root that hooks near the end."

"I have not heard of it."

"It's a rare kind of plant that doesn't grow on the Frontier. It's not found in the East, either."

"Not much of a surprise that it's from the Feral Lands."

"It's quite rare there, too. At least, according to Andilee's best books on the subject. Of course, our depth of knowledge regarding the West is limited. Now, hookroot behaves a lot like I suspected. It can be administered up to three days before a reaction occurs, and once it starts, it moves very fast. Depending on the dosage, it can kill the infected anywhere from a few minutes to an hour or two, at most. From the sample of Xarad we examined, Andilee thinks he had been given a severe dosage. But here's the crucial thing about hookroot—it's benign on its own. I could eat an entire root right now and it would just sit in me for two or three days before I passed it out."

"Then how did the killer—"

"Hookroot requires a catalyst that forces it to release its poison. So, even if Xarad had ingested the hookroot days before, even if someone not on your team facilitated that part of it, one of your team gave him the catalyst during the attack. In fact, the large dosage of hookroot combined with the sudden physical action of fighting—action which caused his blood to flow faster and distribute the poison faster as well—probably left him only a very short time to live. This catalyst is called sour-bale and it can be a liquid or a powder. The question I have for you—which member of your team spent time with Xarad during the attack?"

"Couldn't the whole thing actually be somebody from the town? They would have given him the hookroot when we first arrived to help and then the catalyst shortly before the attack."

"And why would that happen? Why would they want to kill the people who were helping save them? Did Xarad or anybody in your group ever have contact with the townspeople before?"

"No. None of us had ever been there."

"Then I think it's doubtful that they decided to murder one of you upon arrival. I know you want it to be true, I know it's hard to accept that one of your own caused this, but that fact hasn't changed. So, please think back to that battle—who had the opportunity to give Xarad the sour-bale?"

Axon took a final bite of the grava and set the core on the table.

She stepped over to the window, the sunlight spreading across her dark skin as if it spread open her memories. Her body grew still and her face grim.

"All of them," she said.

"All?"

"Xarad was assigned to protect Bellemont, so they had plenty of time together. I recall seeing him with Henlio when they helped get the townspeople to safety. And he was with Pilot when I was off fighting a witch. There were also several times when the chaos of battle meant any combination of my team could have happened. And near the end, all four of us were crowded under Bellemont's shield. So, yes, all of them."

Of course that was the answer. Had she been able to provide only one name, they would have had their killer already. It would be over. He could ride Stick home with a clear conscience and the King's reward. Instead, all of the suspects had to have spent time with Xarad.

He considered a more direct approach. With the King's blessing, they could have Bellemont, Henlio, and Pilot detained by the Royal Guard. While in custody, Zev could go through all their personal belongings and search for the catalyst. According to Andilee, sour-bale was rare enough that it would have no other purpose in any team member's possessions.

But Zev kept silent. The chances of the killer being stupid enough to still have the catalyst on hand were slim. Detaining the team but failing to find the killer would result in a demoralization of Axon's trusted friends right when she needed them most—as they headed after the Beast. Plus, and this was the biggest obstacle to the plan, the King would never agree. To detain three of the triumphant heroes only days after they had saved the city could cause a public outrage that would lead to far greater problems.

"Your Cassun Nine must hate me," Zev said.

"Oh?" She turned back, her brow down, her mouth taut. "Are we to have a religious argument?"

Waving off her sudden anger, he said, "I can't let this end with the killer undiscovered. I won't." He paused—his mind whirlpooling through possibilities that might lead to an alternative. But he ended up right back in the same position—with only one choice he could stomach. He swallowed against his drying mouth. "If you're willing to have me, I'd like to stay on. Into the West. Into the Feral Lands."

She shook her head right away. "The King will pay you like I promised. I certainly wish you had figured out who killed Xarad, but it is not your problem anymore."

"You hired me to solve this."

"I hired you because you have a reputation for intelligence. You've successfully handled a small number of situations, and it was wrong of me to assume that you were capable of a much larger problem. Take your payment and go back to your farm."

Zev gripped the table. "I can find your killer. I just haven't had enough time. Look what I've managed in just a few days—we know how Xarad was killed, what poison was used, and a rough timeframe for when it all happened. If I join you, there will be several days of travel ahead. I can finish my questioning of your people, and with more information, my chances for success grow significantly. I might even have the whole thing finished before we hit the border. Please. Let me do this."

Axon's eyes roved up and down Zev as she weighed her options. "If you come with us, it won't be as easy as before."

"That was easy?"

"You'll be expected to pull your weight in camp. If I have to outfit another person, then I demand you be a true member of the team— even as you stand back and observe."

"I can do that."

"You'll have to fill Xarad's role—protect Bellemont when she casts spells, join us in our fights, everything. We are going up against the Beast, and while I do have the Water Blade, that does not guarantee that we will win. And it certainly doesn't guarantee that we will all live through the battle."

He stepped closer to her. "I want you to succeed. I want you to stop this terrible threat to us all. That can't happen if you're stabbed in the back. Your chances of victory are slim while you have a traitor on your team. Allow me to come, and I'll be the only one you can know for sure is watching out for you."

Axon turned away and headed to the door. Zev kicked at a chair. He had to find something that would convince her.

Over her shoulder, she said, "We've got to get your workhorse outfitted and you need supplies."

Before she had finished talking, Zev rushed out the door. "Thank you," he said.

"You can thank me by making sure I don't get killed."

CHAPTER TWO

The following morning, Zev had to readjust the saddle on Stick three times—his hands kept shaking as he tightened the straps. He wanted to be noble and brave about riding off toward his death, but his brain repeatedly questioned, mocked, and frightened him. It would start by pointing out that nobody would care if he backed away. Nobody would think less of him. So why do this? He should take the King's money, go back to the farm, and figure out his next step in life from the safety of his porch. But he did not like the idea of leaving a murderer to go free.

His brain then argued that he needed to stop acting like he was a brilliant mind stuck amongst ignorant fools. Yes, he had solved a few simple issues in the past. No denying that. But clearly, the murder of Xarad posed challenges far beyond his meager capabilities. Otherwise, he would have found the killer by now. Going off to the Feral Lands only delayed his inevitable failure. But he did not hold himself up as some super-mind, and he did not think the problem was beyond his capability. In fact, after working with the King's chemist, he thought he had made a significant step forward. A little more time to question those who were potentially guilty might be exactly what he needed.

His brain finally pulled out the biggest threat it could fathom—

going off with the group meant agreeing to die in a few days. He was no fighter, and Axon had stated it clearly that he would be expected to fight. She had made him welcome but only after he stood his ground to join the team. She didn't really want him around. Besides, did he remember that little taste of the Beast and magic he had experienced? He wouldn't be able to hide behind a stack of supplies the next time. Only a fool would hurry off to die for nothing. And that was exactly what he could expect to gain from all of this. Nothing.

Of course, Zev believed he would gain a great deal—particularly, helping to save the entire Frontier. More importantly for the rest of his mind, for the parts that mulled over Xarad's death time and again, he would finally acquire some peace—for his mind and for the people. That's what he would gain.

Rebuffed with this argument, Zev's brain would cease the fight and let him prep Stick. But only for a short time. Soon, it would start up again, arguing that nobody would care if he backed out.

Thankfully, Henlio came over and dropped off Zev's portion of supplies—food, water, a blanket, and more. The King had his craftsman customize a sleeve for Zev's rifle that tied on the back-right of the saddle. Zev made sure to load the weapon as part of his packing procedure.

And soon, far faster than he liked, the job was done. He had no more getting ready to do. Any moment, he expected Axon to arrive with the rest of the team, and they would head out. They would ride west with danger on the horizon. But danger lurked amongst them, too.

When the team finally pulled together, the morning still had a few hours left to it. Axon did not want a big farewell from the city that would slow them down on their first day out. Plus, Zev suspected she no longer wanted hero-attention. As much as she clearly enjoyed having the Water Blade at her hip and the admiration that came with it, the reality of the fight ahead required her to return to a warrior's focus. He also noticed a bitterness develop with all her praise— perhaps public adoration did not please her so much after experiencing it.

Before they rode off, however, King Robion arrived at the stables. A dozen others followed him—assistants, valets, advisors, and those who required his attention or decision on a matter but could not wait in the castle. The few city folk who were awake peeked around corners or from windows to watch the King approach.

He strode right up to Axon and clasped her hand. "I've tried to think what else I could give to help you on your journey, but after the Water Blade, what more could you need?"

"You've been more than generous to us all," Axon said, trying to stare back with a firm countenance. But Zev noted a softness in her eyes.

"You have all the supplies you wanted?"

"Please, Your Highness, we have everything we could ask for. You and the wonderful people of Ridnight need not give anything else. It is our turn to earn your generosity once more."

He held his gaze on her for any extra few seconds before breaking into a broad smile and addressing the rest of the team. "All of you embark on the most important task Ridnight has ever asked of any soul. And not just Ridnight. The entire Frontier is indebted to you and your bravery. Many of our fine people will never know what you face, what you may sacrifice, what you will endure in taking on the Beast. But they will know that their lives and prosperity are owed to the great heroes that saved this wondrous land."

As he spoke, he made sure to give a hardy clap on the shoulders of Henlio and Pilot. Zev, however, only received a kind nod as if the King knew Zev did not really belong with this group. Perhaps Axon had confided in the King about Zev's true purpose. Perhaps royalty simply had a nose for the place a person fit. If so, the King also had a sense of humor—he gave Bellemont a hug that made her stiffen like a child forced to endure the embrace of an unknown relative.

"Mount up," Axon said, partially to get them moving and partially, Zev suspected, to save Bellemont further embarrassment.

The King stepped back and offered a final, gentle bow of his head. All of the people behind also bowed. Moments later, Zev followed the line of horses out of the castle, out of the city, and onward west. Just like that. The steady clop of hooves became the only sound as the team settled into their thoughts for the days ahead.

He could have used the whole city cheering them on as they left. He wouldn't have minded a slight delay due to a few celebratory toasts and enthusiastic songs. Perhaps that was one reason a woman like Axon led the team. If Zev had control, they might never have made it out of the city gates.

But they were out, they were on their way, and this time, Zev refused to fail. Which meant that the hour for subtlety was over. Before, when riding with them toward Ridnight, he had tried to act like a quiet, useful team member. Part of the group. New to the team and therefore reticent to put himself forth. That had been foolish. None of them would open up given the short time they expected to be with each other.

Yet he could not simply say that he was here to uncover which of them had murdered Xarad. So, while he no longer wanted to play the team newcomer, he would still require a deft approach as he attempted to question these people more directly.

Letting the morning air fill his lungs, he brought Stick alongside Pilot's horse, Majesty. Might as well get started right away. Before he could say a word, though, one of those new four-wheeled contraptions zipped up the road. The driver of the horseless cart laughed as he passed the team with ease, gently pumping his legs to make the vehicle move faster.

Pilot snorted and spit to the side. "I thought we were far enough away from that Eastern crap."

"It's going to be harder and harder to avoid."

Looking back as if a wall of new gadgets from the East mounted high into the sky, Pilot said, "Why can't they just leave us alone? The Frontier is a good place without all of that stuff." He glanced down at Zev's rifle and shook his head.

"It was a gift from my brother, but I agree with you. A horse is all you really need, and you can't become friends with a horseless cart. Sure, the cart gets you around, hauls your things, but a good horse does all that and becomes part of your life. It's a real relationship. Who is ever going to care about a machine?"

"Exactly."

Zev thought he had Pilot ready to open up, but the man grew quiet and gazed at the road ahead. He had to be careful. Push too hard and he would lose any chance of getting a word out of the man. Back off too much and there might not be another opportunity.

His leg bumped against the rifle and that brought to mind his brother. He recalled a simple idea that Marcel had told him once— whenever he needed to get a business deal moving forward and the other side appeared shaky, he would tell them a story of his past. "Something that would make me seem like one of them." Marcel promised that it always worked, that it relaxed the other side, that it got them talking.

Without a better idea on hand, Zev said, "My brother sent me this rifle as a bribe."

Pilot turned his head. "Yeah?"

"He runs the family business with my father. They want me to be part of it, too."

Adjusting his hat, Pilot's face opened wide. "Hold it. Your last name is Asterling, right? As in the clothing people?"

"That's us. My father worked hard as a shoemaker and my mother was a tailor. The quality of their work got the eyes of kings and queens and all of that. Built a great reputation. When the monarchies of the East fell, my parents invested in those new market exchanges and did well. My father expected me and my brother to take over."

"But that's no life for you, huh?"

"I sold off my interest and left for the Frontier. That world back there is changing so fast nobody is taking the time to understand what they're doing. For my brother, it's all about making money. Nothing wrong with money, but out here, you know there's more. You feel it in the clean air we breathe. You hear it in the sounds of birds and the rushing waters of a river. There's the animals, the land, the people. There's fighting for what's right."

Pilot looked into the distance again, but Zev saw a different face on the man. He was not ignoring Zev, but rather, he considered the words now. Perhaps he thought back through some memory. Zev wondered if he should let Pilot stew with those thoughts but reminded himself—no time for subtlety.

"Sometimes I wonder if I'll ever go back there at all. Even just to visit. What about you?"

Pilot snapped his attention on Zev. "Me?"

"You spent time in the East. Were you born there? Family to go visit?"

"Of course, I was born there. Any idiot can see that. Which means I got family there, too, right? I thought you were smart."

"I only meant—"

"I know, I know." Though Pilot chuckled, Zev could still hear the bite underneath. Pilot leaned his head back to warm under the morning sun. He smiled. "I even understand you wanting to go back even if you don't like your family."

"I like my—"

"Sure you do. Just like you're excited to go out west and fight the Beast."

"I'm not saying—"

"I don't know why you asked to come with us, but you're nervous about it. That's obvious. And it's okay, too. None of us want to be in this fight—maybe Axon, but none of the rest of us. It just is. This is where we ended up, and we got to do our best to make it worthwhile. Make sense?"

"But if you have family you love back east, why not go be with them?"

"Besides stopping the Beast from taking over the Frontier and then being a threat to them in the East?" Pilot laughed even as he leaned closer and spoke quieter. "Listen, you're in a tough spot, and I understand that. Nobody wants to be the new guy, let alone the new guy replacing the old guy that died."

"If you're going to tell me to relax and take my time, that's the problem—we don't have much time left."

Pilot raised his eyebrows as if that had never occurred to him. "You are in a unique predicament."

"I'm not trying to win you over. But a few days from now, we are all going in for probably the biggest battle of our lives. I'd like to know that I've done everything in my power to make sure we all can work together at our best. Learning about each other fosters camaraderie which is an important part of a group like this."

Pilot slapped his shoulder. "I take it back—you *are* a smart guy. Okay, okay. You want to know about me? I'll tell you the full truth." Once again, he leaned closer only this time he had a sardonic grin on his face. "Back when I lived in the East, I was a soldier in the Army."

"I can't picture that."

"Neither could the Army. Actually, I was a good soldier back when the government used its military simply to protect our land. But then they started liking the idea of going on the offensive, provoking attacks, and invading the Frontier. Said they were trying to prevent a war by stopping the Frontier before it could get the idea of a war started. Seemed stupid to me. Have a war so you don't have a war—makes no sense."

"I remember some of that happening—the build-up. But they never actually went to war with the Frontier."

"They would have. Trust me. I was training for it day after day. Only thing that stopped them was King Robion. He had the smarts, the charisma, the kingly power to talk the Eastern government off that ledge. I'm sure he had to give up quite a few things, too—probably some of the silver mines along the border.

"But, during all of that build-up, I may have been a bit too loud about my disapproval. Eventually, there was a mutual agreement between me and my superiors that I should leave the Army. Not long after, I started getting harassed by local authorities. Sometimes just words or being asked to leave a bar. Sometimes a few punches. I could have handled it. But then they went after a few very close friends— people more family than family to me. And that started it off."

"Started what?"

Pilot rested his hand on Zev's shoulder—his grip tighter than before. "Let's hope you never have to find out that answer. I'll say this, though—when it was over, I knew I had to leave the East. If I stuck around there, they would have found some excuse to kill me. So, here I am. Free in the Frontier with the sun warming my face and a mission I can believe in. What more can a man want?"

Though Pilot thought himself clever, Zev had no trouble deciphering what had happened. Angered by the attack on his friends, Pilot must have flown into a rage and retaliated against the soldiers. He clearly ran from the East. And from the way he often looked in that direction, worried some soldiers might appear any day, he most likely killed one of them.

Was that uncontrolled rage what caused Pilot's trouble? Could that have been behind the fight with Xarad over a woman? Could a man enraged like that think straight enough to deliver both parts of the poison?

"If you ask me," Pilot said, "all of us are seven colors of crazy. Even Axon. I mean look at it—she's not been dealing with Xarad's death at all. He wasn't gone for a day and she replaces him with the first guy we come across—no offense. Whole thing is rotten."

Zev hunched over Stick as he squinted ahead. Pilot had a point. Axon had made some odd choices. Something did not seem right. Was there a possibility that *she* had murdered Xarad? If she had, she could then have hired Zev in an effort to look innocent. But she would have made Zev's purpose clear to the others in order to shift doubt. Unless she feared they would see through that.

The more he thought about it, the more it seemed like a viable thread of inquiry. After all, she had put more obstacles in his investigation than anybody. She refused to let him properly examine the body. She had insisted that they push ahead to the castle in the middle of the night, thus lessening the amount of time he had to question the others. And when he offered to stay on with the team, to see this through to its end, she tried to dissuade him. He didn't like the thought, but until he could prove otherwise, he had to keep her in his list of possible killers as well.

Pointing to a hand-painted sign, Axon said, "Landbreak Bridge—half-a-day to go."

An arrow on the sign indicated the direction of the bridge—one of only a few paths across the massive chasm separating the Frontier from the West. As they rode by the sign, Axon's words hit Zev's ears with the dull finality of a coffin thumping into the ground.

CHAPTER THREE

Over the course of the day, Zev relaxed as much as possible under the long, endless travel. He had read plenty of stories of adventurers going off on amazing quests and encountering terrifying trials, yet nobody ever spoke of the incessant boredom that filled the time between those events. Nor the incessant pains running up the backside from spending too much time straddling a horse. The only good to come of it all—he had plenty of time to think. Much of it he spent going over the details of the murder. He had an abundance of suspicions regarding each member of the team, but no one person stood out as a stronger candidate than the others.

He tried speaking with Henlio at one time, and later Bellemont, but found far less success than he had experienced with Pilot. They weren't rude to him, but they were not forthcoming either. Bellemont, in particular, answered in short, monosyllabic words that offered no significant insight into the situation.

The further west they traveled, the more Zev noticed how the foliage drifted away. Soon, they had entered a downward slope that had little to display beyond sporadic bushes and sparse rocks. Dust and dirt filled in the gaps.

Visible ahead—though easily another hour or two on horseback—

Zev saw the Great Gap. Looking left and right, a fissure in the land stretched to the horizon. Most suspected that the land had pulled apart, leaving behind a deep chasm. From far enough away, it mimicked a jagged-toothed mouth. But as they headed closer, it transformed into a far simpler yet more sinister image—a ragged line of demarcation. As if the Cassun Nine had slammed their collective fists upon the ground to make sure Nualla, the Beast of the West, never crossed over.

But the Beast had done so.

Zev's feelings did not improve by the time they reached Landbreak Bridge. He spotted the tension in Pilot's hands and in Henlio's stiff back. Apparently, he was not the only one. Axon and Bellemont, however, both appeared eager to enter the Feral Lands, even excited.

With the sun lowering to the horizon, only a few travelers could be spotted—though Zev suspected only a few travelers ever crossed this bridge. Why would anybody want to go into the Feral Lands unless they had to? Even the bridge itself appeared unwelcoming.

The Frontier side had been constructed of stone. The road across looked straight but bumpy as it stretched far into the distance—the entire bridge would take several hours to cross. Approaching along a road that paralleled the jagged gap, Zev could see the arched stones beneath with its long stone posts that reached so far below they were swallowed in the darkness of the chasm. Hard to believe all of that ancient stone could support them. Peeking over the edge, staring into the deep, perhaps endless plunge, Zev's sense of balance looped around him. If not for a tight grip on Stick's saddle, Zev worried he might fall over.

But that only accounted for half of the bridge. The Dacci had constructed the other half and it showed. Though Zev could not see the details, he had experienced enough of the Dacci already to understand what he did see—bones, decaying cloth, and probably an unhealthy amount of bile and excrement. These objects of waste and death held together by unseen forces to form a bridge with no underlying support. It simply floated in place.

"Rumor I heard," Pilot said, "is that the Beast needed over a hundred Dacci witches to get that thing to stay up. Pulled all of their teeth, too. They say if you listen at night, you can still hear them screaming."

Zev smirked. "Guess we'll find out soon enough. I doubt we can make it across the entire bridge tonight."

Axon did not pause at the head of the bridge nor did she make any speech. They had reached the threshold into the unknown, a moment Zev thought deserved acknowledgement, yet she simply rode on. The others followed without hesitation, leaving Zev to wonder if this was another mark of his inexperience. Perhaps all great warriors did not pause for such things. Following their lead, Zev guided Stick onto the bridge.

It was wider than he had expected. In fact, four horses could easily walk side-by-side without teetering on the edge. But, of course, Axon led the way with Henlio and Bellemont next. Zev and Pilot brought up the rear. Zev figured this served both to protect the team in an ambush as well as to leave room for anybody coming the opposite direction.

Several wooden posts with torches bracketed the sides for a short run at the start. As they pushed on, Zev noted that each post bore one of the symbols carved for each of the Cassun deities. He did not know them all that well, but if he needed to, he supposed Axon would instruct him.

But after the wooden posts, the symbols continued—only these were not carved wood. Crude drawings of dark symbols had been made directly on the stone. Some looked like vicious faces, others were jagged like the chasm they crossed, and still others depicted creatures Zev had never encountered before and hoped never to encounter in the future. With the sun setting, he could not be sure, but some of the symbols appeared to have been drawn in blood.

A morbid silence fell upon the group as if they rode in a funeral procession. The rhythmic hits of hooves against stone became a somber drumbeat. Zev had hoped to attempt another conversation with Henlio or Bellemont, but that was impossible under these circumstances.

At regular intervals, metal posts had been erected for a torch to shed light on the bridge. Glass panes surrounded the torch to protect it from the winds that occasionally blew across. At the base of several of these posts, witches had left behind the remnants of their spellcasting. Or perhaps they simply had to relieve themselves and created little piles to be used for spells later.

Zev tried not to be disgusted but failed. Bad enough they had to sacrifice their own teeth, but to make them handle feces and carrion seem like a greater barrier. Then again, if the rumors were to be believed, a skilled witch could cast a spell for almost anything—so, perhaps the trade-off seemed worthwhile to them. Of course, the greater the spell, the more one had to sacrifice.

No wonder the Dacci could not simply use a spell to take over or even magically end a battle in an instant. Considering the number of witches required to put this bridge up, the sacrifice to win a war would be near-endless. And that did not even account for what Bellemont had said about the need to hold the same image in each caster's mind.

He wanted to shake off these thoughts of witches and their magic, but when he looked to the side, he saw only a wall of darkness. The empty chasm had no torchlights, no campfires, no reflections, nothing to provide even a hint of its jagged edges. Even if under a full moon, Zev's suspected he would be staring out at pure darkness.

"Up ahead," Axon said, her voice cutting through the night.

Zev gazed forward to see the bridge open into a large circle with torches around the edges and a fountain placed in the middle. Several small buildings had been erected—horse stalls, general stores, food stalls, and a few that looked to deal in less reputable wares. Several horses with feed bags stood to one side while another part of the circle had been reserved for parking horseless carts. Two of them faced out, ready to ride while one of the owners puttered with the wheels. Half of the circle had the gray stones Zev had become accustomed to seeing everywhere. However, the closer they came to the circle, the easier he could see that the other side had a dark, glossy quality like black marble.

Answering Zev's question before he asked it, Pilot said, "It's the halfway point. We'll stop here tonight, and in the morning, we'll tackle the rest of this bridge."

"It's also the border, isn't it?"

"That's right. You're looking at the beginning of the Feral Lands."

Although there were at least a dozen people mulling about the circle, the place remained relatively quiet with the murmured softness usually reserved for worship. Zev wondered if he might see some of that as he dismounted Stick. Only a few stalls away, somebody had erected a mini-Temple for the worship of the Cassun Nine. Axon answered that thought right away. After securing her horse, she headed straight over to pray.

An elderly man, the temple Shul, had been sitting nearby. Zev thought he was a sleeping traveler, but the man shuffled over to Axon and whispered a prayer. He placed a prayer cloth atop her head and stepped back. Her hand patted her necklace of nines as she bowed.

On the opposite side of the circle, on the Dacci side, a statue had been erected from tree limbs, bones, and a dark liquid Zev decided it better not to know anything about. Bellemont, however, approached the idol with a mixture of curiosity and reverence.

"Is that what the Beast looks like?" Zev asked.

"We don't know for certain," Henlio said from behind. Pilot stood next to him and the two watched Bellemont with the same mixture of curiosity and wariness. "It doesn't look like the bits and pieces we fought already, but I don't think we've had to face the real thing yet."

Pilot said, "Must be hard—not belonging anywhere. She's not from the East, not from the Frontier, and certainly not from the West. That's the kind of thing that might turn a person crazy."

"Just because she acts like she doesn't belong doesn't make it so. She can cast spells. She certainly smells like one of them. And look at her now—no hesitation. Goes right up there and starts praying to the Beast. If you pay attention, you'll see that we have more to worry about than just fighting the Beast."

"You better watch what you say. Axon hears that, and I don't care how long you've been friends. She won't let anything or anyone upset the balance of the team. Axon will defend that to her last, dying breath."

"Then it's up to you and me," Henlio said, "to make sure she doesn't have that last, dying breath."

Zev stood with his arms folded and his attention routed on Bellemont. But he could not stop hearing the discussion behind him. Part of him wanted to whirl around and chastise these men for talking about one of their own that way. Part of him wanted to lay into them for their bigotry against the Dacci. Bellemont was one of the Stolen—none of this was her fault. She was just a young woman trying to find her place in the world.

But as these thoughts swam through Zev's mind, his opportunity to act floated away. Henlio walked over to one of the food stands while Pilot staked out a spot for the team to sleep for the night. Zev stood alone. His arguments, his suspicions, his urge to stand up for what's right—it all amounted to nothing more than a lost opportunity.

Another thought hit Zev. Another opportunity. Only this one lacked nobility. However, he had been hired for a specific job and that had to take priority.

"Be honest with yourself," he muttered. The truth then—more than anything, more than loyalty to a job or a person, more than the money, he wanted to satisfy that itch and know who had killed Xarad.

While Bellemont remained before the statue of the Beast, Zev meandered toward her horse. After gazing over the entire circle to make sure none of the team members had noticed him—or anybody else, for that matter—he flipped open her saddlebag and rifled through her possessions.

The stench struck him first. Nearly knocked him unconscious. For Tiq's sake, he had been in overused slophouses that smelled better.

Opting to breathe through his mouth, he continued his search. He found all the expected things—food and supplies and such—but then came upon three notable items. The first was a vial of a dark, oily substance. It also smelled awful and had a lightning symbol scratched along the glass.

The second item surprised him—the split skull of a trubat similar to the one he had found in Henlio's saddlebag. Was Bellemont stealing from the others or cursing them? Possibly Henlio gave Bellemont the skull. Possibly they had entered a relationship that Henlio hid through his bluster. Regardless of the reasons, the question remained—why?

The third item chilled Zev's heart. It was a letter written in a shaky hand. Though he could not take the time to read the entire letter, he caught snatches enough to worry him. Phrases like *your sisters await* and *test your enemies until you are sure* and *never trust another.*

Zev thrust these items back into the saddlebag and rejoined the group. He did not think he would sleep at all that night.

CHAPTER FOUR

When morning arrived, Zev did his best to hide his exhaustion as they saddled the horses, mounted up, and got underway. He hung toward the back of the group, not wanting anybody to see the concern on his face. Stick tried to press forward—Zev thought the old creature had taken a liking to Pilot's horse, Majesty—but Zev reined him in each time.

That awful smelling vial plagued Zev's mind. As they crossed the latter half of the bridge, he wondered if all the Dacci witches had such vials. He could easily imagine how that liquid would harden into the mortar that bound the bridge. Perhaps it needed a touch of magic, but it certainly looked and smelled the part.

The next several hours crossed in quiet. The clop of horse hooves died in the air. All sound had lost its echo, and Zev tried not to let the unnatural shift unnerve him. Yet he gripped Stick's reins tighter and could not refrain from scanning his surroundings for threats.

By the time the sun hung directly overhead, they had reached the end of the bridge. Axon made no attempt to commemorate the moment with a speech, though she did look back at the group and offered one firm nod. As she led them onward, Pilot glanced back at Zev with a goofy grin and tip of his hat.

And then they were in the West. Simple as that.

Though the lands were called "Feral," Zev thought them more desolate than anything else. Long, quiet empty spaces spread out around them. The gray and brown cracked earth had been dotted with rocks and crevices. Odd looking plants—many with aggressive thorns or rough surfaces—poked through the dry ground, yearning to bring life to this dead land.

Henlio hummed a gentle tune. Zev did not recognize it and suspected it to be the man's own creation. But he only managed a handful of bars before Axon halted, turned around, and faced him directly.

"There is nothing but danger ahead of us," she said. "The further west we go, the stronger the Beast will become. Do not be deceived by the barren desert around us. It is not empty. We are being watched. Our enemy is calculating against us. The moment the Beast thinks it has the advantage, it will attack."

Henlio stiffened upright. "My apologies."

Not another word was spoken the entire day. Even the horses held back their usual noises. That evening, the team made camp near a red hider tree—a rough barked, thin and tall tree that sprouted three enormous leaves from the top, creating a sliver of shelter beneath. If three or four hiders could be clumped together, they would make an effective shade against the hot sun of the day and any unexpected evening weather. But the trees were scarce and most often singular.

Pilot and Bellemont tossed together a quick stew of cho beans and root vegetables. They all ate in silence. Recognizing how tired everybody must have been, Axon said she would stay up for the first watch. Nobody argued. Without another word, they cleaned up and settled in for the night.

Zev could not recall ever feeling so exhausted before. His thighs and backside ached from long hours in the saddle. Being quiet all day had left his mind plenty of time to go over the murder—again and again. He kept hoping for some inspired insight, but he merely replayed the little he knew and felt any possible answer slipping further away. Resting his head on his pack, his eyes closed, and he let his thoughts disappear.

Hours later, Zev woke from a fitful sleep. Sweat dampened the collar of his shirt, and as he sighed relief for waking, he felt his brow was also soaked. He sat up. The dream would not come back to him, and perhaps that was a good thing. Besides, he didn't need to recall a dream in order to know what bothered him.

The team slept soundly, spread around the embers of their fire. Though the moonlight was dim, the openness of this barren land offered little to block that light from reaching the ground. Zev had no trouble stepping away to find a place to relieve himself.

Sitting with his back to the fire, Henlio kept guard. He grunted to acknowledge Zev's presence, but otherwise, kept vigilant on his duty. After Zev finished urinating, he knew he would not be falling back asleep—at least, not any time in the near future. So, welcome or not, he sauntered over towards the wide rock Henlio sat upon and took the edge next to the man.

"Nervous?" Henlio said.

Zev nodded with a bashful smile. "Can't say I've ever done anything this brash before."

"Axon does tend to pull out the reckless side of people."

Zev thought about the way Axon had come into his life. "She does, at that. I have to say though, I feel like I've let her down. I feel like I've botched everything up. Here I came in to be part of this team, and everything I've said to you and Bellemont especially, every attempt I've tried to put out a hand towards you, you've all slapped it away."

Henlio smirked. "Yet here you are trying again."

"I'm not trying to be pushy. It's late, I'm up, and I thought ... I don't know."

"You've got to understand—"

"Oh, I do. I didn't realize at first how much Xarad meant to everybody. But I see now that his loss hit you all quite hard. So, I'm sorry." Zev kept his head hung low and stared at his hands. He didn't dare glance at Henlio. He wanted to, wanted to see the effect his words were having, wanted to know how much harder he could push, but he had to trust his instincts.

With a dark tinge to his voice, Henlio said, "He was a special boy—not the smartest or strongest or anything such as that, but he was full of hope for what we could accomplish. To me, he was everything we fight for."

"Is that why you dislike Bellemont so much?"

Henlio snapped his head toward Zev, and for a moment, Zev thought he had gone too far. But then Henlio kicked at the ground and tossed a rock into the dark. "I don't like someone who I cannot tell what side they're on. Honestly, I think that's one reason I've been unwilling to talk to you before."

"You think I'm fighting with the East?"

"Of course not. But you come from the East. You use a rifle. In the end, I don't know whether you're going to be loyal to the Frontier or to the world you came from."

"I'm not good with a sword. That's all." Of course, that wasn't all. The specter of his father and brother followed him like the moonlight.

With a shake of his head, Zev refocused on Henlio. Questioning the man was meant to be about Xarad and finding answers. He could not let Henlio alter his course. "I have an odd question for you."

"Odd questions are what help a man through a long night of guard duty. Proceed."

"Well, I don't want you to think I was snooping through your things, but I did notice as we were unpacking that you had a little skull. I thought that was a Dacci thing—carrying around bones and such."

"That is completely a Dacci thing. That trubrat skull doesn't belong to me. I thought somebody had been fiddling with my saddlebag—two or three times now it looked like it had been tampered with—and when we got near the bridge, I noticed the bad odor. When I saw what was in my bag, I knew Bellemont had been up to it. She would of course claim that it was some type of protection spell or something, but I want none of it. I tossed it back in her bag. She can have it."

"Maybe she felt bad about Xarad. Maybe she wanted to do a better job of protecting the rest of us."

"I don't care. Xarad was like a brother to me. Pilot, I can do with or without. And nobody's more important than Axon. Xarad, though—for Bieck's sake, he was everybody's little brother."

Zev hoped one last push would get the man opened up. "It's strange to say that because I got the impression you two were not so close. That maybe Xarad was one of your least favorites of the team."

Henlio scowled. "Who said that? Pilot? I've seen the two of you talking. Let me tell you something, that man does not know this team so well. He's more like you—from the East. He does not know the kinds of things Axon and I have been through."

"That's right. The two of you fought together."

Henlio squinted as if the memories he sought were painted on the backdrop of the night. "You haven't really been tested yet. You've been in a few skirmishes, but an all-out battle—that's a whole different animal. Where we're headed, you may just end up seeing that kind of violence, and if you do, you'll learn that the people who experience it, we don't want to talk about it."

"I didn't mean to pry." Zev reminded himself to stay quiet. Let Henlio feel the need to fill that space with his own voice.

"The Beast, back then, fought more conventionally. Maybe that's not accurate. Maybe it was the influence of the soldiers or the witches. Maybe it was testing our way of fighting. But the Battle of Alapia marked the first real struggle we ever had with the West.

"I can still see Axon charging down on her horse, breaking hard toward all of us, waving her hands and shouting. She had been patrolling when she saw the witches. It's strange, though. I'm sure there was plenty of time after she went by me because somehow our forces were there to meet the enemy, but I don't recall any of that. To me, she flew by and the next thing I know we were swinging swords and fighting off all kinds of weird little creatures that the witches kept making. I'd kill one and another would pop right out of the ground. Some looked like giant frogs with extra limbs. Some were rolling abominations of teeth. You'd look in one direction and see slithering, horrible visions from nightmares, so you'd turn away only to be attacked by something equally as repulsive coming from the other side.

"For a while, it was oddly fun. That probably sounds terrible, but once you've been in a few real battles, you'll understand. Axon and I would pass each other during the fight and we'd laugh. At one point, she leaned close and whispered to me—*I'll beat you at this.* So, we kept score on who killed the most creatures, who killed the weirdest creatures, anything like that. *I got one with eight eyes. Well, I got one that was a giant tongue.* That sort of thing. We kept it quiet so as not to disturb our allies, but it helped cope with the strangeness of it all.

"Anyway, we fought on and it felt like it never would end. I remember being so tired that I wanted to simply drop my sword and be done with it. I had just killed this grotesque creature that looked like a four-headed baby with claws sharper than a jaur's teeth. Somehow, I had gotten to the bottom of a hill, and when I looked up I was surrounded by one horrible mutation after another. They lunged at me. Tried to get a hold of me. But I fought them off. Still, I knew I couldn't last much longer. You can probably guess what happened."

"Axon?"

"Axon." He took a swig from his canteen. "She blazed on in and cut down anything that dared move. In one motion, she dismounted her horse so that the animal barreled through a wall of creatures, and she still managed to slice apart another as she ran towards me. That sweet woman dug her shoulder low into my gut and lifted me up, carried me right out of there. Saved my life." After a pause, Henlio leaned over and put a firm grip on Zev's knee. "You want to know how it is I look at Xarad? I would be his Axon. I would cut through a mountain of monsters to save him." Gripping Zev's knee tighter, Henlio spit out into the dark. "At least, I was supposed to."

Pushing away from Zev, Henlio scooted to the edge of the rock, leaned his elbows on his knees, and watched the darkness in the distance.

Zev did not move at first. He wanted to; however he thought it would be rude to simply slip away. But after a short time, he gave

Henlio a deep grunt—the man's preferred method of communication, it seemed—and headed toward the pack he used as a pillow.

He tried to organize all the information he had gleaned, but it slipped away from him. Part of him recognized that he had heard important things, yet he held the distinct impression that something got by him. He should have asked something else. Some key question or nugget of information went unaccounted. And he wondered if Axon's faith in him had been misplaced. Perhaps he was not as smart as she hoped.

As he reached his pack, he heard a rustling of clothes off toward his right. Looking up, he spotted a dark figure rushing away. A quick survey of the camp told him everything.

Bellemont.

Zev checked over at Henlio. The man was lost in his dark memories. Pilot and Axon had not stirred. He considered waking them up, calling for Henlio, anything like that, but he held back. If he made a commotion, Bellemont would know right away that she had been discovered. Anything of value he might learn about her from this excursion would be lost.

"Okay, then," he whispered. "It's up to me."

CHAPTER FIVE

If not for the desolate landscape, Zev would have lost Bellemont long ago. The dark strips of fabric that made up her clothing blended with the night almost completely. Only a few glints of moonlight or strange shifts in the way it hit the ground allowed him to keep his target in view.

The further they went from the camp, the less confident he felt about his surroundings. Small rocks and oddly shaped holes snagged at his feet, threatening to topple him over. He moved like a dancer unsure of the choreography but determined to keep pressing forward. Sounds carried far. At least, the things he heard could be attributed to Bellemont—he hoped. But then, if he could hear her, she could probably hear him. Did she already know that he followed her?

A shutter rippled across his skin. He should have brought his rifle. He should have woken Axon and told her what had happened.

The terrain became rockier. Zev stumbled on more stones than before. Bumping into a few larger rocks, ones reaching his shoulder or higher, he could feel the shadows pressing in on him. How far had she led him away?

Just as he became accustomed to the new landscape, the ground sloped downward. Soon a soft murmur of life filled the dead silence. A harsh odor hung in the air with all the charm of a stagnant bog.

Witches.

As he followed Bellemont further down the slope, the smell intensified and the noises became clearer—voices, activity, the crackle of fire. Skirting around a ridge of towering rocks, he caught sight of life. He jumped back behind the rocks as his pulse sped up. Peeking his head around the end of one boulder, he saw Bellemont's destination—a Dacci encampment. No—more than that. Letting his eyes rove over the grouping of temporary structures, the guards and soldiers, the witches, the mothers carrying babies, the running children, the older men using canes—this was a village.

In a section that looked like the common area, Zev noticed two pools in the middle. One with water—perhaps the equivalent of the community well, an essential fixture in the barrenness surrounding them. The second pool was filled with a thick, fetid muck. At first, Zev thought it to be composed completely of the oily substance he had found in Bellemont's carved vial. But he watched as children walked up to the edge, squatted, and defecated into it. Strange to put a form of outhouse next to drinking water. But then a woman—possibly a witch—approached and began filling several large containers with the reeking concoction.

The whole thing turned his stomach and part of him hoped never to learn the purpose of that pool. But another part of him could not hold back his curiosity.

Bellemont approached the edge of the village. Though she held her head up and her shoulders back, projecting all the confidence of a woman seasoned by battle, her steps were slow. Sturdy but slow. Cautious.

A small group of children were the first to notice her. One of them scampered to an adult and pointed at the approaching stranger. The adult motioned to others, and like cracks forming through ice, the calm of the village broke into pieces. All activities stopped. All eyes focused to the same pinpoint—Bellemont. Two Dacci guards rushed forward, stood before her, and crossed their spears so that both pointed ends threatened her directly.

Bellemont stopped. Zev could hear her speaking but not discern her words. He thought about edging closer, but with the limited light, he feared losing his footing and getting injured.

Moments later, a Dacci witch emerged from a hexagonal structure in the back. Her long strips of black cloth hung low, brushing the dirt on the ground, and she had a yellow stripe painted over her head-piece. Those villagers that stood in her way bowed their heads and stepped back as she walked by. When she reached Bellemont, the guards raised their spears and moved to the side.

From his vantage point, Zev could not tell much about this witch. Her traditional Dacci garb, including the veil, hid all but her eyes— and he was too far away to notice any fine details. She could be young or old, missing an eye, wrinkled, blind, or any number of things. However, he surmised she had lived a lengthy time to have earned the reverence the villagers paid.

The witch walked a circle around Bellemont, raising and lowering her left hand as if pointing out interesting aspects and strange defi-ciencies of this new specimen that had approached the village. However, Zev heard no sounds to suggest she had been speaking. When she halted in front of Bellemont, the witch leaned forward and made a loud sniffing noise. Her shoulders shook and she coughed.

Probably too clean for the likes of her, Zev thought.

He chastised himself for thinking such a thing. He had to be careful or he would end up being more like Henlio. Being different was not evil. *Smelling* different was not evil. And these little comments, whether snide or humorous, only served to widen the divide. After crossing the Landbreak Bridge, he thought the divide between the Frontier and the West was wide enough.

Bellemont dropped to her knees and dug through her bag. The villagers stepped closer. Keeping her head low, she cradled the trubrat skull as she pulled it out. With her wrists pressed together, she set the skull across her hands and raised it over her head. And she waited. In a swish, the witch swiped the skull and lifted it high in the air. Her loud voice carried well across the open land. "Nualla has told you to find us, and you have succeeded. Welcome, sister."

The villagers all clapped and several moved in close. Two small women hastened over and helped Bellemont back to her feet. As they brought her further into the village, the children crowded around her.

Zev figured it would be best to report back to Axon. He had enough information to paint a clear picture for her. As he stood, he dislodged several rocks that tumbled downward. Despite the noise of the crowd, one of the guards glanced up the sloping land. Just Zev's luck—one of the guards had to have good hearing.

"There," the guard said, pointing.

As Zev turned to race away, he caught a glimpse of Bellemont looking in the direction of his disturbance. He could not read her expression—anger or concern—but he had no time to worry about it, either. He turned upward, scrambling away.

The guards gathered beneath him, rising up the slope with skilled steps, calling out orders as the villagers paused to see the outcome of yet another unexpected event that night. Zev heard his own breath and felt the stones cutting up his hands as he scrabbled higher.

When he bumped into a solid object that was not a rock, he knew he had failed. He had no idea how some of the guards got ahead of him—perhaps they were stationed around the rim of the area—but as he gazed up at the Dacci soldier, as the soldier used the butt end of his spear to daze Zev with one solid hit, Zev managed one last thought as he felt certain he would be killed—*at least I know who betrayed us.*

CHAPTER SIX

Zev cried. They had tied him to a wooden post which held up the fabric forming the ceiling and walls of a hexagonal tent. Blood trickled from a cut in his forehead and mixed with the tears on his cheeks. This was not the life he had sought when he left the East. This was not what he wanted when he had agreed to help solve a murder.

When the Dacci had caught him, the guards dragged him through the village toward his current prison. Children pelted him with jagged bones. They spit on him. One boy with a mean glint in his eye threw horse dung, but his mother smacked him upside the head and admonished him. As the guards lugged Zev away, he watched the boy pick up the dung and respectfully drop it in the dark pool.

They tied Zev to the post—tight enough that he could no longer feel his fingers—and they left him. And he waited.

He waited, and he cried. The tears came unbidden—just a swelling in his chest that gushed up his throat and forced itself out. If his father could see him, the old man would have scowled before launching into a lecture, the sum of which amounted to *I told you so.*

The longer the Dacci took to come in, the more frightened Zev became. At first, it was the simple fear of being caught and the danger that had put him in. But then he got to thinking. Dacci witches needed time to build up their sacrifices before they could cast a spell. Perhaps they worked on something big to torture him with. His mind dived into the depths of every horror he could imagine. In the end, he reminded himself, they would be able to imagine far worse. They had more practice.

He thought of his brother. Shortly after his eighth birthday, and at the urging of Marcel, Zev snuck into his father's office and stole a book. Marcel had promised that the book would teach him how to be a man and that his father would be proud when he discovered what happened.

Zev did not understand the pictures in the book—other than they were all of nude women and men twisting around each other—but his older brother sure found it fascinating. Together, they hid in a tree and giggled over page after page. Until their father caught them.

Marcel went into the office first. Zev flinched at the yelling of his father and the muted cries of his brother—all the time waiting out in the hall for his turn. Waiting. He had been terrified back then. But he would trade that terror for his current state of panic any day.

At some point between the tears, the frightening memories, and the numbing wait, Zev passed out. He only recognized this because the noise of people entering the tent startled him awake.

The witch with the yellow stripe entered first followed by Belle-mont. A Dacci soldier, sword in hand, stood at the doorway. Finally, a stark woman entered—her blonde hair tied back tight and her head scraping the ceiling fabric.

She did not wear any of the traditional witch garb. No strips of black and no veil. Instead, she wore a tan tunic with a white sash that tied around her waist. Her dark skin and narrow eyes stood out against the ring of white stones threaded across her forehead. More than anything though, Zev noticed how clean this woman smelled. Like morning flowers.

The witch and Bellemont knelt on the ground only a short distance from the soldier by the wooden door. Zev thought it strange they bothered with a crude, wooden door when the walls and ceiling were made of fabric. But then, so much of the Dacci was strange.

The tall woman stepped right up to Zev. "I am the Dacci Inquisitor," she said.

He noticed she had all of her teeth as well as a comely face. "You seem kind of young for this type of position."

"Oh? You know so much about us?"

Zev did not miss the clenching of her fist. He had not intended to speak at all, but his mouth had moved faster than his brain. He had to be careful about that. "My apologies. I did not mean to presume."

The Inquisitor grinned. "So much of your people's problems come from that very statement. You *presume.* Do you know why my people are superior to yours? Or do you presume that not to be the case?"

Trying to find an answer that would not anger the Inquisitor, Zev opened and closed his mouth three times. Finally, he kept it shut and looked helplessly toward Bellemont. She locked her focus on the Inquisitor.

"Your people can be clever, I freely acknowledge that. You've created some interesting toys, but everything you hold sacred is built upon lies. And that is where we diverge. Your people use a foundation built from the Cassun Nine—invisible deities that exist somewhere, I suppose, and do nothing more than sit around waiting for you to praise them and beg for favor. You build your temples and your statues and you anoint other people—your Shuls—to act as a conduit to your gods. It looks fanciful and organized, but all it has done is push you away from a god that is real and solid.

"Your buildings, your tools, your weapons, even your food—everything you do is set up to remove you from the world you live in. Even your floors. Here, beneath you, it is the ground itself that we live on. But your people bring in stones and wood to separate yourself from the soil that gives life."

"From what I've seen, your country is nothing but dead land." Zev winced. *Keep the mouth shut.*

As before, Zev saw the Inquisitor's muscles tense, but her voice remained calm. "My people have stayed true to what is real. We stay connected to the land that gives us life. And we believe in a true deity —Nualla. He is a being that is real. We can see him. We can be touched by him. We offer him what he needs to live, and he provides us with power. It is the promise he made and has always kept. This land you think is so dead overflows with his life. Beneath the surface lives Nualla. Everywhere you look, he is there. I don't mean that in a silly, imaginary way like you speak of your gods and goddesses. I mean it quite truthfully. As Nualla grows he consumes what is above. If you travel far enough west, you will find areas he has not grown into yet. But we have no need of that.

"Nualla provides."

"From us he asks for that which we don't need, whether from our bodies or our activities. The bones of our dead and the waste of our living—we give these to Nualla and he returns with power. True magic. From that, we can create everything we need or want. That is a real god."

"You're in luck. I don't believe in the nine, either. I'm an atheist."

"Just as bad." She turned towards the witch but continued speaking to Zev. "There are only two reasons we have tied you to this post instead of killing you. First, you brought us Bellemont. She has made it clear that you helped her travel and find a way to us. For that, we are appreciative. And second, you can help us achieve victory for Nualla." She bent down and lifted Yellow Stripe's chin. "I want you to take Bellemont and teach her the true ways of the Dacci."

The witch stood and bowed. "To Nualla and you, I give my word."

The Inquisitor stepped over toward Bellemont. "You have a good heart. And now that you have seen this man alive and unharmed, I want you to go with Saatchi. Listen to her, learn from her, and you will one day be a great Dacci witch."

Bellemont stood and attempted to mimic Saatchi's bow. Saatchi placed her hand on Bellemont's back, gestured with her head, and guided her new student out of the tent. A motion from the Inquisitor sent the soldier outside as well.

The whole thing struck Zev as an orchestrated performance put on for the benefit of Bellemont—to ease her conscience about the pain they intended to inflict upon him. He watched as the Inquisitor's fingers tightened into a solid fist once again. His pulse quickened and his chin quivered.

The first strike came in hard and fast. Her fist slammed into Zev's gut. If not for the ropes binding him to the pole, he would have doubled over and crumpled to the ground. He wanted to cry out but could only gasp for air.

"That's better," the Inquisitor said with a sigh. From inside her tunic, she pulled out a small leather belt rolled tight and tied. "Because you don't believe and because even if you did, your gods don't actually exist, you may not understand the reality of the world. Nualla is not invading your lands because he wants to rule over you. He is not invading your lands because of some false aggression on your part. You see, he's not invading your lands at all. The land cannot be divided that way."

She untied the belt and spun it open. Zev lifted his head to see a row of bone needles, bone knives, and a few instruments he did not have a name for and did not want to know their purpose.

"Borders between lands—that is a fabrication of your minds. There is no reality to it. Nualla lives beneath the ground and feeds as he needs to. And, quite simply, there are not enough Dacci to produce enough food. But when he takes over the Frontier and the East, when he destroys your notion of the Cassun Nine and your ridiculous beliefs in kings, when you see the reality of our world, then Nualla will be able to feed on all the bounty that awaits him. But like any true and blessed god, Nualla never just takes. You will all receive the benefits that he gives us Dacci. Some fortunate ones of you will even become powerful witches capable of incredible feats of magic."

She ran her fingers over the bone instruments. Like a master chef choosing the perfect utensil for preparing the perfect meal, she deliberated. Her fingers came to rest upon a slim yet jagged tool. As she pulled it free, Zev's stomach tightened. He did not want to scream or cry or make any sound that would satisfy the torturous bloodlust he saw in her face.

"Now, I'm going to ask you questions, and though you may want to resist, the faster you give me honest answers, the better this will go for you. I will take your silence as understanding but you will have to speak eventually. I want you to know that this is not pointless. If you give me the information I need, then with Nualla's help, I will be able to succeed in reaching the inevitable conclusion. You understand? You cannot win against a true and real god. Nualla is real and true and will destroy you if you resist. Eventually, Nualla and the Dacci will win this war that has yet to begin. You cannot change that. However, if you cooperate with me, if you answer the questions that I have, we may be able to speed the process and thus save many, many lives. Perhaps we can avoid the war entirely."

Zev closed his eyes. He tried to fight off the shivers of fear that coursed through his muscles. He had no desire to suffer, but he had to be able to live with himself. Maybe the Inquisitor was right. Maybe his betrayal would save lives. But maybe not.

"I see," she said at his lengthy silence. "Then let's begin with some-thing simple. How many people are in your party? How far out are they located? These should not be things difficult for you to share—we can find them out numerous ways."

When he did not answer, he felt burning on his chest. His eyes snapped open. The Inquisitor had raked the jagged edge of her bone blade across his sternum. The wound stung more than hurt, but he suspected that was the intent. Just a warning. Or a promise of what would be coming down the road should he not comply.

Yet despite the relatively minor wound, Zev's mouth opened and he cringed at the desperation he heard. "Don't do this to me. I can't— I'm not a fighter. I'm not here to harm you. Ask Bellemont. She's been with us the whole time. You can get all you want to know from her. I'm sure she can't wait to tell you."

The pity in the Inquisitor's eyes wrinkled Zev's heart. She actually felt sorry for him. Or perhaps she felt sorry that she would be able to break him so fast.

With the corner of her mouth twitching upward, she said, "I have too much respect for Bellemont to ask her to betray those that helped her return home."

Whipping around with a growl on her lips, the Inquisitor swung her arm overhead and slammed the jagged bone into Zev's chest. He screamed until his voice cracked. When the sound broke into nothing, he shook in the silence from his strained throat. Tears raced down his cheeks.

The Inquisitor stayed close, her face pressed up tight to be both intimidating and intimate. With the slight pressure of one finger on the end of the bone, she could use small motions to rake daggers between his ribs.

"If you think waiting for Axon to save you is a strategy, you will fail. Nualla will see to that. Oh, you weren't aware that I knew her name? And Henlio? I've known them for a long time. I was at the Battle of Alapia. I watched as they galloped about on their horses, laughing as they played their little game. Neither laughed much when we nearly killed Henlio. Perhaps we will get our chance to remedy that sooner than I expected."

She wiggled the bone in a short circle and Zev shrieked. When she stopped, he felt the world growing fuzzy around his head. He tried to remember the things she had said—something important.

"You are far weaker than I wanted. I'm going to have to watch how much I hurt you."

He did not understand why she said that until the fuzziness thickened around his head. She saw it—he was close to passing out. And as his eyes closed and his mind shut down, he knew she had said something that stuck with him. But the words floated away along with all other thoughts.

PART V
AXON

CHAPTER ONE

Barely two days into their mission and it had all fallen to
pieces. Axon stomped through the dark looking for signs of
Bellemont or Zev and fuming at Henlio for falling asleep on
guard duty. She had known the big brute to be reckless at times, even
foolhardy, but never so careless. The disappointment pressed against
her heart and strained her trust.

But she needed him. The only other member of the team, Pilot,
looked ready to leave, too. She always knew he'd been running from
something in the East, but she thought distance and time would quell
those fears. If not that, then she hoped he would be loyal to the
mission.

That was her pride. Nobody cared about the mission but her.
Bellemont only wanted to get back to the Feral Lands. Zev wanted to
find Xarad's killer and get paid. Even Henlio came along simply
because she had asked him to do so. Maybe because of the King, too.

At least in the current situation, Axon thought Pilot could be
trusted to keep watch over their camp. She questioned his loyalty but
not his honor. He would not derelict his duty. If he intended to leave,
he would do so at an appropriate time and with a formal declaration.

Unless—if he was the one who had killed Xarad, then guarding an empty camp provided the perfect opportunity to escape while every-body ran around in the dark. If only Zev figured things out before they had left Ridnight. If only.

She should have said *No* when he insisted on coming into the Feral Lands. He didn't belong here. She knew it then but didn't listen to her inner-voice.

Her eyes narrowed against the cold night. If anything happened to him, she would unleash her full rage upon this land. And with the Water Blade in her hand, there wouldn't be anything left of the Beast for the Dacci to pray to.

Henlio approached from her right. His gruff groans as he thumped closer identified him long before she saw his woolly beard. "No sign of them off that way," he said. "I'll keep searching, but I don't think we'll find anything until the sun rises."

"If you do find anything, you get me."

"You think I wouldn't?"

"I think your dislike for Bellemont might overrule the part of your brain that knows better. Until we know what actually is going on, I don't want you rushing off. We have a mission to complete, not personal problems to solve. Understood?"

"You should think better of me."

Her hand snatched him by the collar so fast that he stumbled. "Understood?"

"Yes, yes. I understand. I will not go after Bellemont on my own. Now, if you'll please let go of me, I'll get back to searching."

She released him, and he wasted no time dashing off into the dark.

What am I doing? When they had left Ridnight Castle with the King coming down in person to see them off, the pride had swelled within her like a capped geyser waiting to burst. She had earned the Water Blade. She had earned the King's trust. And she had set out like a legend of old to save her people. To protect all they held sacred. To stop these other worlds from crashing in and changing the one they loved so dearly.

Perhaps her mother was right. Perhaps she had been foolish to think she could be something other than her birth dictated. If she had been born to become a legend, she would have picked a better team. Instead, Bellemont and Pilot had merely waited for the opportunity to reach the Feral Lands. Change had been built into their group which meant failure had been built in as well.

She thought about the military drills she watched while growing up. The King's Guard always appeared so orderly, so controlled, so complete in its unchanging rules and behaviors. A person could count on any member of the Guard to have been trained the same way, to uphold the same values, to be a part of a greater unit.

Perhaps that was where she had gone wrong. She should have taken the time to train Bellemont and Pilot. And Xarad, too. Better training might have saved his life.

She stopped walking and knelt on the ground. She needed guidance. Her goal remained the same, but how to achieve it? Should she accept that her team had already fallen apart, that they may not wish to come back together, and that she should fight the Beast alone? Or should she hunt down Bellemont and Zev, bring them back to the camp, and force the group to become a unit, to work together like the King's Guard?

She closed her eyes and offered a short prayer to Qareck, Lord of All Existence. The answer came to her fast. She needed to find Zev. Simple as that. Find Zev and bring him to safety. Then, if Pilot or Bellemont wanted to leave, she could not force them to stay. She had no authority, and even if she did, what would be the point? She needed people she could rely on when she faced the Beast, not people searching for a way out.

"Thank you, Qareck."

As she started to rise, the world swirled into darkness around her. Sharp pain struck the center of her back, forcing her shoulders to spread her chest forward. A vicious force yanked her into the air, and the sky billowed with fire. Thunder rumbled over the crackling lightning as Axon's body turned until she faced the ground that shimmered far below.

The Beast lifted his serpentine head as oily tendrils snaked across the land. He continued to rise until he towered over her. The smell of death and decay swirled around him.

The unseen force that pinned her in the air spun her over so that she could look directly into the blood eyes of the Beast.

"I know you won't listen." His voice shook the air around her. It vibrated against her skin. She wanted to cover her ears, but her arms were not free to move. "Go home. Gather those you care for and leave my lands. You have my word that you will not be harmed, if you leave."

"If I leave, you'll follow. You've already tried to invade our lands. You'll try again. I can't allow that." Her heart hammered and she had no doubt he saw the fear in her eyes.

"I only take what was taken from me." The Beast lowered his head and moved closer. His red eyes glowed upon her, radiating heat and anger. "You must be gone. Come after me and you and all you love will die."

"Axon?" Henlio rested his hand on her knee.

Axon opened her eyes. She knelt on the ground in the dark. Looking around, she found no sign of the Beast. No evidence that she had floated in the air.

"Are you okay?" Henlio asked.

Standing, praying Henlio did not see the shake in her legs, she nodded. So—not a vision at all but a direct communication from her enemy. More proof that she did not know what she dealt with. A magic sword was fine, but her arrogance would be the death of them all.

And yet, to turn back would be to spit upon all that she had done, all that she had convinced others to do for her. To leave meant Xarad died for nothing.

"The Beast knows we're here," she said.

"You warned us of that when we arrived."

"He knows exactly where we are. Not just that we are in his lands and not just because the Dacci are watching and reporting to him. He knows you and I stand on this very spot."

"Then why aren't we fighting the Beast right now?"

"Perhaps it's the same thing that kept him from attacking us fully at the city walls. Perhaps the Beast is stretched too far. I don't know."

"Or perhaps he's simply luring us deeper into a trap. Like an ambush—it's better to wait until the entire party you want to hurt is well beyond your ambush point. Then you can block off the exit, block off the front, and have all of your enemy in the killing field."

Axon gave Henlio a firm slap on the back and tried to sound relaxed. "Wouldn't be the first time you and I fought in that kind of situation."

Henlio offered a bitter laugh. "I kind of hoped we were done with that."

"Come on. We have to find Zev and Bellemont. If we're going to be ambushed, we'll need more than just the two of us to survive."

Henlio's beard widened as his smile grew. "Exactly why I came over here. I've found their trail not far to the left."

Axon had the urge to smile, but instead, she chose to simply gesture for him to lead the way.

CHAPTER TWO

Crouched behind a ridge of rock formations, Axon looked upon the Dacci encampment. *Zev, what were you thinking? Once you followed Bellemont here, you should've come back to camp right away.*

Henlio pointed to a long, rectangular tent on the outskirts of the camp. Axon nodded—clearly from the Dacci soldier guarding the building, it either held all the weapons or would be central to the command structure. The center part of the camp had been set up to act like a village. But the outer ring of buildings had a much more militaristic positioning. Plenty of soldiers in those outer areas, stables for the horses, and not a single child. The "villagers" stuck to the center of the camp.

"Are they using their own people as a shield against attack?" Henlio asked.

"They have no reason to expect an attack. It's not like a war has officially begun. I think this is simply how they do things here. The soldiers and the villagers live together. The soldiers protect the village, and the villagers probably provide food and such. Qareck only knows how the witches fit into all of this."

Pointing toward the center of the camp, Henlio said, "A waterhole and an open outhouse right next to each other? Disgusting."

Axon hunkered down with her back against the rocks. Her jaw tightened as she thought over everything she had seen. "I owe you an apology. I should have listened to you from the start. Bellemont didn't care about us. She was just using us to get back here. And she killed Xarad to do it."

Cocking his head, Henlio said, "You are the leader of this group—no apologies necessary. As for Bellemont, why would she kill Xarad? Wouldn't that make it harder for her to get here? If we had discovered that she committed the act, we would never have brought her this far."

"She had to prove herself. You think those Dacci witches would take her back easily? She's a Stolen. Warped and ruined by whoever raised her in the East or on the Frontier. But killing Xarad—maybe that gives her the credibility she needs for the Dacci to accept her."

"You think she killed Zev, too?"

Axon had been thinking exactly that. She turned to look at the camp again. "That larger tent—the hexagonal one. It's in the central village side of the camp but has a guard."

"I see it."

"If Zev is alive, he's probably in there."

"But what if—"

"If he's dead," she said as her chest hardened and eyes turned cold, "then I'll burn this place to the ground."

The odds looked bad. Two of them versus an entire encampment filled with soldiers and witches as well as regular people and their children. Worse—Bellemont was familiar with how Axon worked. She would know that Axon would be responding, especially with Zev either imprisoned or dead.

"I can't order you to go with me," Axon said. "But I'm not leaving without Zev—dead or alive."

Henlio snorted and spit to his side. "Is this really a question?"

"In that case, here's the plan—the only way we can possibly survive is by taking advantage of our small numbers. Bellemont has only been in this camp for a handful of hours. They can't possibly trust her completely. So, if she tells them there are only two of us, chances are they won't believe her. We use that to our advantage."

"How exactly?"

"I'm going to walk straight into the camp. They will never believe I would do that without a lot of support hidden nearby."

"And that is supposed to be me?"

"Your bow and arrow skills improved any?"

Henlio's beard widened. "They'll be good enough."

Axon did not find that as comforting as she suspected Henlio intended, but it would have to do. After taking a few minutes to spot good locations for him and to prepare her mindset, she stood with a strong breath. "If we get the chance to kill Bellemont, that's not a bad thing, either."

"If Wiq wills it, it shall be done."

With a hard nod, she headed down the slope. She walked with the Water Blade ready, making no effort to appear harmless. Its blue glow surrounded her and where the Blade dripped in the ground, she heard a sizzle like meat on a spit. She strode forward as if she had already conquered the place.

A voice in the back of her mind berated her for taking this risk. She had a duty to her King and her people—destroy the Beast. Compared to that, what was Zev?

But she walked on anyway. After all, if she could not take on this encampment, save her teammate, and escape, then the chances of her beating the Beast were slim indeed. With Henlio in a support position, her odds improved significantly.

She chuckled. Not hard to get significantly better when the starting position was abysmal.

Two guards spotted her and raced over with spears leading their way. The bones used for their armor made a hideous clacking like the dead rising under the moonlight. Axon stepped one foot back and lifted the Water Blade. The thin, cold line of her mouth pulled the guards up short. Seeing the shimmering sword caused their breath to shiver and their feet to stumble. She stepped in, cut their spearheads off, pivoted to the side, and swung her sword at one guard's neck.

But she stopped the Blade before decapitating him. Droplets of water trickled off its bright metallic surface and onto his shoulder. "I want to speak with whoever runs this place," she said.

From the edge of town, Axon heard an old woman's voice. "You can let the man go. We are here to listen."

Axon peeked over her shoulder. Four Dacci witches, each with yellow stripes on their heads, stood in a row. Axon lowered the Water Blade. With a short motion of her shoulder, she dismissed the guards. They had the intelligence to scurry away.

As she approached the witches, her footsteps scratching the dirt and rocks beneath her, she noticed the entire camp had grown silent. Children peeked out between tent flaps while adults stood like statues to observe events. Even the wind had died down so that fires did not flicker as much or as loud.

The four women before her all stood with near uniform build and stature. They all wore veils to cover their mouths. Only their eyes drew any distinction—Big, Blue, Narrow, and Black.

"You are not welcome here. Leave."

Because of the veils, Axon could not tell which woman had spoken. Indeed, the more they spoke, the more she became convinced they were trading off sentences, possibly even individual words. Unable to discern which one of them led the conversation, Axon decided to treat them as one unit.

She said, "I would love to leave you. But you've taken one of my men."

"You stole many of our kind."

"No. I brought her back."

The witch with blue eyes stepped forward. "Are we expected to be grateful? Your people have stolen hundreds of our children, and you have returned one. Your kings have done all in their power to eradicate us. And every generation you've pushed us further and further west. You even created your own religion in an attempt to erase ours."

"My king had nothing to do with this. The Stolen were from another time. My king, and those like him, put a stop to that horrible practice."

"Yet you only return the one."

With a grim motion, Axon tried to acknowledge this terrible fact while not giving any ground. "I would gladly return more if I knew where they were. But if we argue the past, we won't get anywhere. I can't change what those before me have done. Neither can you."

"Don't be so sure what I can and can't do."

"If you could reverse time, you would've done so."

Blue chuckled. "You've made your speech. Now leave." As she spoke, the other witches swished their feet to create small piles of dirt in front of them. They pressed holes into the piles to form small craters.

Axon said, "The man you've taken has nothing to do with the grievances between our people. He's not even from the Frontier."

"It does not matter where he's from. He is with you. And you do not roam our lands for innocent reasons. You are here to start a war. You have come because you don't like the way we live. You think of us as backwards, antiquated, ignorant fools chanting in the wild. You think your ways are better. So you wish to come and change it all for us. But did you ever ask us if we want to change?"

Axon's thoughts stuttered. For a moment, a stream of doubt weaved its way through her heart. But she remembered Xarad's corpse on a table in Zev's barn.

She had not come here to start a war. The Dacci had done that when they coaxed Bellemont into killing Xarad. The Dacci had started the war when they attacked Ridnight. Axon came to the Feral Lands not to start a war, but to stop it from going too far. Kill the Beast, kill the war.

"You know nothing of my people," she said, the fight in her voice snapping at the silence of the village. "They have no interest in hurting you. They don't seek to push you west. They are farmers and merchants. They are good people who care about their children just like you."

"They stole our children."

"Their ancestors did, and that was wrong. But if you want those of the Frontier to apologize, if you want them to repair the damage their

174

ancestors have inflicted, why provoke war? Why not come to our King and speak with him?"

"You think we have not done so?"

"I think you are ruled by the Beast." The moment the words left her mouth, Axon knew she had made a grave mistake. The widening eyes of the witches and the audible gasp of those watching nearby confirmed her thoughts.

All four witches dropped to their knees. As Blue set about making her own crater of dirt, the other three filled theirs with bones and bile and foul smelling matter they carried with them. They mixed their ingredients and set about casting their spells.

Axon stepped back, raising her sword while the crowd thickened—adults and children emerged from their tents, congregating in an arc as if gathering to watch a show. Several soldiers positioned nearer the witches, brandishing swords and spears to protect the spellcasting.

The fact that Henlio had not fired an arrow did not speak well. All the time she had been talking with the witches, Dacci soldiers were probably circling the camp. If they had not captured Henlio yet, he certainly was in no position to help her.

Movement to the left caught her eye. Two witches stood before a large pile of dark slop.

Guess I'm not the only one who thought to have side support.

In unison, the two witches raised their arms and the ground rumbled. A small fissure formed in the dirt before the yellow-striped witches. Bones of different shapes and sizes poked through. It happened fast. Faster than Axon could comprehend. If not for the fact that she witnessed it, she would have been hard-pressed to believe what she saw—a creature formed from bones and nothing more. It rose piece by piece, bone by bone, until it stood three people high with a head larger than Axon herself.

It opened its jagged-tooth mouth and bellowed a curdling roar.

CHAPTER THREE

Though she knew it would become a problem later, Axon offered quick thanks that the creature before her did not breathe. No foul heat, no rank odor, nothing repulsive washed over her while the bone-bred thing produced its impressive roar. Impressive enough that the adults grabbed their children and hastened back to their tents. No matter how good the show, nobody wanted to die watching it.

The bone creature straightened and examined its own body. Three arm-like appendages—two on the left side, one on the right—connected to a relatively large but human-shaped rib cage. Two spines ran down the back and sprouted into a tangle of short bone tentacles.

While the creature swung its arms in the air, quickly gaining better control with each swing, Axon settled into a fighting stance and flexed her fingers for a more comfortable grip on the Water Blade. One Dacci soldier—brave and stupid—charged from the crowd of soldiers. She held a rusty sword overhead as she sprinted toward Axon—perhaps thinking she could defeat Axon while the creature stole all attention. But her scream rattled in her throat, and even the bone creature paused to watch.

Unfortunately for the soldier, Axon did not fear an overeager yet obviously green fighter. She sidestepped the attack with ease, slid her back foot around like a dancer, and used the momentum to slice the Water Blade fast and smooth. When the soldier stopped running, her intestines billowed out of her side. Nobody came to help her.

She did a strange thing, though. Instead of crumpling over like most soldiers, forming a fetal ball and trying to push her guts back inside her body, this soldier opened her arms wide and dropped flat against the ground. She even wriggled against the dirt as if forcing the land to enter her body.

A thick, dark substance oozed up from the cracked terrain. It surrounded the fallen soldier, and she moaned in pain. But she lifted her head to look at Axon. And she smiled like a lover lost in ecstasy.

Several villagers lowered their heads as they raised their arms and mumbled words Axon could not hear. But the time for understanding such things would have to wait. The bone creature had decided it controlled its body well enough to fight, and Axon had no choice but to pay attention.

The first attack came far swifter than she had anticipated. For such a massive creature, it did not appear to be slowed at all by its size. Perhaps a result of magic.

In three successive blows, its arms pummeled the ground. Axon danced out of the way from each strike, but she knew playing the evasion game always resulted in losing. All it took was one mistake or a little bit of luck on her opponent's side and she would end up a blotch of meat in the dirt.

From the safety of their tents, the Dacci children laughed and jeered. The parents used more verbal taunts, employing word combinations Axon had never heard before. But she knew the tone well—hate, derision, mocking defiance. Many more Dacci simply cheered the bone creature.

Covering a large distance on its bone tentacles, the creature whipped its arm down hard. Dirt and stone burst into the air, raining projectiles that Axon had no hope of escaping. They pelted her like hail. Coughing from the dust and rolling the pains out of her neck, she repositioned for the next attack.

She blotted out all distractions, locked her focus on her opponent. She watched close as she sought a strategy or a weakness.

Despite its speed, despite the magic keeping it together and allowing it to move, it still existed in the physical realm. It still followed the same rules her body followed—mostly. With a human opponent larger than herself or faster, oftentimes her best approach involved the upper-body. *Watch the shoulders, and when they moved, the rest usually followed.*

She held her ground and stared up at the massive creature. If the witches allowed it a mind of its own, it did not seem all that bright. And if one or more of the witches controlled it, they did not know much about fighting. When the next attack came, the creature gave away its intent with a broad shoulder move.

Axon had no trouble evading. This time, however, she pushed off her feet and slammed back into the arm with the Water Blade. The Blade flashed bright blue and water droplets splashed like stinging sweat as she notched a divot into the bone.

The creature did not rear back. It did not cry out. It did not react at all.

Great. It doesn't even feel pain.

She reset her stance and remained focused on those shoulders. When they moved, so did she. Slewing under the attack this time, she slashed across the bone arm—one, two, three hits before the creature pulled back.

This would not do. Even if she managed to cut the arm off, it had two more. And the damage she had inflicted did not appear to slow it down in the slightest.

Off to her side, she noticed several Dacci adults with buckets scooping black slurry out of the dark pool. They scurried across the ground and dumped the sludge in an ever-growing pile before the four yellow-striped witches. Like insects, they skittered back and forth. Axon wondered if the new pile of foul smelling crud would fuel the bone creature longer.

The bone creature!

She turned her head as the creature's arm descended upon her.

Thrusting her arm up to absorb some of the blow, her body dropped as the heavy bone hit true. A bright flash and she tasted dirt. Spitting out the ground, she found her face flat against a rock and her head throbbing.

As she forced herself to a standing position, Axon heard the high-pitched voices of excited children as they broke away from their tents to see the action. Turning in a circle to find the bone creature, Axon spied several Dacci soldiers rushing off into the dark. If Henlio had managed to escape their previous attempts at him, more trouble would be on its way soon.

Killing the witches would stop this creature, but she saw no way to get to them—too many Dacci soldiers guarded them. Finishing her turn, she saw the creature's arm flying down once more.

Axon managed to jump back, but she misplaced her footing and lurched to the ground. Rolling fast, she popped to her feet. She couldn't get to the witches, and there was no chance she would tire this thing out. It probably couldn't tire at all. Which brought her back to the original strategy—dismantle the boney creature.

Perhaps because the witches had grown weak as the fight prolonged or perhaps because the bone creature itself had some sort of will, it launched into a series of attacks filled with rage and frustration. Axon had seen this kind of behavior before—a flagging opponent attempting to end a fight quickly through brutal aggression. It was a risky strategy, admittedly not much of a strategy at all, because success only happened if the assailant landed a lucky blow. The fierce power behind the attack could often lay out a person. The risk, however, was that most of the strikes were sloppy and left one open to counter-attack.

All of that theory was good for Axon's intellect, but as one bone arm after another slammed into the ground, as Axon dodged in one direction only to have to pivot back the way she had come, it became clear that this creature's brutality could go on far longer than Axon could evade its strikes. She managed a few thumps, chipping away more bone fragments, but nothing significant. Though she had excellent stamina, she did not have magic spells to back her up. The only magic she bore was the Water Blade, and it did not appear too effective against the creature.

Slick with sweat, breathing hard, and with her heart pounding against her ribs, she searched for any opening to cause lasting damage. At this rate, she would lose. She could only hold out for so long before making a fatal mistake. Better to take the high risk while still in control of her body.

Two arms clubbed the ground, and instead of weaving away, Axon leapt into the air and landed on the thick bone of the left. With a blank expression on its skull face, the creature lifted its arm. Axon hacked away with her Water Blade even as the ground receded beneath her—chopping over and over as if breaking up a log into kindling. She straddled the arm, holding tight with her knees, feeling cold wind brace her skin, and not daring to look anywhere beyond the task at hand.

Before the creature could flick her off, she jumped onto its rib cage. Instinct guided her. Climbing down a short distance, she pushed off and rolled to the ground. She had not managed to sever the bone completely, but it hung limp and useless.

Still not enough.

The creature charged her as the crowd collectively uttered a thrilled gasp.

"I've had enough," Axon said and she launched forward. Racing toward the creature, she bared her teeth and growled.

The Dacci watching must have thought she had lost her mind. Perhaps the bone creature thought so, too. It seemed to hesitate.

Lowering its head, it opened its mouth and roared. But as it pulled back, readying to strike with its thick arm bones, Axon sprinted forward. She hurdled onto one of the creature's tentacle-legs and hopped up towards its two spines. Climbing the sets of vertebrae like a ladder, she entered the creature's chest cavity. Protected by its ribs, she had no fear the creature would clobber her. At least, it could not do so without crushing in its own chest.

As the crowd pointed and shouted, she expected the soldiers to intervene. They did not move. They would never stop protecting the witches. Or perhaps they feared meeting the same fate as the earlier soldier.

That just made things easier. Holding onto the creature's spine with one hand, Axon used the other to cut across the bones. She chopped and hacked and walloped the ribs and sternum. She screamed her rage as she laid waste to the creature's skeletal structure. Larger and larger fragments of bone flung off. And when she finally turned her attention to the spine, the entire bone creature came crumbling down. Sounding like a drumline of bones, the creature fell apart onto itself. Despite the damage she had done, the few ribs that remained intact thankfully protected her from the falling debris.

Silence settled over the encampment.

Axon staggered to her feet and emerged from the wreckage. Nobody spoke. Not even the children. Fear froze them.

Axon nodded and suppressed a grin. She turned back toward the bone creature. Her chest swelled. She had done that much. And if she could take that whole thing down on her own, maybe she had a chance against the Beast after all.

The Dacci began to clap. Slow at first, but soon a rising group of voices chimed in. The cheering and applause became undeniable. Frowning, she turned back—why were they happy that she destroyed their monster?

The answer came quick. The Dacci were not looking at her nor were they applauding her. They all watched the four witches.

In front of these women, the Dacci had created a long pile of filth. Perched atop the pile, each witch had placed three of her own bloody teeth. Three. Axon shivered.

She glanced down at her Blade. She expected it to be covered in dirt, bone dust, and gore. But unlike a normal sword, this one showed no signs of wear. It looked clean as new. Its glow brightened. It felt stronger in her hand. But as the four Dacci witches convulsed, as they changed before her eyes, Axon was not confident the Blade would be enough.

CHAPTER FOUR

The witches screeched their anguish. One stretched her arms high above her head as her spine cracked backwards. Another jerked her pelvis to the left while her shoulders shuddered violently. All four moved in a spastic dance choreographed by a madman. The witch with blue eyes opened her mouth and saliva slobbered out as she gagged. A long tusk emerged followed by a thick-skinned appendage that blocked all her sounds.

The Dacci soldiers guarding the witches stepped back. Those villagers who had been applauding now rushed to put distance between them and these fearsome creatures. Axon, however, sprinted ahead.

She could not let these witches finish their transformation and fight her. Four against one—not the kind of fight she wanted to be in. Especially when her opponents had become bizarre mutations.

One guard discovered his courage and attempted to stand between Axon and the witches. But Axon did not stop. As he pulled out his sword and adjusted his shield, clearly expecting Axon to stand ready and fight, Axon blasted forward. She tucked into a roll and as she came up, the Water Blade cut through the man's knees with a blinding blue flash. He toppled over, shrieking as blood spewed from halved legs.

Before he even hit the ground, Axon resumed her charge. The remaining soldiers scattered further back, putting their spears and swords in front to protect themselves. But as the witches continued their transformation—the skin of one turning a mottled gray while another sprouted several arms from her waist—Axon rushed by the far left side.

With one stroke she removed the head of Blue Eyes and did not stop moving. By the time the shocked expression on the rolling head settled, the remaining three witches tried to take a defensive posture. But instead of attacking, Axon rushed off into the crowd.

Chaos erupted.

The Dacci villagers screamed and shouted as they dispersed in all directions. Several soldiers regained their courage and tried to thread through the confused people, but the panic surrounding them blocked every possible way.

Once Axon saw she had evaded the initial attack by the guards, she ducked down the first alley between tents that she found. From afar, the layout of the camp had appeared orderly and purposeful. But on the ground, the tents formed a haphazard maze.

Racing up one pathway and dashing across another, she poked her head through the flaps searching for Zev. A woman carrying a baby ran by, caught Axon's eyes, and begged for her life. As if Axon would slaughter a baby. No point in trying to calm the woman down. Axon rushed for the next tent.

Turning down another pathway, she saw two Dacci soldiers with swords. They spotted her and barreled forward. She looked back the way she had come—two burly men blocked the passage. They did not notice her. They were hiding from where they thought the threat came. But if they saw her, their fear would make them dangerous. The only other path led off to the right, but the screaming woman with her baby had gone in that direction.

"Guess I fight."

The narrow confines forced the guards to attack one at a time. If they charged side-by-side, the likelihood of injuring each other increased substantially. The first one came on with two sloppy, nerve-fueled attacks. Axon did not bother blocking. Simply shifting her body kept her safe.

Upon the second miss, the guard stumbled forward. Axon raised her knee and let the man drop into it. Groaning, he doubled over and grasped between his legs.

She struck the back of his head with the Water Blade's pommel. This kept her blade pointed toward the true enemy—the second guard. He had more patience and skill—after all, he stood back to be second and balanced his feet in a firm stance. If Axon had stabbed the first soldier, this one would have attacked while she was busy removing her Blade from a dead man. Keeping the threat of her Blade evident saved her life.

She stepped forward and bent at the knees, lowering her body, strengthening her balance. No point in watching this man's shoulders. He would not give away his moves. Not from there. But the eyes—his eyes might give away his secrets.

An anguished voice straining like animal skins made thin enough to see through, called out from the head of the passageway. "Leave her to me."

Both Axon and the guard gazed down the path. A monstrosity stood before them—mounted on four spiked legs, a hard umber carapace led up to a torso lined with two vertical rows of eyes, and at the top, the witch's face absent all but a jagged-toothed mouth.

"What in Nualla is that?" the guard said.

The witch barreled down the path, her legs clicking against bits of stone like a field of insects waking for the night. The guard's sword hit the ground as he raced away blubbering madness. Axon lowered into her fighting stance once more and raised the Water Blade.

The witch's head angled back farther than made sense. Extra rows of teeth descended from the roof of her mouth as she hissed a horrible, guttural noise.

Holding for the right moment, Axon put all her weight on her back foot. Her front foot positioned to take the shift the moment when she would launch forward. She adjusted the height of her Water Blade. As best she could, she ignored the twisted horror in front of her—saw it as no more than a straw dummy to practice upon.

The witch raised her arms revealing jagged claws lining the skin and hissed once more. Axon shoved off with her back foot, screaming to generate more power, and thrust her sword forward. The Blade slipped through the creature's skin with satisfying pressure, but the witch's momentum whipped Axon off to the side.

Axon held tight to the Blade, yanking it out as she tumbled against a tent. The witch continued forward several steps before turning back. Her hard shell smacked Axon in the side and the foul stench nearly knocked Axon worse than the attack.

The witch's hand covered her wound as oily black blood dribbled between her fingers. "That hurt—a little. Looks like you are hurt more."

Axon did not feel any pain. She scanned over her body, taking quick inventory, and saw no blood. When she stood, she felt a strange twinge in her hip. With one hand she explored the area and discovered one of the witch's thorny claws embedded in her skin. She plucked it out and tossed it away. "It'll take a lot more than that to slow me down," she said.

"You're in for a surprise." With a soft chuckle and a slight hobble, the witch clicked her legs against the ground as she slipped down an alley. Axon did not think the witch would die, but she clearly wanted out of the fight. And why not? She had two other sisters roaming this encampment with their own monstrous bodies ready to fight.

Though the panicked screams had died down, plenty of commotion still filled the air—children crying, soldiers barking orders, and the odd grunts of the witch creatures. The longer Axon remained in the camp, the more danger she faced. With a slight limp, she hustled down the passageway. She returned to checking tents and avoiding alleys that led to frightened screams.

At one point, Axon watched a blue-green snake creature with a witch's head slither by. The witch did not notice her, and that was fine. The next tent she reached had a shabby, wooden door. She opened it and her body released a mountain of tension. She had found Zev. Alive.

He had been tied to a pole and clearly abused. Filthy, sweating, bleeding, and battered. Worst of all—Bellemont knelt before him. She had a fetid smelling pile of slop in front of her.

"You killed Xarad," Axon said, leading with the Water Blade. "Tortu can damn me to an eternity of suffering if I let you kill Zev, too."

Zev lifted his eyes. His mouth opened with bloody drool, but he could not form a word.

"It's okay," she said. "I'm going to get you out of here."

Before Axon could move on Bellemont, the entranceway behind her cracked into pieces and ripped outward. Standing in the doorless doorway, Axon saw the last witch—a muscular creature made of metal. Nothing more. Whatever trade-off the witches had to make, this one poured everything into muscle. Axon had never seen such an overly-developed and ultra-defined physical form before.

Trusting her brute strength, the witch barreled forward, throwing metallic punches at Axon. She missed the first two but connected on the third, lifting Axon off the ground and tossing her through the air. Holding her fists together, the witch thundered ahead with the intent of bringing her brutal strength down upon Axon. But the Water Blade flashed out as Axon rolled to the side.

Where the Blade hit the metallic witch, sparks flew in the air. A sharp sizzle followed the scraping of metal. Back on her feet, Axon saw a glowing band of melted iron across the witch's arm.

"Almost ready," Bellemont said.

Axon pointed her Blade at the witch. "I will stop her. No matter how many times you attack me. She is not going to kill my friend."

"Axon." Zev's weak voice seemed to amplify in her ear.

She looked to Zev's bruised face—a horrible mistake. She felt the fist smash against the side of her head as her own thoughts warned of her lapse in judgment. Her body floated to the ground. In the instant that transpired, she saw Zev's eyes widen. Bellemont stood, stepped toward him, and wrapped her arms around his neck.

With a sharp crackle in the air, a puff of smoke, and a putrid odor, Bellemont and Zev vanished.

All went dark.

PART VI
ZEV

CHAPTER ONE

In the span of a heartbeat, the world flipped. The air ripped out of Zev's lungs as his bindings disappeared. His ears popped. With a cool rush of air across his sore body, he collapsed onto a hard stone surface.

He could not move. His muscles refused. With his arms no longer tied, they flopped forward, stinging with a thousand needles as blood flowed through his veins once more. The cold ground pressed against his face, and when he opened his eyes, he saw the wide stretch of Landbreak Bridge leading to the halfway circle.

Bellemont stepped into view and squatted beside him. "Don't try to move. Flashing to a new location is hard enough when you're in good health."

He tried to speak but his jaw would not work properly. His muscles cramped. Tighter. They wouldn't stop. Vibrations rippled down his arms, his waist, his legs, into his toes. Just a shiver at first, but soon, with ferocious abandon, his entire body jerked and spasmed.

"You'll be okay," Bellemont said. She shoved something awful tasting in his mouth. "So you don't bite your tongue."

Her veiled face gazed down at him, but only for a moment. Everything blurred before a blinding white flashed like staring into the sun. He glimpsed the Dacci Inquisitor as she cut him, poked him, and burned him. Her smile engulfed him. An evil smile. One that enjoyed the pain she had caused.

"Come back to me." Bellemont's voice—so far away. "Fight your way back to me. Axon needs your help."

Axon.

His eyes snapped open. Drenched in sweat, he struggled to breathe. Bellemont cradled him and stroked his wet hair. At least his body had stopped shaking.

She removed the foul object from his mouth—just a stick. "I need you to trust me. I can make you better."

From inside the black shreds she wore, Bellemont produced a small pouch. Picking at the knot that had tightened over time, her eyebrows narrowed downward. "This wasn't supposed to happen. Nobody was to get hurt. This wasn't the plan."

The knot finally released and she pulled out a small glass vial of a dark, oily liquid—a vial with a distinct lightning symbol scratched on the side. Zev's heart jumped into a full-on panic. He tried to wriggle free, but she kept him in place with one arm. He clamped his mouth shut as she used her teeth to pull off the stopper.

"Calm down. I'm not going to hurt you."

He cringed at that black liquid, yet his brain told him Bellemont spoke true. She did not mean to hurt him. She could have done so many times over. Instead, she had taken him away from that awful tent.

His brain told him to trust her, but the rest of him demanded he take flight. If only his muscles would obey him. Yet even if he could stand, even if he could walk, he would not have lasted long enough to get to the end of the bridge.

"Open your mouth. I won't lie—this stuff tastes horrible. But it will heal you."

She gripped his jaw and forced it open by pressing her thumb and middle finger against either side. After dumping the oily contents into his mouth, she wrapped her arm under his chin and pulled up.

Tossing the empty vial aside, she used her free hand to pinch his nose.

Once again, she had told the truth—the liquid tasted vile. Not only did it have the bitter taste of spoiled meat, but the liquid had texture, too. Gritty at parts. Lumpy at others. When he swallowed against his will, his stomach tried to toss it right back.

But Bellemont refused to give in. She held him tight until after a few moments, his body relaxed and that disgusting liquid settled.

"That is a gift from Nualla. It will heal you. It'll take anywhere from moments all the way up to half-a-day depending on how bad your injuries are. So until you can take care yourself, you're going to have to rest your faith with me." She turned his head so that he looked directly at her. "I did not kill Xarad. I didn't kill anybody. And I didn't betray anybody, either. You've got to believe me."

Zev wanted to nod, wanted to open his mouth and explain that he had figured that much out, but he lacked the energy and the strength. Instead he closed his eyes.

"It'll have to do," she said.

He thought she said something more, but his mind drifted off into a blissful darkness. For how long, he didn't know. But when she eased him back to the stone before walking off, the pain ratcheted his eyes open.

She promised to be back. True to her word, she returned shortly. "I'm afraid they're all out of horses. So, I paid for one of those horse-less contraptions. I hope you don't mind."

With Bellemont's aid and the early healing effects of the oily liquid, Zev managed to crawl onto the backboard of the horseless cart. Bellemont positioned herself in the driver's seat and took a few moments to look over the machine's operation. As the owner explained the vehicle to her, Zev's vision went in and out of focus. He finally recognized that they were at the halfway point across the bridge—but then his brain reminded him that he knew that already. Only a few people walked around the area. Most curled up on the edges to sleep through the night. Sleep sounded good. Pleasant. So little felt pleasant lately. He thought he would rest his eyes for a bit.

With a jolt, he lifted his head. Two things struck him immediately —one, they were driving somewhere in the Feral Lands; and two, he felt tremendously better.

Rising up to his elbows, he opened his mouth and tried to speak. A rasping sound came out at first, and Bellemont glanced back at him. Her eyebrows lifted and widened her eyes.

"You look much better." She grabbed a canteen from a basket built into the side of the machine. "Drink this before you try to speak."

Zev unscrewed the top and sniffed its contents. Smelled like water. But even if it was more of that horrid tasting liquid, he could not deny the results. Swigging back a mouthful, he discovered cold water. His throat loved the caress of cool liquid and he let out a long, satisfied sigh.

"Keep drinking. And if you get tired, go back to sleep. We still have plenty of time before we reach Pilot."

Zev noticed a strange light in front of the machine that stayed there no matter how they turned or what speed they went. Had Bellemont sacrificed another tooth for this light?

"I hope you understand that you are not in any danger with me," she said. "I didn't want to hurt anybody. I swear to Nualla. I just wanted to meet my people. Find out where I came from. I figured I would help you all until we reached the Feral Lands, and then I'd spend some time in a Dacci village. That's all. I had no idea they were going to do any of this. I'm truly sorry for what they did to you."

"You saved me," Zev said in a gravelly whisper.

"I shouldn't have had to. Everything's gone wrong, and I don't understand why. You know, I thought that maybe I could be Dacci, that maybe they would accept me. But the rumors are all true. Once you're a Stolen, they never want you back."

"So talkative."

"Sorry about that, too. The stories I had heard were that the Dacci tended to be quiet and mysterious. My Stolen parents always complained I talked too much. So I've tried hard to be more Dacci-like. And, not to be rude, but I didn't want to talk to you at all at first. I didn't like you replacing Xarad so quickly."

Ignoring the pain, Zev sat up straighter. The twined threads unknotted in his head. Could it be that simple? One question would make it clear beyond doubt. "Did Xarad know you were in love with him?"

Bellemont's shoulders stiffened. "That's absurd. Why would you think that?"

"Mostly a look I caught—or really that I didn't catch. I didn't quite place it at the time, but whenever Axon spoke of Xarad, you would try to hide your eyes. It made me think you were guilty, but nothing else added up to you being the killer. So, what were you guilty of?"

"Not—"

"You're blushing, now. That tells me everything."

She shook her head. "I could never have told him. We fought alongside each other. That's intimate in a way others don't understand. I would never risk losing that. I couldn't."

That was all he needed. Gripping her shoulder, Zev said, "Hurry. Axon's in danger."

"What do you think we're doing? I saved you from the village so that we could get Pilot and go save Axon and Henlio."

"No. Not Henlio."

"We don't abandon our people."

Zev shook his head. "He's the one who killed Xarad. He's betrayed you all."

CHAPTER TWO

Driving across the flat Feral Lands should have been easy on Zev's healing body, but every bump jostled him to the bone. He wondered if the unpleasant drive came as a result of Bellemont pushing the speed as fast as possible or the poor crafts-manship of the horseless cart. He wanted to blame it on the latter, but he suspected the former. As the sun lifted over the horizon, he rested his head back. At least he would have some warmth soon.

"I'm trying to be respectful," Bellemont said, shouting more than necessary to be heard, "but you have got to explain to me how Henlio killed Xarad. And don't try to pretend that you've passed out again. The mixture I gave you should no longer be causing that. Besides, talking to me will help you keep your mind off any pain you're feeling."

Zev doubted that last part, but he figured it would be a good idea to share his information, too. It would give him a practice run at explaining it—he would have to tell Pilot and Axon eventually, and he wanted to be as clear and concise as possible. Plus, his throat felt much better. Talking would not cause the raw soreness it had before.

Rolling onto his side so that Bellemont could hear him better, he said, "Henlio is an agent of the Beast. Excuse me, of Nualla. There were a lot of things pointing to this. His anger towards you—I couldn't find any reasonable explanation for it. His saddlebag—he stole that skull from you and claimed you planted it on him. Pilot's saddlebag—Henlio stole that vial with the lightning bolt and tossed it in there. Anything to confuse me. But in the end, he wanted to shift blame to you and to cover up the odor that followed him because of his association with Nualla."

"Odor? What odor?"

Zev tried to hide his embarrassment. He sought a delicate way to explain when he finally settled on the blunt truth—no time for delicacy. "Surely you've noticed that the Dacci smell of all the death and, well, defecation that they work with."

Bellemont's head rocked back and forth. "Of course, I know."

"Then why did you—"

"A joke. I thought we could ease a bit of the stress."

Zev had to keep reminding himself that the real Bellemont acted very differently than the one she had portrayed before. "Anyway, Henlio was doing everything he could to make me think you were the spy for Nualla."

"Not a bad choice. Considering I'm Stolen."

"Exactly. But that was all a side matter. A cover-up for the murder he committed. A murder that had not been planned. His real purpose was probably to use his position as Axon's right hand in order to spy for Nualla and ultimately attempt an assassination of King Robion. Xarad must have figured that out, so Henlio killed him."

"Maybe that's why Xarad acted so strange around Henlio."

"How so?"

"He'd get stiff and cold whenever Henlio was in the area. I always thought it was out of fear—Henlio could be a bit of a bully. But now I'm thinking Xarad knew something was wrong."

"Possibly. I wish you had trusted me earlier. That kind of information would have been helpful."

"Axon brought you in to find out who killed Xarad, didn't she?"

"It wasn't for my fighting ability."

Bellemont grinned. She leaned forward and rolled her shoulders.

As she turned her neck from side to side, little cracks and pops followed her movement. "I'll tell you whoever built this thing has no idea how uncomfortable it is to drive for long periods." She resettled and continued on. "Everything you said about Henlio is very suspicious, and I completely believe you, but I can't say that it all adds up to him being a spy for Nualla."

"There's more. The attack on Ridnight was too easy."

"Easy? How can you call—"

"All the attacks on us since I joined your group were too easy."

"You don't know what you're talking about."

"Think about it—Axon and Henlio sneak into the enemy forces that have built a wall around the city. Despite your spell, they were surrounded by dozens of witches, many if not all who were more skilled than you, yet not one of them notices anything. Then Axon and Henlio fight the giants. At one point, Henlio fights three giants all by himself. I'm sure he's a great warrior, but I don't see how he could have survived that without injury unless Nualla did not want them to harm him. Then, in a matter of moments, Axon and Henlio saved the city. They killed a few giants, came after the witches, and it was suddenly over."

"The witches were the ones creating all that magic—the wall, the giants, all of it. Once they fled, nothing would stand."

"But surely there were more witches surrounding Ridnight City. If they had wanted to, they could have put up a serious fight against two warriors. Maybe they had an inkling that you were off in the distance somewhere casting spells, but they had no reason to believe there was anybody else. No, their actions don't make sense. Unless it was all a show."

"You think they were faking?"

"If Henlio's original goal was to kill the King, they had to create a reason for him to gain access to the King."

Bellemont nodded. "So by defeating the attack on the city, there would be a big celebration in our honor, and Henlio hoped to get a private audience with the King to be thanked or maybe given a medal."

"Something like that. But Henlio never got the chance. He didn't expect Axon to immediately tell the King she wanted the right of going after the Water Blade, and he certainly didn't expect her to succeed. Before he knew what had happened, we were all packing up to leave."

"But couldn't I still be the killer? Or Pilot? All of this applies to us, too."

"But you loved Xarad. You loved him so much you kept it secret to preserve the camaraderie you had as a fighting force. I suspect you were jealous of the girls that Xarad and Pilot fought over, but not enough to commit murder. And not in such an underhanded way. If you killed Xarad, you would have wanted him to know exactly why he was dying. As for Pilot, it's not so much that I have evidence that he did not commit the murder as the evidence against Henlio just keeps piling up. See, once we headed out to the Feral Lands, Henlio had to find a way to lead Axon to that Dacci village—to a trap. They knew we were coming. They had been writing letters to you, trying to help him bring you in."

"Those letters were a trap?"

"I think so. I didn't get to read them. I only glimpsed a part of one."

Bellemont stiffened. "You searched through my things?"

"Sorry. But I was looking for a killer."

With a turn of her mouth, she acknowledged his reasoning—though he could not tell if she accepted it. "I reached out to the Dacci through a friend. They told me the stories of Stolen being rejected were just stories. They told me they wanted me to rejoin them, become a sister witch to them, and I believed it."

"They preyed on your desires."

"They'll regret that."

"I suspect Henlio knew about the letters and found a way to tell the village about our movements."

"Except I brought us all to the village. If I hadn't gone there—"

"Then he would've had to find some other way to lure us there. But it's not too hard for him to have figured out that you were going to sneak off at some point. We all knew one of the reasons you were with us was to see the Feral Lands. It's only natural." Zev grunted as he sat up. "The real key to it all, however, came from the Dacci Inquisitor. She gave it all away. When she was hurting me, she spoke of the Battle of Alapia. She told me about a game Axon and Henlio played during the battle and how disgusting she thought it was. But there was no way she could know about that game. Even if she had overheard them, she could not possibly have called it a game. And only two people knew the details—Axon and Henlio. So, it could only have come from Henlio."

"I hear everything you're saying, but it's still hard to believe. Henlio has been loyally at Axon's side for as long as I've known them. Longer than that. I don't see why he would betray everything for Nualla. At least with me, it made sense that you were suspicious. I was once Dacci. But Henlio—I don't know."

"I don't know why he did this, either. For now, let's focus on saving Axon. We do that, and she'll make sure to get the answers out of Henlio. Though, I'm not sure I want to see that happen. It's going to be ugly."

CHAPTER THREE

*Z*ev woke when he felt the horseless cart slowing down. They approached their camp—Stick, Majesty, and the other horses grazed nearby—but they saw no sign of Pilot. Bellemont parked but remained seated.

"What do you think?" she asked.

Zev swung off the back and hopped to his feet. "I think I feel great."

"That's nice, but you'll still need rest. You have to be careful. Until the mixture has completed its healing process, you'll injure easily."

"Haven't you noticed? I always injure easily." As if his body wanted to illustrate the point, a sharp stab of pain rippled up his side. Zev grimaced. "I'll be fine. Let's focus on Axon."

"Which brings back my question. What—"

Pilot emerged from the dark on the opposite side of the campfire. "I thought I heard your voices. Good to see you both back. Where's Axon? And Henlio?"

Zev strode across the camp to his pack. "That's a long story." He checked over his rifle and stuffed his pockets with ammunition. "Get yourself ready. We're heading out immediately."

"Wait, wait. You can't come in here like that, arming up, and not tell me what's going on."

Bellemont grabbed her saddlebag and threw it over her horse. "Henlio is a murderer, and Axon is in trouble. Need anything else?"

"Oh. In that case, you can tell me on the way." Pilot pressed his hat on his head, grabbed his own saddlebag, and prepped Majesty.

In short order, they mounted their horses and headed off. Everybody made sure to have their weapons ready—and in Zev's case, loaded. Bellemont reminded them to also pack food and water. They had no idea how long it would be until they returned to the camp.

"Why don't we just take that thing?" Pilot asked, pointing to the horseless cart.

"Not enough room for all of us," Zev said.

Bellemont added, "Where we're going, that thing won't do well. Too rocky and too many narrow passages. Trust me—your horse is going to do a lot better."

She led the way. Zev and Pilot hung back, keeping pace as Zev detailed all that had transpired. He started from the moment he had followed Bellemont out of the camp and finished with their recent arrival driving the horseless cart. Telling the tale used up most of their travel time.

In the end, Pilot only said, "Huh. I wondered why my pack smelled so bad."

As they neared the Dacci camp, they dismounted, tied their horses, and approached on foot. Crouching behind the rocky ridge, they waited and observed. Zev did not spot any movement. Nothing at all.

"Am I missing where everybody is?"

"Not a soul there," Pilot said.

"But we had a big fight," Bellemont said. "Axon took on a lot of people, and there was panic. Four witches made a huge creature. It doesn't make sense."

With rifle in hand, Zev walked down the slope toward the quiet camp. He did not mean to be brave or courageous or foolhardy, but he could hear time clicking in his head. Axon was in trouble. The longer they spent trying to figure out where she was, the more time their enemies had to hurt her. Wincing, he recalled how much pain the Dacci Inquisitor had caused him. He remembered thinking that he did not have the stubborn strength of Axon. The Inquisitor had no trouble breaking him, but Axon—she would break eventually but not before the Inquisitor had put her through all kinds of horrors.

He tried to shake off the nervous tingling on his skin. He watched every shadow, every tent flap, every flicker of a torch—searching for hints of what had happened. The dead that he had heard fall during Axon's assault were gone. At least, he did not see any evidence of them —not even bloodstains.

Bellemont and Pilot walked behind, and he could hear their shock. When they reached the camp center—the pool of water looked nearly as dark as the pool of waste.

"Come here," Pilot said.

Zev turned back. On the edge of the circle, half-in and half-out of a tent flap, Zev saw a dead man. The dark and oily sludge they had all come to know surrounded the body, bubbling as it dissolved the corpse. Long strands of filth strapped around him like slick ropes and pulled the shrinking pieces of corpse into the ground.

"It's Nualla," Bellemont said. "He feeds on all that we throw away."

Watching the Beast in action, Zev started to comprehend more of what he had been told—of Nualla's enormity, of how it stretched out across most of the Feral Lands. How would they ever defeat such a creature?

A breeze picked up and what had been an unpleasant but tolerable odor became a fetid stench that turned Zev's stomach. "Let's keep moving. We've got to find where they took Axon."

"What if they didn't take her anywhere?" Pilot said, watching the dark strands pull the last of the body underground. "That is part of the Beast, right? Maybe he was displeased with whatever went on here and wiped them all out."

Bellemont shook her head. "He doesn't work like that. He only takes what is offered or what is left behind. That's the core promise between the Dacci and Nualla. He only takes what is offered, and he only gives what is asked."

"I know you're technically Dacci, but you're also Stolen. You might not know what the Beast really does."

"I know more than you do, so at least that gets us a little further."

With a raised eyebrow, he said, "You weren't as mean when you were quiet."

Zev said, "Stop bickering and start looking around." To Pilot, he added, "If she is dead, we'll find that out, too. Unless you're looking for an excuse to leave us and continue running from your past?"

Pilot's glare hardened. "I gave my word to her that I would be part of this team and that's what I will do. I'm no coward."

"Then let's get searching."

Zev poked his head in one tent after another. Most looked like abandoned homes—sleeping areas with personal items strewn about as if the owner had left unexpectedly. The tents reeked of sweat and grime. But even as he tried to turn his nose up at these homes, he saw small beds for children and dolls made of cloth scraps. An unsettled sorrow lodged in his chest as if he had no right to look in these tents, that he had somehow perverted their sanctity.

But when he came across an opening to a hexagonal tent, his heart pounded up to his throat. Using his rifle's muzzle, he pushed aside the fragments of a wooden door that had been torn apart. The post he had been tied to stood with all the callousness of the Inquisitor. It mocked him with his own blood staining the wood. It shamed him with the scars where the Inquisitor stuck her blades into it hoping to intimidate Zev. And she had succeeded at that.

He turned to the side—near the spot where he last saw Axon—and he threw up. He did not think he had anything left in him, yet gobs of saliva and the remnants of his last meal burned up his throat and splattered against the ground. The next instant, he watched as the Beast pushed through the fouled dirt, taking his vomit with its dark, oily embrace.

Sanctity? These people allowed him to be tortured in the name of this fecal-eating horror. Where was there any sanctity in that?

Outside the tent, Zev pushed on. The deeper into the camp they walked, the more bodies they saw—each one in a state of decomposi-

tion encouraged by the Beast. He came across a large snake-like creature with blue and black skin and the head of a Dacci witch. The
Beast's oily fingers spread across the witch, slowly coaxing her corpse
into manageable pieces.

Bellemont called out, "Over here. I found someone alive."

Zev and Pilot dashed through the passageways toward the back of
the camp. Bellemont stood before a rock formation similar to the one
on Landbreak Bridge—a simple area designed for praying to Nualla.
An old Dacci man sat in front of the statue. His long, white hair
pasted to his forehead with sweat. His labored breathing and his unfo-
cused gaze left Zev with the impression that the man would not be
alive much longer.

"Finally, finally," the man wheezed. "Didn't know if I would survive
long enough."

Bellemont said, "Who are you?"

The old man snorted. "I'm the warning and the taunt. You are fools
to keep going. You cannot save your lady friend."

"Then she's alive," Zev said, trying to keep his emotions in check.

"Oh, yes. The great Nualla is not done with her."

"Where is she?"

The old man gazed up at the stone edifice. "I am the bait and the
blockade. Or maybe I'm the bluff—maybe I am here to waste your day
so that you can never save her." He laughed until he coughed and spit
phlegm onto the ground.

"He's mad," Bellemont said.

As the old man laughed harder and louder, Bellemont walked up
to him and slashed open his neck with a small knife. Blood poured
down his front. He gazed up with a thankful expression as a gurgling
sigh escaped his throat. When he collapsed, he pushed himself
forward so that his blood would splash across the ground—a final gift
to Nualla.

Bellemont looked from Pilot to Zev. "Perhaps the Dacci are right—
quiet is better."

Zev clenched his jaw. "He was our only source of information.
We've got nothing now."

Pilot stepped beyond the dead man, beyond the statue, and squatted on a section of dirt that looked recently disturbed. "It's time I show you the reason why Axon wanted me on this team. I'm going to track her." Standing, he added, "Get our horses. She's out there, and I'll find her."

CHAPTER FOUR

Pilot led them now, his face deliberate as he studied the ground searching for prints in the dirt, broken ends from the low plants struggling to survive, displaced rocks along their path, any sign that he could track. Zev would have found the operation frustrating if not for the fact that he saw no other course of action. It helped that Pilot said the Dacci were making it easy to follow them. "I think they want to be found."

Perhaps they do.

Zev could think of numerous reasons to keep Axon alive. Chief among them—luring the rest of the team to their slaughter. A familiar part of his brain enumerated the arguments for turning back. He was not a fighter, he was injured, barely healed, he had uncovered the killer which had been his main purpose all along, he had nothing left to prove. Yet he walked on. Because weighing against all of that was one simple name—Axon.

The gradual downward slope took a sharper incline. They descended into a small canyon—the rock walls straight and tall like a fortress. Most of the canyon was wide and easy to navigate, but a few sections became so narrow they had to ride single file.

Time drifted.

At length, Pilot said, "We're close."

Bellemont frowned. "How can you tell? This canyon looks the same as it did when we first dropped down here."

Pilot halted his horse and waited for the others to join him. He gestured to listen. Zev obliged, and to his astonishment, he heard soft chanting echo off the canyon walls.

"From all I ever learned about the Dacci, their villages are a far distance for one another. So, unless you have reason to believe there's another village nearby, this is where they took her. Either way, we'll find out shortly."

The further they traveled, the louder the chanting became. It had a surprisingly melodic pattern. Not pleasant, but Zev suspected he would be hearing that tune in his dreams for years to come.

After traversing another narrow section, they passed close to the canyon wall on the right while the left side dropped off into darkness. Keeping the horses calm with soothing words and gentle strokes, they slowly made their way down. Amplified by the canyon's acoustics, the chanting engulfed them, and Zev thought those strange sounds would trouble Stick more than the narrow confines of the walk. But Stick proved sturdier than the other animals, never once fidgeting, complaining, or attempting to turn around. Zev reminded himself that not being an actual horse meant Stick did not necessarily react like an actual horse. He was his own animal, and a good one, to be sure.

At the bottom, Pilot dismounted Majesty and gestured for the others to follow. In a whisper, he said, "Wait here."

Keeping low, he hustled around a towering rock form. Zev checked over his rifle once more. Nothing had changed, but he could not stop himself. When Pilot returned, he wore a boyish grin.

"I saw her. She's okay. Come on."

Following Pilot, they hugged the canyon walls until he waved toward the ground. Zev lowered to his belly and crawled. Bellemont followed suit. Like snakes, they slithered up toward a low hill of dirt and rock.

The chanting had grown enough in volume to confirm Pilot's

assertion. Once Zev looked over the hill, though, he did not see any reason for Pilot's jubilant attitude. The scene before him looked terrifying.

Here at the bottom of the canyon, the Dacci had carved an enormous temple into the wall. Round towers connected by jagged balconies poked out at impossible angles—probably held sturdy by magic. Faces and events had been carved in tableau, becoming more intricate the closer they were to the ground. The entire area had been restructured into wide steppes with low rock walls lining the edges. At the bottom, the villagers and camp soldiers had spread into a crowded arc, all facing the curved salt-marble stairs leading up to the temple dais.

With their backs to Zev, he knew he could watch without fear of being spotted. And there was a lot to watch.

The Dacci repeatedly dropped to their knees, head to the ground, as they chanted their song. As the unsettling music cycled through, they returned to their feet, lifting their hands to the sky. Back and forth they continued.

On the temple steps, two guards with jagged swords and spears watched Axon for any dangerous movements. Axon knelt three stairs below the flat-topped dais. Her head hung low.

Crossing the dais, Zev saw the Dacci Inquisitor—the same woman who had tortured him. Though she now wore an outfit of white strips mingling with red and yellow, with a headpiece clearly denoting her as some type of religious leader, Zev saw the sadistic grin of his torturer. If she was what the Dacci considered holy, then Nualla was nothing but a demon.

The Inquisitor stood much taller than Zev remembered. At first, he thought this was due to her being up several steps from Axon. But the longer he watched, the more convinced he became that the shadows he saw beneath the Inquisitor were not shadows at all but tendrils of the Beast.

Confirming his thoughts, the Inquisitor spread her arms. The chanting ceased and a hush came over the crowd. When the Inquisitor spoke, it was not her voice. Instead, she spoke with a guttural, gurgling sound as if her tongue did not move properly. "I am Nualla, and this vessel is my priest."

The entire Dacci congregation dropped to the ground, their heads pressing into the dirt and rock.

"My loyal believers, I see through my priest's eyes and I hear through her ears. I am with you even as I am everywhere." The Dacci congregation uttered the first few notes of their chant. Nualla via the Inquisitor said, "You have brought me a great treasure today. With this woman in our possession, our future becomes clearer."

Zev's dream of racing in and saving Axon fell away. This would never work. With only the three of them, they were doomed before they even left their camp.

Pilot rolled on the ground until he stopped next to Bellemont. He whispered into her ear, she nodded, and he rolled back. Bellemont scampered off to the left, keeping low, keeping quiet.

Peering over the ridge, Pilot weighed a thought or two, and rolled over to Zev. "I've got an idea," he whispered in Zev's ear. "Take up a position on the right by those two huge rocks. See them?"

"And then what?"

Pilot winked. "Then watch me be brave. Or insane. Haven't decided which one yet. Just be ready to shoot, if I need it."

Zev wanted more information—any information would have sufficed—but Pilot rolled away. He considered following Pilot and demanding an answer, but too much noise might get them noticed. Swallowing down his frustration, Zev huffed and scurried to the right.

The large rock formations offered plenty of cover, and the new position amplified the Beast's voice more. At least when Pilot's plan got them all killed, Zev would hear it coming clear enough. He peeked over the lip and found that the new position also provided a new angle on the scene—one that allowed him to see a man standing on the dais but far enough off to the side that he had been hidden earlier.

That man—Henlio.

Not only did the traitorous bastard stand by watching the woman he betrayed be humiliated and probably executed soon, but he did so with a smug expression. He smoothed his beard, and whenever Axon shifted on her knees, he sneered. Zev aimed his rifle with care, lining up Henlio for a perfect headshot. Whether or not he succeeded did not matter—he knew he could only make the shot by pure luck—but he simply wanted to squeeze the trigger and watch Henlio's satisfaction disappear.

Zev kept his finger off the trigger. Saving Axon meant infinitely more.

The Beast pushed his priest upward, lifting her into the air on a pillar of sludge. "We have waited for many generations while those that this woman defends became a scourge upon the land. They look down upon you all because you are willing to serve me. Because you create life and beauty out of death and disgust. While they take all our world offers and reshape it into something unnatural, you help me expand throughout the world as a natural being. As I was born to do. As you were born to do."

Zev could not take his eyes off Henlio. He thought of all the signs pointing to the betrayal, yet he had missed each one. If they did not save Axon, Zev knew he could only blame himself. She should never have been in that position. Had he figured out that Henlio was the killer even just a little bit earlier, Axon's life would not be in danger.

As Henlio turned to gaze across the Dacci crowd, Zev's heart sank. A bit further behind Henlio, a woman stood—a Dacci witch with a white stripe down her head. At her side, Zev spotted a distinct blue glow. The Water Blade. The white-striped witch had the Water Blade.

PART VII
AXON

CHAPTER ONE

As the Beast continued to speak through the Dacci Inquisitor —Axon refused to consider her a *priest*—the tension in Axon's shoulders, her arms, her legs, even her toes threatened to snap her in two. She wanted to burst to her feet, take out the two guarding her, and lunge right by Henlio. She pictured the scene with ease. The white-striped witch's face would startle as the Water Blade jumped to Axon's hands. Axon would slice across the witch's neck, spin back, and cut Henlio—the traitor—in half. Confusion would soar across the crowd like a roll of thunder, and she would use that moment to attack the Beast, pull it from the ground, and hew it into pieces.

But she did not move. All the heroics of her imagination amounted to the same as all her real heroics of the past—nothing. So what that she had fought off Dacci witches and giants and sludge walls? So what that she had faced the Godwalkers and survived their trials and earned the Water Blade? What did any of it matter now? Her life rested in the hands of her enemy. She had failed. Even if the Beast decided to let her live, she would forever walk the streets of Ridnight with her head hung low. She could hear her mother's shame and disappointment echoing in her head.

"Look at this brave woman," the Beast continued, and his rapt audience leaned in. "A great warrior and a great leader. Her only mistake was to fight for an unworthy side. Arrogance takes over the mind when such a decision is made, and that arrogance has led her to be a fool. It is the same arrogance that we will use against them to our ultimate success." The crowd chanted another round.

Axon breathed deeply, trying to force down all desire to slaughter every Dacci in sight. To do so would not help the Frontier, would not serve the King, and would only get herself killed.

"I can feel the anger and doubt within her. It shakes the ground beneath her and calls out to me. But she must learn. She must believe." The Dacci Inquisitor reached toward Henlio.

The traitor stepped forward, and Axon tried to stand. The guards rested the flats of their blades on her shoulders. When she pressed further up, they shoved her back to her knees.

The Inquisitor gazed down upon Axon, her eyes filling with the Beast's tendrils, and she said, "I, the great Nualla, have such power that you cannot even recognize your closest ally. You look upon this man and see your friend, Henlio. But this is not him. This is a copy that I constructed two years ago. For two years, you have fought at the side of my puppet. You have eaten with, laughed with, argued with a fiction of your friend. And you never noticed. Never knew."

Two years? A sharp steely rage ripped through Axon. She wanted to deny it all, but the moment the Beast said the words, they shuddered with truth. Two years. She had been troubled by the way Henlio turned against Bellemont. She had seen other odd behaviors in the man. But she never once thought that Henlio was not Henlio. Two years—it must have been after the Battle of Alapia.

The white-striped witch sneered, and Axon had no doubt that this woman had cast the spell for Nualla. No wonder she ran off whenever Axon came close to striking her. If she died, perhaps the fake Henlio would die too.

Axon glowered. She should have done something when she had first noticed the changes in Henlio. She should have said something to

Pilot, should have found Zev or another like him to investigate. Something. Another failure.

And Bellemont. Axon had spent most of her time suspecting Bellemont. Why? Because the woman was Dacci? Because she acted strange and different? Axon had always taken pride in treating all people by the same standards, yet she had turned on Bellemont with no solid proof, thought the worst of her, thought her capable of murder.

"See how this great warrior, the best the Frontier can throw at us, see how she crumbles now that she knows the truth. If we can fool her with my puppet version of Henlio, then taking the Frontier and the East will be simple. My Dacci—I recommit to you our ancient pact. You will provide me with the sustenance I need, and I will give you the power of magic. My word is a blood bond that cannot be broken. Together, we will use our power to make more puppets until we have infiltrated the people of the Frontier. When they can't tell the difference between us and them, we will triumph. We will take back our lands with the least amount of blood spilled. For how can they fight when they don't know which one of their own is theirs or ours?"

Hearing the Beast spout his nonsense sickened her. Axon failed to see how so many people could support this ridiculous idea. The Frontier had no interest in destroying the land. They cultivated it. They grew food and built homes and communities. Just because the people of the Frontier did not want to roll in the muck like the Dacci did not mean they wanted to destroy the Dacci. If the Beast and the Dacci stayed where they were, if they honored their borders and did not seek to enslave others, then all would be fine. But to listen to the Beast was to think that King Robion wanted to dominate the Dacci and destroy the Beast.

Axon lifted her head and saw her Water Blade on the witch's hip. The King did not want to destroy the Beast, only stop it from invading the Frontier, and he used Axon for that purpose. Because she wanted the Beast to fall. She would only be satisfied if she knew in her core that the foul creature died under her hand, that it could not harm her people ever again, that it ceased to exist. She craved the sound of her people's cheers once they heard that the Feral Lands offered nothing to fear.

And the answer hung on that witch's hip. The Water Blade. It made the difference.

A new story formed in her head. One in which, like before, she rose to her feet and fought off the guards. But then, instead of taking on the Beast or the Inquisitor or the white-striped witch, she went after Henlio. She would get her vengeance against the traitor, and all else would not matter.

But that path led to nothing. Even if she succeeded, she failed at everything else. However, it got her mind thinking more seriously. With a sudden flutter in her chest, she played out several scenarios, but in each one, she approached it not as a wishful fancy but with true strategic planning.

Pausing to listen to the Beast, she heard him repeating the same points as before—the wrongs done by King Robion, the wrongs done throughout history, the Dacci's right to fight back, the use of the puppets to defeat the Frontier. It all sounded like the conclusion of a speech. And something inside her shifted.

With a click like snapping fingers, she embraced the conclusion of the options in her head. Since she had failed her King and her people, perhaps she could make things better through sacrifice. If she acted now, took out the guards, grabbed the Water Blade, and fought every attacker until she had no more to give—if she did that, then perhaps some small bit of forgiveness could be achieved. Perhaps by taking on overwhelming forces, by facing her enemy with a brave soul, by rousing the hearts of her people with her sacrifice, then she would be remembered.

And if remembered, she might even inspire others.

She inhaled one last strong breath. Ignoring the stench, she planted her foot hard. She felt the soldiers' blades come to her shoulder. As she lowered her shoulders but kept her foot planted, she readied to push off, throw the soldiers off-balance, and start her offensive.

But a familiar voice called out. "Excuse me?" Pilot said as he entered from the back. He moved with steady confidence and a cocky strut.

Like gawking children, the Dacci stared—shocked by the man's audacity. Axon tried to hold back her sudden hope. After all, even though Pilot could be reckless, he would never simply walk into a place like this without a plan. It may not be a good plan, but he would have something in mind.

"Another?" the Beast said. "Come forward and kneel with your partner." The Dacci stepped back, parting a pathway toward the Inquisitor.

"Partner?" Pilot put up his hands. "Oh, no, no. We never went down that road. And I can see you're all busy here. I didn't mean to interrupt, but I was told this is where the crazed gathering of Nualla fanatics meets and I just had to see it for myself."

CHAPTER TWO

Axon couldn't stop herself. She laughed. It was enough to provoke one of the younger, more ambitious Dacci soldiers into action.

He shoved aside his peers and blustered into the open. With his chest puffed up and his jaw set tight, the man blitzed towards Pilot. Axon hoped Pilot's plan went into action soon or the poor Dacci soul would be beaten into the ground—enemy or not, she had no desire to see a kid beaten into fodder for the Beast.

A gunshot rang out. The dirt before the Dacci soldier kicked up, and the young man froze. Unease rippled across the crowd. Most had never heard such a strange noise before.

"I apologize again," Pilot said. "I forgot to mention that I have my men surrounding your little group here, and they are all armed with these fancy new things called *rifles*. Think of them like a good ol' bow-and-arrow that'll take your head off with one shot.

"Now, I've been listening to a bit of your chatter, and I've got to say that I'm not convinced. Nualla makes a big deal of pronouncing how great he is, and somehow that makes everyone here great, too. He says that the only thing stopping all of you from having the lives you dream of is the nasty, despicable people living in the Frontier or in the

East. But I can tell you, it's not true. Those people have no interest in hurting you or the world they live in. Proof of that is right here with me.

"If I wanted to destroy you, I would have had my men shoot you all without warning. Most of you would have been dead before you even heard the shots. Instead, I've given you a cautionary shot. Because all I want is to take my friend back and leave you in peace."

The Dacci Inquisitor's body bent forward, held by the Beast, so that she hung at a sharp angle, nearly upside down, and glowering like an angry tree limb. "You are exactly what I claim you to be. You bluster in here with weapons and threats. If you truly wanted peace, you would have no need for either. You would have walked in here humble. You would have presented yourself by showing respect to my people before begging them for their kindness."

Axon watched the faces in the crowd. Pilot had not convinced them of anything—except maybe that the Beast had been more right than they had originally thought. She scanned the back of the area, searching for hints of where help might be positioned, hints of what Pilot had planned.

The morning sun rose high enough to cut a sharp line of warm light across the top of the canyon walls. Though still in shadows down below, the temperature rose noticeably, and every passing moment, she could see easier. Whatever Pilot wanted to do, Axon thought he only had a little time left. Once the sunlight filled the canyon, the Dacci would be able to spot the true size of Pilot's army.

The Beast uttered a dark chuckle. "You will join your friend on her knees because she will never trust you again. She cannot. She has seen the truth and knows that she can never believe any of her people are really her people anymore. Many of them will be my puppets."

Pilot made a show of laughing harder and darker than the Beast. "Your little copy of Henlio is not as great as you think. I'll concede that it looks like Henlio, even sounds like him, but I knew something was wrong. His behavior toward our Dacci—oh, did you all not know there's a Dacci witch in our group?—well, his behavior towards her changed drastically. Nualla can make a good replica, but he can't know how to act like the real person. And there's that smell, too. Henlio was never the cleanest man in the world, but he never smelled like that. Now that we know you can play this game, we'll find other ways to pick out the differences between real and copy." Feigning a sudden curious idea, he gestured across the congregation. "You should all be worried, though. If Nualla can do this to one of my people, what makes you think he hasn't already done it before? Perhaps some of you are just copies, too."

A shockwave of doubt spread across the crowd. Axon repositioned her feet so she could launch into action the moment she had an opportunity. Though she still did not understand Pilot's plan, she knew to be ready.

The Beast snickered. "You have had a chance to speak. I have even allowed you an attempt to sow doubt. But you can see that the Dacci are tougher than your words. They know to their core that I share with them a deep, beneficial relationship. If they feared that I would make copies of them, then they would cease making offerings to me. Simple as that."

"But they don't know if any here are copies. Maybe that one over there with the long hair—how long has he been acting differently? Or perhaps the woman in the back holding the baby. Did she have the baby in front of everybody? Or did she disappear for a bit and return slightly off? Oh, I'm sure many of you dismissed it as the change of being a new mother, but what if—"

"They have nothing to fear because there is only one puppet—your friend, Henlio. He is our first." With a flick of a slimy tendril, the Beast motioned for the white-striped witch to step forth. "The idea and, therefore, the glory go to this great witch. She thought up creating a puppet, she found a candidate, and she made a grand sacrifice—including seven of her teeth."

A gasp rippled out across the crowd. Axon's relief that all the Frontier was not teeming with assassin puppets was tempered by the reminder that this experiment by the Beast had succeeded. Those assassins would be coming eventually.

The Beast continued, "You see now that there is only one puppet, and just as I created him, I can destroy him as well."

Guided by an unseen cue, the white-striped witch edged back behind Henlio. He made no effort to stop her, but Axon thought she saw recognition on his face—that he understood what would next occur. The witch plunged the Water Blade through Henlio's spine and out his chest.

His skin glistened and his brow pulled down. A sheen of sweat covered his forehead. He looked nauseated. The witch let the Blade remain inside him as she raised both hands in praise.

In a flash, his body fell apart. Simply dissolved into a pile of rancid smelling goop. Some of the clothes he wore had been part of the copy, and they also became part of the sickening pile. But a few items—a belt and his shirt—were real. They poked out of the pile.

Amongst it all, Axon's eyes fixated on her Water Blade. It rested half in the pile with its hilt sticking out as if inviting her over. This was it. She did not hesitate to think. Launching forward, she bolted toward the Blade.

CHAPTER THREE

For a few heartbeats, the world around Axon ceased to exist. No canyon, no Dacci, no Beast. Only the Water Blade. Stuck in sludge, its shimmering color poked through the air, infiltrated her eyes, and mesmerized her—pulling her closer, faster, begging to be reunited. Her fingers stretched further as her hand pleaded with her arm to reach that weapon. Once she grabbed hold of its comforting warmth, once she let its weight tense her muscles, once she let its glow reflect her heart—only then did she recognize that all around her had become pandemonium.

During her run for the Water Blade, Zev had opened fire. His first shot kicked dirt near the stairs Axon had knelt upon. His second shot struck one of the guards, ripping a hole through his spine, and dropping him as fast as the witch had dismantled Henlio.

The Dacci scattered. They were already stressed from the mayhem back at their camp, and this sent them careening out of control. From the top of the temple steps, Axon saw numerous adults clutching children as they raced to the edges of the canyon. Others hurried up the incline toward home. Only the soldiers remained focused, and there were plenty of them.

Her well-trained brain kicked in, reminding her to focus, too. A lot of threats remained. Including—

Axon whirled around to face the white-striped witch. The revolting woman pulled off her veil with one hand while raising the other like a claw. Blood dripped from where she had yanked free one of her few remaining teeth. The air around her clawed hand ignited into white flames as she threw gobs of mystical fire.

Instinct guided Axon's hand. She flipped the Water Blade up, and though she could tell she had missed the block, the Blade spewed out its blue, shimmering material. The drips of magic splashed upon the witch's fire and stopped it like a rainstorm on a field aflame. As long as Axon came close to her desired target, the Blade made sure the block counted.

She saw the shift in the witch's eyes. That cocky confidence dropped into sudden concern. She had only two teeth left that Axon could see. Would she attempt to cast a spell?

Her hesitation cost her. Axon leapt forward, screaming all her anger toward this one witch. Drifting across the stone, her heart cried out for all the pain caused by this toothless hag.

Axon inhaled hard and bellowed, "For Xarad!"

Though the witch fell fast—one strike from the Water Blade did her in—Axon had the satisfaction of seeing defeat in her eyes. This thorn had been worn to nothing, and now Axon had removed it.

But she had no time to wallow in triumph. A group of Dacci soldiers encircled Pilot. They jabbed in the air, far from striking him, and they spit at him. But none dared be the first to attack. They could overtake him with ease, but whoever ran in first would end up dead. Unsurprisingly, no one wanted to be first.

More gunshots. They came in bursts of two, then a short pause, then two more. Each shot flashed fire from the source. A woman wearing a metal helmet ordered a group of soldiers onto the ridge. "Stop those things," she barked and her soldiers rushed into action.

As Axon surveyed the situation, two soldiers tore up the stairs intent on taking her apart. They never made it to the top. She stepped forward, her intense focus intimidating on its own, and she used the Water Blade with efficient and merciless speed. Two sharp motions, two severed limbs, two screaming soldiers tumbling back down the stairs.

Despite the terrified villagers, despite the gunshots hitting the ground or taking down the occasional soldier, despite Pilot's situation or Axon standing tall with her Blade, despite it all, the majority of the soldiers clumped together a distance removed from the action, frozen like statues. Axon thought they were scared. But when she heard the heavy panting breaths to her side, she knew she faced something worse—something sinister.

The Dacci Inquisitor still watched over from the end of the Beast's stalk. Her skin had cracked like bone-dry land and blood drew tiny lines across her face. How long could the Beast control her before it killed her?

As a new thought struck Axon—that the soldiers standing around waiting were being controlled by the Beast—the world kicked into full speed. She had been standing next to the Beast, listening to the battle building up, yet it had only been a breath or two. She had not noticed.

Glancing down, she wondered if her experience had been part of the magic of the Blade? No matter. Such thoughts were meant for calmer times. She had a battle to win. And that meant killing the Beast.

Swinging the Water Blade back and ready, she lunged toward the oily limb holding up the Inquisitor. The bleeding woman gazed upon Axon, and with her, all of the soldiers not actively fighting shifted their gaze upon the Inquisitor in unison like a swarm of birds changing course.

As if flicking away an insect, a tendril snapped up from the ground and swept Axon's legs out from underneath her. "No," the Beast said as an afterthought.

Axon's training and experience saved her from hitting the stone too hard. She controlled her fall, striking the surface with her side, and bounded back to her feet. Resetting her stance, she launched into another attack.

With a sharper tone, the Beast repeated, "No." Another tendril shot up from the ground. Axon evaded the limb and hacked at it as she dashed by. But two more broke out and knocked her down once again.

"You should stop," the Beast said. "You do not understand what I am, so you will fail. And I don't want to see you dead—not yet."

Axon pushed back to her feet. "You want to copy me, don't you? You want to use me like another puppet."

"Look across all of those Dacci. Your friend holds them off well through fear. Your other friend with the rifle—I know there is only one out there—he won't last much longer. When he is caught or when his toy no longer works, the one in the ground will be swarmed by my soldiers. But why should more die than have to die?"

"Because you're so merciful? You want to destroy the Frontier and the East, take over, because you want peace for all? Is that the lie you want me to believe?"

"Let me show you."

Four of the soldiers huddled below rose into the air on pillars of the Beast's dreadful muck. As they rose higher like perverse flowers pushing up through the soil, Axon grasped that the soldiers had not been standing idly by. They had been clustered together, giving themselves to the Beast, allowing him to take control of their bodies—of their lives—as he saw fit. Their faces opened into horrified gasps as their bodies cracked apart and monstrosities composed of oily muck emerged.

Axon's rage and desperation inundated her body with new power. Ignoring her pains, she blazed across the dais, wielding her Water Blade, bellowing her frustration. The Beast tried to swat her aside but she dodged his foul limbs when they burst through the ground.

Twisting her torso and causing a circular spin upon release, Axon generated as much force as she physically knew how. Relaxing her muscles to add speed to the energy and tensing at the final moment, she unleashed all of her power into one vicious swipe of her weapon. Blue flashed like lightning. Vapor hissed off of the Water Blade as it buried into the Beast's trunk holding up the Inquisitor. Axon had one shining breath of satisfaction. One moment where she could envision her success.

A mouth opened up around the Water Blade—a black hole like a knot on a tree. The Beast regurgitated a thin green and brown liquid. It spewed over Axon, and she stumbled back, maintaining her balance despite the slick surface.

With weapon in hand, she spit the nauseating substance off her lips. Forcing the bile rising in her throat back down, she said, "You're a liar. You say you want peace, yet look at what you're doing out there."

She gestured toward the men circling Pilot. She had more to say, but the words stuck in her throat. Nobody had hurt Pilot—he could not leave the circle, but he had not been attacked, either. Another group of soldiers marched Zev out of the rock ridges and had him join Pilot.

Even from a distance, Axon spotted the change on Zev's face. More determined, more seasoned. Having been captured by the Dacci, she expected him to be frightened. But his eyes spoke of anger and frustration. Perhaps even a touch of shame.

She recalled how Bellemont had saved him—she knew now that had happened—and the way he tried to warn her. He must have known at that point that Henlio had betrayed them. He had accomplished all she hired him for, yet he and Bellemont had returned. For her. And she could not help them.

Soaked and stinking, the reek of bile covered her body and infiltrated her nose. Fitting. She deserved no better. Certainly not their loyalty. They came back for a failed warrior. A prisoner.

Pilot and Zev stood with as much courage as they could muster—and it was impressive—but Axon knew the two of them were not strong enough to fight off those Dacci soldiers. Not all of them. Perhaps if she stood in that circle, too, there would have been a chance. Perhaps not. But this way—

"What are you going to do with us?"

"You still refuse to accept what the Dacci have learned long ago. I am the world. All that you experience comes from me. I am a terrible and benevolent deity. And if you provide me with what I ask for as tribute or sacrifice, then I provide for you. That is my pact. It is that simple."

"I understand completely the deal you have with the Dacci. But we of the Frontier want only our freedom. We want no part of servitude to you. And I'm sure those in the East feel the same way."

The Inquisitor's body shivered. "You are too ignorant to understand. I'm not giving you a choice. You will accept. The only decision I leave in your hand is whether you will join us of your own volition or if countless people will die until you bend your knee."

Axon tried to find that spark within again. She wanted to roll her shoulders back, puff her chest, and jut her chin. She wanted to see her father's approving grin and her mother's shocked outrage. She wanted to hear the cheers of Ridnight. But she saw none of those things. Instead, she saw the Beast's dark tendrils crawling over her father's face. She watched her mother's body dissolved into the ground by fetid sludge. She heard the anguished cries of her people in sorrow.

The Water Blade held her arm in check, and seeing her team surrounded by the enemy caused her knee to quiver.

"You hesitate. Then I'll give you another choice—pick which of your two men will die."

She looked from Pilot to Zev. None of this made any sense. She had defeated the witches and the giants. She had taken back Ridnight. How could she have ended up here? Yet if she fought back out of spite, others would die, too. Her knee tried to bend even as she tried to keep it straight.

"I will kill one of them and ask you to bend your knee again. Fail that, and the other will die, too. Fail again, and I'll find others to kill. I will destroy everything until you do as I command."

"You only prove you're no god. You only show you're a monster." The words sounded strong and brave in her head but they drooled out of her mouth—weak and lazy.

"I think the smart one should go first. Zev. Yes, I think he's the perfect candidate."

"No. Stop."

"Then you see it the way it is. Bend on your knee, vow your allegiance to me, and we will save all your people. Defy me and I will kill—"

"You don't have to kill anyone." She could not imagine this moment had really happened, yet as she lowered her body, as her throat tightened, she swallowed down the futile desire to leap forward and attack the Beast. Her knee dropped, and she bowed her head. Tears welled in her eyes.

This was all wrong. None of it should have ended this way.

With a pop in the air, a bright light appeared like the sun breaking through an overcast morning. Axon stopped to gaze upward as did all the people below. A small figure drenched in yellow and golden light floated overhead.

Bellemont?

Her eyes blazed. While she continued to wear her black strips of clothing, she had removed her headdress and veil. Her hair fluttered behind. Blood covered her chin, and she smiled to reveal the three gaping holes from the teeth she had removed.

Three teeth! Axon thought before praying to Qareck that Bellemont could handle the power of the magic she now unleashed.

With outraged pride, the Beast grabbed several more of his soldiers, split their bodies into sludge creatures, and pushed them higher into the air. They became dark flowers on oily stalks. But Bellemont brought her hands together over her head—a clap of golden lightning issued forth and a resonating tone echoed across the barren lands. The gruesome stalks holding these creatures in the air severed at the bases.

The creatures tumbled to the ground. When they struck, the blow woke them from their stupor. Many scattered toward the edges of the canyon, leaving behind trials of sludge. Other soldiers yet to be ripped apart raised their weapons and darted toward those circling Pilot and Zev.

Axon shouted and soared down the stairs. With the Water Blade held up, with her focus on those with bloodlust in their eyes, she sprinted across the canyon floor. Though she had lacked the strength and skill to use the Water Blade against the Beast, she knew there would be no problem taking down these foes.

The first she cleaved across the legs as she ran by. The second made a feeble attempt to attack her. She had no trouble parrying the sword, spinning to the offside, and digging her Blade into the man's ribs. All without losing her stride.

The third soldier had seen her coming. He raised his sword and shield. Though he shivered like a newborn, the placement of his feet suggested he could handle a fight. He made one mistake, though. He attacked first.

Leading with his shield, he swung his sword, aiming across her neck. He might as well have written a detailed prophecy of his intentions. Axon slid onto one knee, under the swinging blade, and thrust upward. The Water Blade ran through his lower jaw and out the top of his head, sprouting blood mixed with droplets of water.

"There's your bent knee," she said, glaring back at the Beast.

The striking down of these three Dacci soldiers ignited the rest. Or perhaps the Beast had finally let them go. They heaved their weapons up, showered the air with their yelling, and broke into action. Most turned toward Pilot and Zev. A handful launched after Axon.

Blazing claps of golden lightning pulverized the ground with the crackle of falling timber. Dacci soldiers were tossed in the air. Two burst into flames. A protective ring formed around Pilot and Zev that no soldier could get through without being hit by Bellemont's magic.

Axon engaged two soldiers, cutting open the gut of one while being struck in the back by the other. Fortunately, the soldier who scored against her had a toothless mace for a weapon. Painful, damaging, but seldom deadly.

A dark, scaled claw emerged from the ground beneath Bellemont —part of the Beast. But as it shot through the air, threads of its oily skin folded off and stretched toward Bellemont. Not as a threat. Rather, they entered her eyes and mouth and nose. They fueled her power, which she continued to unleash upon the soldiers.

Axon gazed up and smirked. *Smart, Bellemont, smart.* The pact between the Beast and the Dacci meant that any Dacci that gave a proper sacrifice would receive the power of the Beast to fulfill a magic spell. Bellemont was Dacci. Stolen, yes, but Dacci nonetheless. She had made a great sacrifice and the only way the Beast could not give her the power she asked for was to leave—but to do so would be a violation of the pact. The Dacci would see the Beast as a fraud. As Axon recognized the situation, the Beast appeared to do so as well.

"You have cost me soldiers," the Beast said through the Dacci Inquisitor. "You have gained time. But you will not destroy me today. Not ever. Soon enough, I will take the land that is rightfully mine. I will grow strong and I will be the only deity of power. But I promise not one of you will live to enjoy your minor victory."

The Beast disengaged from the Inquisitor, and as her body traveled to the floor, all the Dacci paused to stare at the dais. Had they been abandoned? Had their great god failed them at the first sign of difficulty?

Axon wondered the same thing when the Beast shot out numerous dark limbs. Like spears, they flew out of his torso and skewered the remaining Dacci soldiers.

Axon did not think she would ever forget the horrified shock on those soldiers' faces. Fast and brutal, the Beast decimated them all. They slid to the ground with their blood draining out and their eyes bulging wide. The Beast's spears dissolved into liquid and fell through the cracks in the ground until there were no more. The scaled claw pulled back, disappearing below the surface.

Axon shook her head. Rather than admit defeat, the Beast had killed off his forces so that they could not spread the word of his failure.

Bellemont drifted down next to Axon. A dim amber aura framed her body. Pilot and Zev jumped over the dead bodies and weaved their way around until they could join the group. The Dacci soldiers were all dead. The Beast was gone.

Axon reached out towards Pilot. He grinned and put his arms out to embrace her. But she slapped him in the cheek. "That was a stupid thing to do. You don't lie about your strength when you are standing in front of an entire group—not when you don't have any strength to lie about."

"We had to do something. It may have been stupid, but it was the best I could come up with. Besides, from what I heard, you walked right up into a Dacci encampment."

"What I do and what I tell you to do are distinctly different things."

"Clearly. But at least it worked. We're done with the Beast."

Axon glanced back at the dais. "I doubt that. But we don't have to deal with it today." She gave the Water Blade a short shake as if testing its weight. "Gives me time to learn how to use this thing properly."

Zev stepped forward and put out his hand. "I'm just glad we were able to get to you in time. Once I figured out Henlio had killed Xarad, I had to let you know."

"You're a smart man. But next time, could you be a little smarter and a little faster?"

"I'll try."

Pilot snorted a laugh as he clapped Zev on the back. "Don't kid yourself. You're not planning on staying with this outfit. There won't be a next time."

Reddening, Zev said, "I suppose this really isn't where I belong."

"Of course," Axon said. "You have gone far beyond what anyone should have asked of you. I appreciate your help. All of you."

"Indeed," Bellemont said.

Zev raised an eyebrow and cocked his head toward her. He did not understand what went between the two, but he certainly had a sense that they were having a private conversation through facial expressions.

Axon gestured at Pilot, but before she could speak, a strange noise stopped her. A series of liquid gurgles and cracking bones—a sound she had heard many times on the battlefield after disemboweling an enemy. She noticed Pilot, Zev, and Bellemont all scanning the area in horrified disbelief. She clutched her necklace, closed her eyes, and recited the names of the Cassun Nine. She knew what she would see, but hoped it would not be true.

Turning around, Axon looked upon the Dacci Inquisitor standing tall on the dais. In her hand, the Inquisitor held one of the Beast's dark limbs. She bit into it like a drumstick, and as she chewed, a new tendril snaked out of her legs.

Like a blind worm, this tendril wriggled further and further out, growing longer as it moved so that it always remained connected to the Inquisitor. It searched for food. It fell upon one of the soldiers Axon had killed on the dais stairs. More tendrils shot out of the Inquisitor, and this nest of slithering snakes hauled in all the energy, all the blood and bone, strength and muscle, every last piece of flesh until nothing remained.

"The Beast is still here," Axon said.

"That is not Nualla," Bellemont said.

"Doesn't matter. She's not a Dacci witch," Zev said. "She has all her teeth."

Bellemont shook her head. "She has sacrificed something far worse. Her life."

The tendrils multiplied. Those that had already finished on the stairs split to find more corpses to devour. They branched out like fast-moving roots of a tree, reaching, reaching, with no end of corpses in sight.

One thick root poked from the Inquisitor's side and slithered across the dais. It wrapped around the white-striped witch's corpse and dragged her back. With a sharp motion, the Inquisitor separated the witch's head from her body.

Axon stood still and watched as the Inquisitor's skin glowed a dark and dangerous blue. The Inquisitor jolted, grimaced, and gritted her teeth as her bones crackled—making room for her to grow.

And she did grow. Taller. Stronger. Adding muscle and even more limbs.

Then she wore the head of the white-striped witch like an ornate hat. Blood coursed down her face and her cracked skin soaked it in with pleasure.

Scratching his chin, Pilot said, "Well, this doesn't look good for us."

CHAPTER FOUR

A xon pointed at Bellemont. "You're glowing orange. Does that mean you still have some of that magic left?"

"You think I sacrificed three teeth and probably a few years off my life just for one strike? I'm smarter than that. What do you want me to do?"

"Cut apart as many of those worm-things as possible."

Bellemont's dim aura brightened into a vivid, noonday shine. She lifted into the air, clapped her hands together, and sent golden blades of light cutting through the slithering tendrils.

Pilot stepped forward, sword in hand. "You want me to go in straight or flank her?"

Axon turned to Zev. "Pilot and I will attack from either side. You stay here in the middle and shoot her as many times as you can."

"Not a good idea," Zev said. "The only reason I hit anybody at all was because they were crowded together. Chances are I'm going to kill one of you instead of her."

Axon stepped up to Zev and grabbed his shirt. "Either shoot the Inquisitor and get your revenge or go help Bellemont."

Using his nose to point behind Axon, Zev said, "Um, Pilot just left."

Axon glanced over her shoulder to see Pilot springing off towards the Inquisitor. She shoved Zev aside, uttered a few foul words, and rushed for the dais. Up ahead, Pilot sliced several tendrils in order to reach the stairs. The salt-marble now looked more like a volcano spewing a river of oil off the dais, and Axon had no doubt Pilot did not want to put his foot into that grime.

"I'll help," Bellemont said, soaring overhead, smooth and silent like a cloud. She clapped her hands, cutting a hole into the stairs and through her own silence. Axon knew what would be on Bellemont's mind just as she knew there would be no stopping her—she needed to set things right, she needed to show her people another way, she needed to make sure Xarad did not die for nothing.

Bellemont sped toward the Inquisitor, pulling her hands back, ready for a powerful clap. But the Inquisitor flashed out her left hand. Her fingers extended into thick, brown tentacles that latched around Bellemont's head. A surge flowed back upon the Inquisitor—she flinched—but she had no trouble maintaining control. Whipping her body in a circle, the Inquisitor whirled Bellemont in a wide arc. She tossed Bellemont into the carved canyon walls and watched as the girl flailed against the stone, falling toward the hard surface below.

Having reached halfway up the stairs, Pilot attacked next. He had run out of safe places to put his feet, but the rush of fighting propelled him forward. He managed three strong steps before the dark muck beneath him exploded outward. The Inquisitor shrieked. He flipped backward, banged into the ground, and continued a painful series of rolling hits down the stairs. When he reached the bottom, his face bruised and bloodied, Axon stepped over him to start her own assault.

Using the Water Blade, Axon carved a path up the stairs. She did not bother running—the Inquisitor knew she would be coming. Though the Inquisitor's eyes were a solid mass of sludge, Axon knew the Dacci saw everything. She could feel that twisted gaze cover her skin.

"Your master has abandoned you," Axon said, keeping her eyes on the tendrils nearby while also holding steady focus on the Inquisitor. "He slaughtered all these people and turned you into a monster. For what? So that he can run away like a coward."

"You are arrogant and idiotic. Nualla gave you a chance. Gave you an opportunity to join the right side. The righteous side. All of his people below sacrificed their lives so that I may become powerful enough to protect him and our kind."

"What kind of all-powerful being needs to be protected by you?"

"He never claimed to be all-powerful. If that were true, he would simply make the world what he wants it to be. That's how you should know your pathetic gods are false. They cannot do what they claim."

Only two steps from the top of the dais. That was when Axon saw the tilt in the Inquisitor's shoulders. A slick pole of foul matter sprang from the Inquisitor's belly. It slammed Axon's head. She never had time to react. Moments later, her vision cleared enough to find that she sat at the bottom of the stairs with ringing in her ears and foggy thoughts rolling in her head.

"When I kill you," the Dacci Inquisitor said, "you will become part of me. Part of Nualla. And when we cross over to the Frontier, when we behead your King Robion and rule your lands, I will make sure you get to see every last drop of blood fall."

With Pilot's help, Axon strained to her feet. They stumbled back toward Zev who busied himself clubbing tendrils that snaked towards him. Bellemont limped over from the side—still glowing but with one eye swollen shut and fresh blood on her chin.

"I don't think we should try that again," Pilot said.

"I don't think we can stop it," Zev said.

Axon snorted hard and spit out a bloody gob of mucus. Rubbing the side of her head, she tried to concentrate. She couldn't get her thoughts to connect. "Something's off here."

"We just got ripped apart," Bellemont said. "That's plenty *off* for me."

Zev arched back and closed his eyes. Sweat trickled into his mouth. "Hold on. Axon is right." Opening his eyes, he turned in a slow circle. "Look around. Why are we still alive?"

Pilot said, "Not really the time for philosophy."

"Everything else is dead. We attacked her and she's made it clear that she could've killed us all. But she didn't. Why?"

Axon said, "Maybe she's stalling to let the Beast escape."

"I'm sure the Beast could move fast enough on its own. It's traveled across the entire countryside without much problem. Besides, we've been here long enough to let it get a good distance from us. Assuming we could find it if we wanted to. No, something else is going on here. Maybe she's simply getting her strength from the easy pickings first. She thinks we hold no real threat—"

"Which we proved just now."

"-- but I think it's something more." Zev turned to Bellemont. "You said that spells are cast with a sacrifice—your teeth. You use your teeth and combine it with various gross things and that's how you get the Beast to give you power. But the Inquisitor did not use her teeth."

"Because she used her life," Bellemont said.

Axon thought back to when Bellemont attacked the Inquisitor. Axon saw their enemy reacting to a surge of energy. She assumed it came from Bellemont. But the same thing happened when Pilot attacked. The Inquisitor screamed out in pain.

"Did any of you see when I got hit in the head?" Axon asked.

"Sure," Pilot said. "Would've been hilarious under different circumstances."

"The Inquisitor—did she yell or show any signs of being hurt?"

"I think so. She did this sort of thing—" Pilot screwed his face up tight.

Axon faced the dais. The Inquisitor stood with her arms out, sending greater numbers of oily-drenched snakes across the canyon floor to feed on the dead, and she swallowed like a woman savoring an exquisite meal.

"This might be our last chance to attack her," Axon said.

"How hard did she hit you in the head? We tried already, and I've got the bruises to prove it."

Zev gave an energetic nod. "Look at the Inquisitor. We're standing right here, yet she doesn't attack. Because she can't. She can fend us off, but she's not strong enough to take the offensive. Not yet."

"But that time will come," Axon said. "If we don't take her down now, then the Frontier has already lost. Between her and the Beast, we won't have time to find the strength to fight her."

"Right now, she's vulnerable. In some way. We just have to figure out how."

Axon rested her gaze on her team as her mind linked together the answer. It popped in her thoughts like a gift. Pausing to kiss one of the strands of her necklace, she spun the Water Blade into a fighting position and strode towards the dais. "We already know," she said. "We've always known."

CHAPTER FIVE

Marching across the brutalized canyon floor, Axon sensed her team falling in line behind her. She steadied her breaths and focused her thoughts. All her triumphs and failures blended into one compacted lump, a stone in her chest. Slapping her palm against her sternum, she shoved that solid feeling deep within. Nothing would distract her. Not her fears. Not her ambitions. Not her family. Not her losses. She had one task only—stop the Dacci Inquisitor.

As they walked by the remaining corpses, Axon explained what they would do. Though she did not look at her team, she could hear their attention. Her confident demeanor spread behind her and captured them in her wake. Her plan would work—it had to.

"You sure about this?" Pilot said, though he did not sound as if he doubted her.

"The Godwalkers told me. I didn't understand it, but I do now. Trust me."

He flicked his hat. "Good enough for me."

The dark tendrils thickened and undulated as they devoured more death, but Axon ordered her team to ignore those horrors. "Only the Inquisitor matters. We kill her, the rest will die."

Bellemont said, "I need a little time to focus my energy. Once I use it like you ask, there won't be any more."

Axon nodded and Bellemont peeled off to the left.

"I know my part," Pilot said.

"Not like before. You don't run off until I say so. You understand?"

"I got a little excited last time. But I'm in this with you."

"Everybody does their part together or we all die."

"Trust me."

Axon gestured off to the right. "Then go."

With a wink, Pilot jogged away. Continuing her march, Axon said, "How many bullets do you have left for your rifle?"

She could hear Zev checking his pockets. "Only four."

"You can't really make this shot, can you?"

"I've gotten a lot better with all this practice. And I'll get as close as I dare so that it's not too hard. But even if I fail—"

"You don't get to fail. We act as one this time. You fail—we all die."

"She won't be able to kill us. You're too good a fighter, and she's still not strong enough."

Axon whipped around and clutched Zev's jaw in her hand. "If this doesn't work, she and the Beast will destroy the Frontier. We will die. If not today, then tomorrow. When the Frontier falls, the East will be next. Your brother, your father, all you knew growing up waits in that shadow. So, you find whatever rock you need to be set up at, and you make that shot. You think about every horrible thing the Inquisitor did to you, all the pain she forced you to suffer. You savor that anger, you swim in that rage, and funnel it all into your aim. The Dacci Inquisitor dies now."

Zev managed to move his head up and down slightly. She let go of him. With a toss of her head, he ran off. Turning back toward the dais, Axon gazed up at the creature – it hardly looked like a person. Dripping that slick substance, wearing the white-striped witch like an ornament, smelling like an animal that died in the a pit of waste, and slurping in all the corpses before they even had time to rot—no, this woman could not be considered human.

"Inquisitor," Axon bellowed, with her arms held wide—the Water

Blade in one hand, the other hand open. "I am Axon, daughter of the family Coponiv, warrior of the Frontier, sent by King Robion to destroy your god. My skin is the night. My heart is the day. My breath is the wind, and my sweat is the water. I am the bringer of your death."

The Inquisitor must have heard a change in Axon's voice. She stepped back. With a flick of her hands, all the wriggling tendrils retracted into her body. They moved fast, but with so many out there, she could not get them in quick enough to free her arms.

Axon reached the stairs, and as she climbed, the dark sludge flowing across the marble parted for her.

"Back away," the Inquisitor said, unable to mask the quiver in her voice.

"You have used too much energy to fight us off to this point. You're weak. Surrender now, remove yourself from the influence of the Beast, and I'll let you live."

The Inquisitor took another step in retreat. "Still a fool. Just because I spread my energy thin fighting you, doesn't mean I can't pull my power into one blow that will rip your head clean off. Your friends may hurt me after that, but you will be quite dead."

"Funny," Axon said. She lowered her hands and adjusted her grip on the Water Blade. "I realized I could do the exact same thing to you."

She thrust the sword high overhead—the signal—and Pilot sprinted from the right side of the dais. He screamed in an effort to distract the Inquisitor. When she did not look away from Axon, Axon's mouth rose with all the joy of a predator about to catch its prey.

Pilot sunk his steel into the Inquisitor's side. Her face broadened, but she did not cry out. Clearly, she wanted to kill Axon, but she could not ignore the damage being done by Pilot. She backhanded him while turning her body and used some of her meager reserves to push the sword out with a black tentacle. The sludge blocked the bleeding. Pilot rolled to his feet, picked up his sword, and attacked again.

Axon continued up the stairs. She concentrated on the Water Blade, imagining all her love and hatred, all her hopes and disappointments, her dreams and failures, all that she had used to form that stone in her body—she pictured all of that emotion and energy flowing into the Blade.

Nearby, Bellemont clapped her hands and sent a blinding arc of light across the canyon from the left. It struck the Blade—knocking Axon back two steps.

The Blade vibrated in her hands. One more member of the team left. *Come on, Zev.*

As Pilot fought the weakened Inquisitor, Axon pressed toward the top of the dais. She heard Zev's first shot but never saw where it struck. The second shot spit up marble several steps in front of her. She had to keep moving, but she knew from working with a bow and arrow that hitting a moving target only compounded problems. The third shot did not come, but before she could worry, she recalled it would take him time to reload.

A sharp, jittering tingle reached up through her arm and back down as if the Water Blade had become a true extension of her body— not simply the way swordsmen spoke of it. Not simply a metaphor. It was part of her. Another limb.

She stepped onto the dais, and her hair stiffened as another jolt of energy crackled off the Water Blade. Pilot swung his sword overhead and yelled as he rushed the Inquisitor once more. She caught Pilot's sword with her hand, wrapping an oily limb around it, and ripped it from his grip. She threw it, spinning in the air until it clattered at the bottom of the stairs.

Zev's third shot hit the carved wall to Axon's side.

"Don't think I cannot see what you're doing," the Inquisitor said to Pilot. "But weakening me a little more is not going to stop me from destroying your idiot leader."

Pilot laughed as he stepped back. "I wasn't weakening you. I was just a decoy."

As the Inquisitor's shoulders stiffened, as she spun around to face Axon, as she lowered and bit into her fury, Axon pushed the Water Blade a little higher so that its bright blue light stood as a beacon for Zev.

The last shot echoed off the canyon walls and Axon stepped forward, ready to bring the Water Blade down fast and hard. The Inquisitor thrust her chest out and a thick, oily mass spurt forward.

Axon felt Zev's bullet strike her leg.

The impact knocked her down and to the side. The Inquisitor's thrust caught the air where Axon had been. As she blinked her eyes, Axon felt the surge of energy from the bullet course up through her body. It filled her chest with warmth. It raced down her arm. It raced into this new part of her, this extension of her arm, this new limb—the Water Blade.

"For the Frontier!" She shoved upward, digging her whole arm into the Inquisitor. The Water Blade part of Axon worked up the spine and through the neck, all the way into the Dacci's skull. Axon could feel all that touched the Blade for it was part of her.

Standing motionless, Axon and the Inquisitor stared into each other's eyes. But Axon caught movement of that dark goo on the ground. Moving toward her.

No.

Releasing the Water Blade, she yanked her hand free and jumped back. Blood dripped down and her fingers tingled as they yearned to be around the Blade again. But instinct told her to be patient. The Blade would return.

And it did.

The Inquisitor grabbed her stomach, and a pleading, hopeless look crossed her face. She let out a soft mew before the Water Blade split her open. The woman's organs and bits of bone flopped onto the dais, splashing with all the blood and sludge that gave her life. The sizzle of the Blade against her skin echoed off into the canyon. Her carcass toppled down the steps, smacking into the marble with wet and vile clarity.

And the Blade dropped to the dais floor—right at Axon's feet.

Most of the oily tendrils feasting on the dead soldiers slipped into the ground. Without their current host, they searched for the Beast to take them back. Those slithering on the dais jumped upon the new source of nourishment before slipping away, too.

Breathing hard, Axon watched the Inquisitor's body dissolve to become one with the Beast below them all. She wanted to take the Water Blade and strike at the muck, but that would only be attacking the edges of a much larger creature. A powerful being that she had underestimated.

Never again.

"Is that it?" Pilot said, blood glistening on his dark cheek.

As Zev and Bellemont worked their way toward her, Axon picked up the Blade. "For today, yes. We've won this first battle. That will have to satisfy us."

"Hey, we're all alive, and we stopped our enemy for the moment. I think that's a victory."

Zev said, "It's better than that. A lot of those Dacci villagers that ran off, well, they're going to spread the word about what happened here. They're going to be very cautious about coming into the Frontier now."

"But they will come," Bellemont said. "Nualla is out there. Weaker after today, more wary, but he has been patient for longer than we've been alive. He knows his chance to take over is close."

Rolling her neck from side to side, Axon said, "He can take all the time he wants to prepare. I'm preparing, too." She stared at the Water Blade and wondered just how much she could learn to do with it.

Stretching his arms overhead, Pilot said, "I don't know how you all feel, but I'm thinking it would be nice to go back to Ridnight. Get a little bit of praise, maybe another parade, and a few other pleasures. I think we've earned it."

"Not me," Axon said. "I'm going to start training."

PART VIII
ZEV

CHAPTER ONE

Zev popped his feet up on his desk, leaned back in his chair, and rubbed his eyes. Only midday and he already wanted a drink. Even with the windows open, the little office felt stifling, and he could feel the beginnings of a headache pressing in the back of his neck.

One year gone. He still couldn't shake the experiences in the Feral Lands. Especially knowing that eventually they would have to deal with the Beast and his ability to create copies of people. King Robion had the word spread to look out for extreme personality changes, and most in the Frontier created code words to authenticate each other. So far, the Beast had yet to show its head or its puppets. But every day that went by quietly only meant a day closer to a terrible noise.

Still, Zev knew better than to dwell on things he could not control. Instead, he had a growing business to run. The moment he had returned home from the West, he paid off his loan with his earnings from the King, then turned around and sold his farm. That money seeded the opening of his office in town. The people welcomed him—the entire Frontier had heard of Axon's exploits and Zev's part in it—but the majority of cases brought to his investigative services were minor and inconsequential.

Still, his office held up as the only local law. Unless the King could free up enough soldiers to create dozens of local police forces, Zev would have to suffice.

His office door opened, and Bellemont stepped in. Even after a year, he had yet to grow accustomed to seeing her in local clothing. A lacy dress down to her calves, pink sash around the waist, and a light collar covering the neck—a far cry from her Dacci wares. She still concealed her head, though she opted for a sensible hat, and she always wore a veil. No need for the locals to see the gaps in her mouth and be reminded of her connection to the enemy.

Bellemont balanced a bowl of soup and a mug filled with ale on a wooden tray. As she set it across his desk, she said, "This should keep you going for the rest of the day. If you need something stronger tonight, let me know. I might need it myself."

"Sit down."

She hesitated—working together had been mostly beneficial, but whenever they reminded the other of the Feral Lands, things often got awkward. She settled on the edge of a guest chair and looked back towards the reception room—her oasis where she helped run his business.

"I'm thinking about writing a book," he said.

That snapped her out of any morose thoughts—he knew that it would. "Like one of those storybooks they read children?"

"I don't think I have the skill for that. But I was thinking about a book on detection techniques. Let people into the thought processes I go through to uncover criminals. You think anybody would be interested?"

She shrugged. "Folks in the East seem to read just about anything."

Mentioning the East brought Zev's thoughts to his father and brother. If he wrote such a book, perhaps they would see it. He wasn't sure if that was a good or bad thing. Neither one had mentioned his newfound fame, though Marcel did send him a gift of ammunition with a note that read: *Glad to hear my gifts were helpful.*

An unsettled silence filled the room. From outside, the sound of Stick trotting in his pasture soothed Zev back. When he bought the office, he made sure to purchase a large chunk of land attached to the back. That caused Mayor Adler several conniptions—the town needed its land—but Zev explained that the Mayor would be a puppet of the Beast right now if not for that wonderful workhorse. The Mayor tried to protest but lost.

Clearing his throat, Zev said, "We're going to be okay. It's just an anniversary. And hey, we were heroes. We saved all these people in the Frontier."

"I try not to think about that day—not just because of what it meant as a Dacci but just the simple day. All those dead bodies, all those intense moments, sometimes it hurts to remember."

"You still having nightmares?"

"Aren't you?"

Zev sat forward, banging his hands on the edge of the table. "We are not going to get sad over our success. Things aren't perfect, I know. Far from it. But we got out of there alive and we succeeded in buying time for everybody. We did more than our part." He stood and rapped his knuckles against the wood. "So, I declare today over. We're going to close up the office, and you and I will go down to Pritchett's Bar. We will have a meal. We'll drink a bit too much and listen to somebody attempt to make music. You like when Pritchett's wife sings for us, right?"

He could tell from the crinkle in her eyes that Bellemont smiled. She said, "That sounds like a wonderful idea. But—"

"No, no, no. We're going to do it."

"You have to see Mr. Fylan first. He's been trying to talk with you for a few days about his son. He'll be here soon."

"See that? We're not useless. We're here for this town. It's a good thing." He picked up the mug of ale and raised a toast. "To helping Mr. Fylan. And afterwards, to helping ourselves."

He drank half the mug down when the front door opened. Bellemont hurried out to greet Mr. Fylan and guide him into the office.

"Oh, I'm sorry," Mr. Fylan said. "I didn't mean to interrupt your lunch."

Mr. Fylan reminded Zev of the kind of old man his mother would tell stories about—a gentle soul living in the woods who would help the heroes of a children's story with important information or much-needed advice. Only this time, the wise old man had come to see him instead.

"How can I help you?" Zev said, gesturing to the chair.

"It's my son." Mr. Fylan proceeded to tell a woeful tale of how his son, Inric, had grown bitter since the death of the boy's mother. "I've seen him being violent towards our livestock. I've seen him take his rage out by simply punching trees. It's not good. Nothing seems to appease him. I've tried talking with him. Tried bribing him. I'd do anything to make him better."

"You think he might be one of the Beast's puppets?"

"No, not at all. You see, the real problem is that I think Inric was like this before his mother died. He's always had a violent streak. Andra's death is just his excuse. He's going down a bad path."

"The boy's sad, and I can't make him forget his mother."

"I don't want to see him on the wrong side of your cell."

Bellemont had introduced the idea of a jail cell recently—another marvel from the East meant to replace castle dungeons—and she had convinced Mayor Adler to have a single cell built. It had only been finished a few days earlier, and so far, it had been thankfully unused. But that would not last for long, and clearly Mr. Fylan thought Inric might be their first resident.

"I don't want to see him in there, either," Zev said. "I want to tell you to go back and speak with him as a man, but I suspect you've already tried that."

"Of course. He is a man—practically."

"Perhaps his inclinations towards violence don't match with the life of a farmer. Perhaps he's looking for a place to take all that anger away."

Mr. Fylan rolled his fingers over the lapel of his coat. "There's nothing I can do about that. Farmers is what we are. All our life is in that farm. It's too late to start something new."

"For you, yes. But Inric is a young man. Perhaps he shouldn't be a farmer."

"Of course he'll be a farmer. That's what our family does."

Zev did not like to brag, and he certainly did not like to draw attention to the more famous people in his life, but he had a simple solution in mind which required a bit of name-dropping. "You know the things I've done?"

"Everybody knows."

"And you know who I did those things with?"

"Of course."

"Well, Axon and Pilot are still friends of mine. They are stationed at Ridnight Castle where they train King Robion's Army. I know it may not be exactly what you want, but I think if you offer the opportunity to Inric, he will jump at the chance to join up. He doesn't want to be in this little town, and I doubt he wants to be a farmer. As a soldier in the King's Army, he will get ample opportunity to let out his aggression in a safe way that will keep him out of a jail cell or a dungeon. And I can promise that Axon and Pilot will watch out for him."

Mr. Fylan frowned. "But that's dangerous, isn't it?"

"Yes. But better he use his violent tendencies fighting for us all instead of fighting us all."

With a somber nod, Mr. Fylan said, "You think you can get him a spot in the Army?"

"Axon wants all the strong soldiers she can get. And I've never asked her for a favor. So, I don't see why she would turn me down now."

Though Mr. Fylan's face did not break, Zev saw the tension lift from his body. It would take a night or two, but the old man would come around. And if he didn't, Zev would let him know about his own father, and how his father denying him a chance to be free sent him off to the Frontier. Mr. Fylan loved his son and would not want to have an estranged relationship.

As he escorted Mr. Fylan out the office door, Zev felt confident this little family's problem had been solved. Another win for Asterling Investigative Services.

Turning back to his desk, his gaze lifted to the rifle mounted high on the wall. More than solving Mr. Fylan's family dilemma, Zev knew all the soldiers would be needed soon. The Beast remained alive. It was out there gaining strength, preparing to attack. War would be here soon enough.

"Bellemont," Zev called. She walked into the office already dressed to leave. He smiled. "Let's go get drunk."

She laughed. Such a sweet, wonderful sound.

Read on for a sneak peak at Book Two of The Ridnight Mysteries - The Waters of Taladoro!

ACKNOWLEDGEMENTS

I've been writing books for twenty years now, and this is the first time I've had a full team behind me to see a story come to fruition. It's been a great experience. Big thanks to John Hartness, Melissa McArthur, Tuppence Van de Vaarst, Joe Crowe, and all the fine people at Falstaff Books who worked hard on this project (many without me even knowing). Extra thanks to Natania Barron for an incredible cover. Of course, to my wife and son for their enduring support. And always, always, always, my deepest thanks to you, my reader. Without you, I'm wearing a straitjacket in a rubber room telling the world I know all about magic systems and parallel universes. Thank you.

ABOUT THE AUTHOR

Stuart Jaffe is the madman behind *The Max Porter Paranormal Mysteries, The Malja Chronicles, The Bluesman, Founders, Real Magic,* and much more. He trained in martial arts for over a decade until a knee injury ended that practice. Now, he plays lead guitar in a local blues band, *The Bootleggers,* and enjoys life on a small farm in rural North Carolina. For those who continue to keep count, the animal list is as follows: one dog, two cats, three aquatic turtles, and seven chickens. As best as he's been able to manage, Stuart sees that the chickens do not live in the house.

ALSO BY STUART JAFFE

The Way of the Power

The Way of the Soul

Nathan K Thrillers

Immortal Killers

Killing Machine

The Cardinal

Yukon Massacre

The First Battle

Immortal Darkness

A Spy for Eternity

Prisoner

Desert Takedown

Lone Star Standoff

The Parallel Society

The Infinity Caverns

Book on the Isle

Rift Angel

Lost Time

Short Story Collections

The Marshall Drummond Case Files: Cabinet 1

The Marshall Drummond Case Files: Cabinet 2

For more from Stuart Jaffe, visit him
on his website — www.stuartjaffe.com

FRIENDS OF FALSTAFF

Thank You to All our Falstaff Books Patrons, who get extra digital content each month! To be featured here and see what other great rewards we offer, go to www.patreon.com/falstaffbooks.

PATRONS

Dino Hicks

John Hooks

John Kilgallon

Larissa Lichty

Travis & Casey Schilling

Staci-Leigh Santore

Sheryl R. Hayes

Scott Norris

Samuel Montgomery-Blinn

Junkle

www.ingramcontent.com/pod-product-compliance
Lightning Source LLC
Chambersburg PA
CBHW020415110726
47899CB00006B/1998